THE LONG ROAD TO LOVING BYRON

ALICIA HOPE

DEDICATION

For my dear beta readers, where would I be without you? xox

ABOUT THE AUTHOR

Once you choose HOPE anything is possible....

Despite living within cooee of the Great Barrier Reef, idyllic tropical islands, and a well-stocked ocean pantry, author Alicia Hope is a self-confessed landlubber and disliker of seafood (I know - what the heck, right?!). She's also a keen horse rider, bass player, and bird watcher, and shares her gumtree-dotted acreage home with an author husband, Frank H Jordan, a feathered larrikin, cockatiel Kewbie Kewberton, and a whole bunch of wild birds, roos, goannas, and pretty-face wallabies.
Her feel-good stories showcase Alicia's love of the land and the natural world, and this is especially true of her LONG ROAD series.

For the latest on her books and writing life, visit Alicia online at aliciahopeauthor.blogspot.com.au, and collect an exclusive gift. :-)

Family Tree

De Brande Barlow / Brande

Fitzwilliam de Brande Barlow

| Edward James Lorienne (1871-1902) | -M- | Elizabeth Anne de Brande Barlow (1876-1902) | Henry Montville de Brande Barlow / Brande(1861-1932) | -M- | Constance Penelope Pickle (1871-1959) |

No issue

Charles Montville Brande
(1890-1952)

James Edward Brande
(bastard son)
(1918-2006)   -M-

Antoinette Grace
(1929-Present)

Michael John Rothbury
(1851-1990)   -M-

Constance Rosalie Brande
(1954-Present)

Madeleine Brande
(1985 Present)

PROLOGUE

L e *Froid Peninsula, Tasmania, 1881*
'What do you see, son?' The well-dressed man leaned back in the saddle to squint into the swaying canopy of leaves above his head.

'One moment, Father.' The boy climbed monkey-like along a sturdy tree branch, stopping to peer through each break in the foliage as he went.

'Take care, lad.' The man dismounted, loosening the reins of both horses so they could pick at the lush grass. When a boyish cry of, 'There it is!' came from above, his face lit up and he barked, 'What?'

'The harbour, Father. I spy the harbour.'

'And the open ocean, do you see it also?'

'Yes, the ocean too.'

'And the port?' When this met with scrabbling sounds

above, the man called more urgently, 'Do you spy the port?' Only grunts and a shower of leaves greeted him. He raised his voice in concern. 'Son?'

'All is well, Father,' the boy called, breathless with exertion.

'Tell me, is the port visible?' The man turned his face away as more leaves fell.

'I ... yes!' The boy's voice squeaked with excitement. 'The port, I see it, Father!'

Clenching a triumphant fist, the man hurried to tie the horses to a low branch before clambering up the tree to join the beaming, jubilant boy.

The two sat side-by-side on the branch, legs dangling, staring out through the leafy canopy.

'Well done, my lad. We have found a most favourable situation.' Ducking his head and widening the gap in the leaves with a hand, the man swept a gaze over the ocean at the mouth of the harbour and up to the bustling port. 'From here I will observe the arrival of ships bearing my timber, as will you and your sons.'

Puffing out his chest, he threw an arm around the boy's lanky shoulders. 'This will be the site of our new home, Edward. Our home, our castle. And our family's legacy.'

International waters, Pacific Ocean, 1902
The stately ship, her name inscribed in elegant cursive

on her foam-flecked hull, rose and dipped in the swell as she rode the squally ocean. The blustery wind carried the scents of fish and seaweed, the creak of marine timbers and slap of salt water against wooden hull, the strident cries of gulls, and raised voices.

Men's voices, audible above the snarling tempest.

'Captain!' The tall figure on the ship's salt-sprayed deck stood legs apart, heavy coat tails flapping in the rising wind, holding a cheroot in one hand and the fingers of the other hooked into the pocket of his tailored waistcoat.

'Aye, sir?' A stocky figure in oilskins, moving with a slight limp, joined the other man on the blustery deck.

'Why are you furling the sails, man? With this gale we could make up time, arrive earlier.'

'But the approaching storm—'

'Storm be damned!' The well-dressed man glared down at him. 'Is your vessel not capable of withstanding a blow?'

'That she is, sir.' The captain rose to his full height and stuck out his chest. 'I'll 'ave you know that since bein' launched in eighty-five, the *Polly Brown* has safely rounded Cape Horn a number of times.'

'Is that so?' The tall man straightened and tugged down his waistcoat. 'Then she is more than capable of maintaining speed in weather such as this.'

The captain eyed him warily. 'We're enterin' a bad stretch, sir, littered with treacherous reefs.'

'Did you not just this moment assure me of your ship's competence? This squall is surely but a trifle when compared to the infamous Cape Horn. Or is it your own competence you call into question?'

'Not at all, sir.'

'Then do as I say.' Bending, he put his face close to the captain's. 'It is a matter of urgency that I return to Australia, and I cannot—*will* not—be delayed by a patch of bad weather.' His voice, his very essence bristled with authority. 'So you *will* unfurl the sails, my good man, and take us there with every possible speed.' Rising to his full height once more, he stood with hands behind his back, booted feet firm on the pitching deck.

The captain stared up at him. 'There's not many would 'ave the effrontery to override a ship cap'n's orders.' But this passenger, standing proud and authoritative before him, appeared unaccustomed to being disobeyed. And beneath the impeccable grooming and fine clothes, indicative of a life of privilege and high social standing, lay a barely concealed iron will, of that the captain was certain. Such a man was unlikely to accept disappointment with anything akin to mildness of spirit.

With a tug on his dripping beard, the captain rasped, 'If anyone 'as the right to do so, it be the man whose timber fills my ship's hold to burstin'.' His tone soured. 'Somethin' what happens less 'n less now merchants are favourin' them new steam ships for transportin' their goods.' He gave a slow, pensive nod. 'A Pacific Ocean storm should pose no serious threat to a ship what's proven 'erself a match for the most challengin' routes known to seafarers.'

Fixing the tall man with a narrow-eyed gaze, he touched grimy, work-roughened fingers to his temple. 'Very well, sir. I will give the order—' His remaining words were torn from his mouth by a snarling gust of wind.

On the horizon, the mounting swell curled into a wave and sprouted an angry white crest, while ahead of it, the ship's newly unfurled sails caught the rising wind and she surged bravely—hopelessly—forward.

As the deadly surge continued toward the *Polly Brown*, its poison-green, frothing threat gained height and ferocity as it bore down relentlessly on the ill-fated vessel. Capable as she was, the ship stood no chance of outrunning the fuming, destructive wall of ocean water. It rose higher still until suspended above its victim like a raptor about to swoop on its prey.

Screams from many throats pierced the ocean water's roar, until the wave descended with a thundering crash, swallowing the *Polly Brown* like an insignificant sliver of driftwood.

1

L orienne Castle, Le Froid Peninsula, Tasmania, 2012

Madeleine Brande stepped lightly onto the circular gravel driveway, tilting back her head to taste the cool air with its hint of salt and sea. Sweeping a gaze over the surrounding vista of cushion-thick lawns, full-to-bursting flower beds, blossom-festooned arbours, and glistening harbour backdrop, she spread her arms wide in delight.

Almost too perfect....

'There you go, Miss.' The bus driver transferred her travel-weary suitcase to the base of the stairs with a crunch. At her thanks he gave a smiling salute, closed the luggage bin and climbed back up for the return trip along the castle's tree-lined access road.

Humping her suitcase up the steep steps, Madeleine

paused between the stone lions guarding either side of the landing to catch her breath. When her ears caught the cries of sea birds she glanced upward, shielding her eyes with a hand.

Were they albatross, those dark specks cruising on air currents in the expanse of blue? From nearby Albatross Island maybe? Tasmania was known for harbouring the graceful, feathered seafarers on its offshore islands. Albatross, thought to carry the souls of dead sailors, like in poet Coleridge's Ancient Mariner....

Instead of the cross, the Albatross about my neck was hung.

Madeleine's spine tingled with anticipation.

How exciting to observe these seafaring "harbingers of doom" in their natural environment....

Behind her the bus trundled off, and a taxi nosed forward with a bip of its horn.

Inside the castle, a man at reception gave a start and twisted to peer through the leadlight entrance doors and past the woman loitering on the landing outside. Seeing the taxi crawl to a stop on the circular drive, he cleared his throat, tugged down his crumpled shirt, and turned back to the receptionist. 'That's my cab.'

The shrill edge to his voice and his wide, freaked-out eyes had the receptionist averting her gaze as she hastened to finalise his payment. Sticking doggedly to the script despite her departing guest's nervy antics, she handed him the receipt and mustered some cheerfulness to say, 'Thank you for staying with us. I hope you've enjoyed your time at Lorienne Castle.'

With a surly, 'Enjoyed? More like survived,' the man snatched the receipt and stuffed it into his pocket. 'It'd be a cold day in hell before I ever set foot here again.' Grabbing his suitcase, he spun on his heel and was about to charge out when the hastily shut case fell open and spilled some of its contents on the floor.

Pausing as if tempted to simply leave them there, he gave a snarled curse and bent to retrieve them.

From where she stood on the landing outside, Madeleine's gaze skimmed over the castle's grey stone walls. The afternoon light made the aged stones shine like old silver. Leaning to press a hand on the wall, she noted the flinty coolness, the chill seeping through her skin to slither up her arm.

Ooh ... ethereal.

She gave a shiver.

To think the Lorienne estate was once in her family ... kind of. Could the connection be reforged if her planned sleuthing produced positive results? Not to re-establish some sort of loose claim to the castle for monetary benefit, nothing that tacky. Her goal was to restore her family's good—and full—name.

If that were possible.

Anticipation sparkled in her brown-gold, green-flecked hazel eyes as she withdrew her hand and bent for her suitcase. Her fingers had hardly brushed the handle when a figure burst through the double doors, nearly collecting her.

The man from reception.

At her gasp and sideways stagger he didn't stop, merely puffed, 'Sorry,' while taking the stairs two at a time.

She watched, frowning, as he darted to the taxi, wrenched open the passenger door, tossed in his bag, and dove inside. Moments later the cab sped away in a shower of gravel.

Wow, someone was in a hurry. Late for a flight perhaps?

Shrugging off her curiosity, Madeleine turned and bumped through the still-swinging doors into the reception area, a screened-off section of the castle's original entrance foyer. Behind the antique, leather-topped counter, the smartly dressed receptionist sat talking on a vintage telephone. At Madeleine's approach the young woman glanced up to nod a 'one moment please' acknowledgement.

With an answering dip of her head, Madeleine parked her case and wandered the room, taking in the collection of sepia-coloured photos and framed pencil drawings mounted on the stone walls. Most featured the castle and grounds, so when her eyes fell on the sizeable oil painting of a gracious tall ship, she moved closer.

A bronze plaque beneath the picture read, *The* Polly

Brown, *a nineteenth century tall ship at anchor in her home port of Lyttelton Harbour, NZ. A three-masted iron-hulled barque, described by many as the most beautiful ship built in Belfast, she was used for the deep water trade and carried timber, salt, grain, and coal to countries around the world. Sadly, in 1902, the* Polly Brown *struck a reef en-route to Australia and sank, leaving no survivors. Among the passengers aboard was Tasmanian timber merchant Edward Lorienne, whose life and valuable timber cargo were lost in the shipwreck.*

Madeleine gave a slow nod.

Edward Lorienne, previous owner of the castle and her great, great grandfather's brother-in-law.

Family ... even if loosely connected.

Moving on to a display of oval-framed portraits, she stopped in front of one featuring a handsome young couple. Their smiles and casual bearing set them apart from the other stern-faced subjects in the stiff poses of the day. The tall, dark-haired man stood casually smoking a cheroot, his other arm around the slender-waisted woman at his side. She was smiling tenderly up at him, her features familiar....

'Really?' From behind the desk the receptionist's voice rose. 'Well, despite what *you* think, not everyone appreciates the vagaries of life in a neo-Gothic castle.' Thumping the phone's receiver onto its stylish candlestick-shaped cradle, she caught Madeleine watching her and reddened.

Setting her lips in a polite smile, she cleared her throat,

flicked back her hair, and stepped up to the counter. 'Good afternoon. Sorry for the wait. How can I help you?' She noticed Madeleine's case. 'Checking in?'

'Yes, thanks. Name's Brande, Madeleine … Maddie … Brande.'

The receptionist nodded. 'Welcome to Lorienne Castle, Miss Brande. I'm Emma, and if I can assist you in any way during your stay, please let me know.' As she spoke, she ran heavily made-up eyes over the new guest.

She saw a slim woman of around her own age, a touch over average height, smartly dressed in jeans and tailored shirt, with her honey-blonde hair in a ponytail and a long, side-parted fringe sweeping the brow of a heart-shaped face. Beneath her natural eyebrows and darkly lashed lids, a pair of unusually coloured—hazel?—eyes tilted upward at the outer corners. And below them, this 'Maddie's' straight, freckle-dusted nose sat above a wide mouth that appeared inclined to grin.

When their eyes met, Emma hurriedly lowered her gaze and moved to a screened-off section of the counter. 'I'll just call up the details of your booking.'

Madeleine's lips twitched. She was used to having people find her direct gaze off-putting. 'Perceptive and striking' was how her mother described the 'Brande topaz' eyes, but Connie Brande was bound to appreciate them, having passed on the shape and colouring to her daughter.

Kris too had admired her eyes, describing them as 'captivating'.

Kris....

No.

Mustn't go there.

'Have you stayed with us before?' Emma's voice brought her back to the present.

'Only been here on a day trip, and promised myself I'd return and spend longer, have a proper look around.'

When Emma gave a cursory nod and bent over the large, old-fashioned guest register lying open on the counter, Madeleine followed her scarlet fingernail as it ran down the list of names. Each entry had room numbers and dates marked against them on the open, gold-edged page. Even upside-down, Madeleine could read the names written in a firm, clear hand.

Mr A and Mrs S Jenkins

Mr P and Mrs J Fox

Mr T and Mrs S Meier

Mr M and Mrs R Singh-Samra

Ms M and Mrs C Brande

Raising her eyes, she asked, 'You still use a manual register?'

'We employ a combination of systems.' Emma turned to peer at the computer screen, saying absently, 'This area, in fact the whole peninsula, is susceptible to power outages, so having a manual back-up system allows us to continue operating when the computer goes down.'

A crease formed in her otherwise smooth brow. 'I've located a booking for a thirteen night stay for yourself, and a Mrs Brande?' She raised sculpted eyebrows at her guest.

'Mum was meant to come with me on this holiday, until a last-minute surgical procedure spoiled her plans. I did phone last week to advise I'd be on my own.'

Emma returned her focus to the screen. 'Oh yes, there's a notation to that effect below your booking.' She straightened. 'I'm sorry your mother hasn't been well. I hope she recovers soon.'

'You and I both. She's the grumpiest patient ever, so it was something of a relief to come on my own.' Madeleine gave an indulgent huff. 'Though she made me promise to report back regularly by email, so she can share the trip from her convalescent couch.'

'Well then,' Emma said with polite finality, 'I trust you have an enjoyable stay.' She handed Madeleine a key. 'You're in room number sixteen of The Lodge, what used to be the castle's stable building. That said,' she went on quickly as though pre-empting an enquiry, 'let me assure you that the room has been completely renovated since Elizabeth Lorienne's favourite thoroughbred, and feline stable mate, vacated long ago.'

'I love that the building has a history.'

'One thing we're not short of here is history.' With a fixed smile Emma recited, 'As a house guest, you're welcome to dine in the castle with the McAlister family ... unless you're put off by the possibility of spectral entertainment. As you may have noticed,' and she arched an eyebrow at the doors the freaked-out man had bolted through earlier, 'it's not for everyone.'

'I don't believe in ghosts, but wouldn't be put off even if I did.' Madeleine grinned. 'They'd make more interesting dinner companions than some I've had. So please book me in for tonight.'

'Of course.'

'By the way,' and she pointed at Emma's name badge, 'I couldn't help noticing your surname is McAlister?'

'That's right.'

'So ... you're a member of the family that owns the castle?'

'I am.' An edge crept into the young woman's voice. 'My brother and I share ownership of the estate with our mother.'

'Oh, lucky you.'

With a tight murmur of, 'Yes, lucky me,' Emma turned away with a smile that didn't reach her eyes.

From: Madeleine.Brande
To: Connie.Brande
Re: Travelogue, day 1

You'll be pleased to know I've arrived safely, Mum, though maybe not so pleased to hear I used the travelling time to ponder your accountant's advice. Oh sure, he makes it sound simple, but what will you do with yourself if you hand over management of the business? The company has been the focus of your life, like ... forever. You'd go crazy without another project to take its place, and finding a sufficiently worthy project would be a serious challenge. That's my take on it, anyway.

Now, the castle. As promised, I won't skimp on details.

Here's an intriguing snippet ... on arrival I experienced a sensation of coming home. Fascinating, though perhaps not totally unexpected.

I'd forgotten how fabulous the views are from up here —you can probably hear my rapt sigh from over Bass Strait. Will send photos but they won't do justice to the rolling green hills, glistening harbour, and wind-swept ocean. And as for the meticulously landscaped castle grounds ... yep, there's another sigh.

My room is in The Lodge, the converted stable building on the edge of the escarpment. Apparently Elizabeth Lorienne's favourite thoroughbred was accommodated right here, back when it was a horse stall.

Are you pulling a face? Silly question, of course you are!

Now while some might not relish the prospect of sleeping in a space previously occupied by equines, I'm thrilled by the sense of history contained within these walls. Can almost smell the scents of horse and hay, and hear the feed-bin snorts and scrape of hooves on cobblestones. And really, the room as it is now bears little resemblance to a stall. It contains a Queen Anne bed, winged armchair (cosy reading spot), French doors to a balcony, and a picture window overlooking the harbour.

Oh, and did I mention my roomy, the handsome grey tabby I found snoozing at the foot of the bed when I arrived? He welcomed me with loud purring and smiles from his feline version of 'Brande Topaz' eyes, so who am I to evict him?

As for tonight, I'm having dinner in the castle's dining room, in the company of the McAlister family and other in-house guests. According to the brochure, I can look forward to a three course 'table d'hôte' meal similar to those served during the castle's heyday. On tonight's menu is cream of mushroom soup, roast New Zealand lamb with Yorkshire pudding, and baked custard with caramelised pears. Following all that, postprandial port and coffee will be served in the gentlemen's drawing room. Yum.

You can probably tell that I've got my 'happy tourist' on, and it feels good after the recent ... upsets. Even though I had to leave you recuperating at home, I'm glad I came on this holiday, Mum, it'll give me a chance to put recent events behind me. And if luck is on my side, I might even discover some clues to unlock long-buried secrets from our family's distant past....

Holidaying AND doing some sleuthing in a castle? How lucky am I!

Luv,

Maddie xxx

2

The sea breeze ruffled the wide legs of her linen trouser suit as she strolled the dusk-gilded path toward the castle, her tabby 'roomy' sauntering by her side as though accompanying her to dinner.

The whoosh of nearby waves against rock and sand only partly filled the evening hush as the insect, bird, and animal inhabitants of the castle's gardens bedded down for the night. From within a deepening patch of shade in the garden came the eerie cry of a curlew, answered moments later by equally mournful cries from the gloom of another corner.

Madeleine gave a delighted shiver.

Once outside the wrought iron gate of the castle's rear courtyard, she inhaled the cooling air and swept one more look around the garden. Murmuring, 'This place is really something isn't it, Puss?' she glanced at her feline companion.

Gone, without even a 'by your leave'.

That's cats for you. Loveable but oh-so fickle.

She gave a fond shake of her head and unlatched the gate. Its ornate metal grating creaked a flinty protest as she pushed through into the shadowy courtyard.

Her soft-soled boots made only faint thuds on the cobblestones as she strode past moss-drenched stone walls toward the hinged metal portcullis leading into the castle proper. It too complained on being opened, emitting a series of deep, indignant groans before closing behind her with a weighty clang.

Once inside the building she paused to absorb its historic, slightly damp and chilly allure. When her nose picked up wafts of warm bread and roasting meat, she licked her lips and set off along the corridor toward the dining room. On passing the butler's pantry she slowed pace to admire the scrubbed bench tops, neatly stacked crockery gleaming from dark timber shelves, antique meat safe, and porcelain canisters standing to attention on an imposing dresser.

When a sizeable brass key ring dangling from a hook on the facing wall snagged her gaze, she paused to stare at it, picturing the dimly lit, secretive places in the castle the keys might unlock.

Then again they could be merely decorative, their

matching locks and therefore their original purpose, long gone.

With a frown at her hedonistic—and yes, overactive—imagination, she continued on toward the open doorway to the left of the corridor.

Flickering candlelight spilled from the room, framing the figure standing in the doorway. Dressed in a Victorian-styled gown, all layers and bustle and pinched-in waist, the woman gave a regal dip of her head at Madeleine's approach.

'Good evening.' She extended a satin-gloved hand. 'I'm Kathryn McAlister, the lady of the house.'

'Madeleine.' They shook hands. 'Pleased to meet you, Kathryn.'

'And you, Madeleine.' With a small, dignified smile, the lady of the house clasped her hands together in front of her fulsome skirt. 'I'd like to welcome you to our beloved castle.' With a graceful sweep of one arm, she moved aside. 'Please, come in.'

As Madeleine stepped into the dining room, a deep voice at her elbow asked, 'Care for a sherry, Madam?' On turning, she saw a man in butler garb holding a sherry glass in a gloved hand, a white cloth draped over his jacketed arm.

A tall and undeniably dishy man.

Dishy! Could there be a more appropriate description for a butler?

She grinned to herself.

'Unless a sparkling sauvignon blanc is more to your taste?' He smiled into her eyes. 'Both the produce of local vignerons, naturally.'

With a twitch of her left eyebrow she answered, 'The sparkling, please.'

'An excellent choice, Madam. I believe you'll find it the perfect aperitif.'

While he set down the sherry glass to extract a dewy bottle from an ice bucket on the drinks cabinet, Madeleine ran her eyes over him. With a hint of five o'clock shadow along his angular jawline and tapered chin, a set of firm but full lips, slightly hooded brown eyes beneath dark eyebrows, and equally dark, slicked-back hair, he projected elements of smooth refinement over an underlay of masculinity.

Nice.

Not wanting to be caught staring when he straightened to pour her wine, she swept a gaze over the room's antique furnishings and fine tapestries. Golden candlelight spilled from the chandelier above the long, intricately carved dining table, gracing the room with a warm, intimate atmosphere. It was easy to picture the countless meals, conversations, arguments—and assignations?—witnessed by these walls.

'Your drink, Madam.' As he held out the champagne flute, along with a linen napkin, the butler's gaze lingered on her face.

'Why, thank you, Jeeves.'

With something akin to mischievous amusement sparkling in his eyes, he touched his forehead in a salute and watched her take a tentative sip.

Seriously tasty, she decided. Both the wine and the person serving it.

'Not dallying with "the help" I hope?' The imagined voice sounded in her inner ear. It belonged to her grandmother, Antoinette Brande.

Her much loved grandmother, whose failing health was never far from Madeleine's mind, and whose long-held wish was one of the reasons she was here....

Shrugging off the imperious internal commentary, Madeleine gave the waiting butler a nod of approval and advanced into the room. From among the group of diners standing by the fireplace, a raised hand gestured for her to join them.

'It appears you're the only Aussie among this multi-cultural bunch,' a smiling American woman announced after Madeleine introduced herself. 'We're the Jenkins, Sally 'n Alan, from the States.' She inclined her head at the tall, craggy-faced man beside her, and then pointed to each couple in turn. 'This here's Mr and Mrs Fox from Britain, and these are the Meiers from Germany, and the Singh-Samras from India.' Once hands had been shaken all round she went on cheerily, 'We were just talkin' about the castle's colourful history, and of course, the ghosts.'

This met with a ripple of self-conscious laughter.

'You all believe, then? In ghosts?' Madeleine glanced around the group with raised eyebrows. Would she be the only pariah? That could be fun too.

They responded with sheepish grins, some head-shaking, and an unconvincing chorus of, 'No, of course not,' followed by, 'Well, not *really*...,' from the more honest among them.

Recalling the earlier scene, Madeleine said brightly, 'A man was leaving the castle as I arrived. He rushed off as though the Hound of the Baskervilles was nipping at his heels. Clearly something creeped him out.'

'That would've been Tony,' Sally said with a knowing dip of her head. 'He got a bit spooked by all the ghost talk ... said he could smell cigar smoke wherever he went in the castle, even though smokin' ain't allowed inside.'

Sally waited for assenting murmurs to die down before continuing. 'From all accounts, there's a whole *bunch* of disturbed individuals in this castle—present company excepted of course—and not all of 'em...,' and she lowered her voice, '... have human form.'

This garnered nods and a breathy chorus of, 'Ooohs,' from the group, and a stifled snort from Madeleine. She sipped her wine as others shared their 'spectral experiences', and sampled the hors d'oeuvres offered by the attentive and somehow also unobtrusive butler.

And then Kathryn rang the crystal dinner bell.

. . .

Candlelight from the antique crystal candelabrum centrepiece sparkled off the glassware, gold-edged crockery, and silver cutlery adorning the table's white, satin-edged cloth.

Madeleine took a chair beside the affable Sally Jenkins, who leaned in to say, 'Don'tcha find the castle simply fascinatin'? I can almost *feel* the history.' She ran her hands along her upper arms as if to smooth away goose bumps. 'So many stories within these old walls. Ancient and present-day.'

'Present-day?'

'Oh yeah, the McAlisters have stories of their own.' She lowered her voice. 'Take Kathryn and her husband,' and she flicked a discreet glance at the lady in question. 'Their marriage went the way of the unicorn thanks to her obsession with restorin' the castle ... so the story goes.'

'Sad for them.' Madeleine gazed down the table at Kathryn, who was listening with an expression of gracious tolerance to the animated guest at her side.

'The husband felt he was playin' a poor second fiddle, apparently.' With a sheepish glance at her own husband, Sally dropped her voice to a whisper. 'And men don't much care for takin' second place to anythin' much.'

A lesson Madeleine had learned the hard way.

In her head, she heard again the angry squeal of tyres and indignant growl of the sports car's engine as Kris roared away from their last fight.

The inevitable lump rose in her throat, and she bent her head to focus on the napkin in her lap, running the hem through her fingers as if to flatten non-existent creases.

Don't go there.

Just ... don't.

Oblivious to Madeleine's silent distress Sally continued, 'And 'specially not to some old buildin' ... if one dares call the castle that,' she added in a hushed tone. 'So with the husband gone, that left Kathryn and the kids to carry on by themselves.' A crease formed between her brows. 'There's talk they might be thinkin' of sellin' up. Could be not all three share the same devotion to the place.'

Blinking, Madeleine pressed the napkin flat against her lap and raised her head. 'Selling up?' She rested her clasped hands on the table. 'So the castle might be for sale?'

'That's what I heard.'

As Sally spoke, the dining room door creaked open and the butler came in, wheeling a laden trolley. When he leaned over her shoulder to serve a bowl of soup, Madeleine caught a hint of masculine, woody cologne.

And like mentholated vapours, the scent cleared her mind of painful memories.

Only half listening to the chatter around her, she watched the butler deliver the remaining dishes.

After a suitable interval he returned to collect the empty

soup bowls, and then wheeled in the main course. Assuming a serious and purposeful expression, he removed his gloves with a theatrical gesture and donned a starched white apron to begin carving the glistening, red-brown joint of lamb.

As he served the meals, unobtrusively re-filling each empty or close-to-empty wine glass while doing so, Madeleine wondered what sort of salary package would attract such a top-quality staff member. One prepared to not only perform the duties of a waiter but also to act the part of butler extraordinaire.

Assuming he *was* an employee, of course....

Once dessert was done with, Kathryn set aside her linen napkin, rose to her feet, and tapped a spoon against her crystal wine glass. 'Coffee and port will be served in the gentleman's drawing room,' she announced, 'if you'd like to follow me.'

Despite being too full to want either drink, Madeleine wasn't about to let an opportunity to see another part of the castle go begging. She joined the group following Kathryn down the corridor to the heavily draped and softly lit drawing room.

After gliding into the room, Kathryn lowered herself into a brown leather Chesterfield wing chair, and with a graceful hand gesture, invited her guests to do the same. 'I have been somewhat remiss in my duties as hostess, I'm afraid.' She gave a contrite smile. 'A situation I will now correct.'

Gesturing toward the butler circling the room serving coffees and crystal port pots filled with the fortified wine, she announced, 'Allow me to introduce another part-owner of the castle. My son, Byron.'

3

Something broke the tentative embrace of oncoming slumber. Blinking, Madeleine lifted her head from the pillow to see the cat kneading the quilt at the foot of the bed.

'Well, hello again.' She yawned. 'So you found the window I left ajar.'

After gazing at her through contented, half-closed eyes, the tabby tucked himself against one of her legs and began a rigorous licking of his grey-striped coat.

With a sleepy, 'Night, puss-cat. Sweet dreams,' Madeleine closed her eyes and let her head fall back into the pillow's softness.

. . .

The oil painting beckoned her from within its ornate frame as she glided toward it through the heavy grey mist. Feeling a damp chill beneath her feet, she glanced downward and saw the embroidered skirt of an unfamiliar Victorian nightgown billowing as she moved. Its white folds glowed eerily in the gloom, and with each step pale toes peeked out from beneath the gown's delicately laced hem.

Barefoot? On a cold stone floor?

The query, coming from the distant, semi-conscious part of her sleeping mind, skittered away into the thickening fog.

Glimpsing an opening in the dimness to her right she turned her head, the movement causing her hair to float around her like a gossamer halo. When the opening morphed into a window, deep-set in the thick stone wall, she approached and saw a castle's battlements reflected in a puddle of still, dark water on the ground outside. Swirling fingers of mist clasped at the vision, shrouding it in a wraith-like embrace until it was concealed from sight.

As she continued her trance-like approach to the painting, misty tendrils followed in her wake like a train of cobwebs.

The canvas bore the portrait of a young woman, expertly captured in textured oils, but whose face was in deep shadow. Madeleine crept closer to get a better look, only to have the shadow deepen and grow larger, swallowing more of the woman's image.

The darkness continued to expand, stretching shadowy

claw-like fingers toward Madeleine as if to also draw her into its dark embrace.

With a gasp she made to leap back but her feet wouldn't respond. They felt cemented to the stone floor beneath them.

The shadow advanced, creeping along the walls and across the ceiling above her, its clinging blackness clouding her fearful, wide-eyed gaze. As its dank mist infiltrated and defiled her lungs, she gave a cry and tried to force herself to move, only to remain rooted to the spot.

All she could do was throw up her hands in a feeble attempt to ward off the encroaching malevolence....

Her quivering fingertips met only warm, dry, empty air. Madeleine lifted her head and opened her eyelids a slit, to shut them an instant later against the glare of early morning light through the French doors of her Lodge room.

It was just a dream.

Blowing a relieved breath through pursed lips, she fell against the pillows to savour the euphoria of relief. As her ears registered the comforting sounds of birds stirring in the garden outside, the hum of a plane going overhead, and the bump and clack of early morning human activity from nearby buildings, her heart rate returned to normal.

What a vivid dream ... make that nightmare. Prompted by...?

She raked fingers through her hair and yawned.

Being here, in the shadow of Lorienne Castle most likely. Of course her mother would say her overactive imagination was to blame, while darling Gran would no doubt put it down to her granddaughter's 'empathic abilities'.

She smiled fondly.

Her mother was probably right.

At a hint of frying bacon on the air, her nose twitched and she grasped at a happier thought.

Breakfast.

Pushing the lingering visions of the dream to the back of her mind, she bent to retrieve her dressing gown from under a ball of slumbering feline. He flicked her an indignant glance before curling himself more tightly into the snug spot on the quilt, earning himself an amused snort.

'Oh, humble apologies, your royal furriness.' She slipped on the dressing gown, not bothering to knot the belt, and padded in bare feet to the French doors. Opening them with a flourish, she was greeted by the dewy brightness of a fine morning.

Unable to resist stepping onto the balcony, she filled her lungs with fresh air while taking in the vista. Her gaze swept over the greener than green hills, glistening harbour, and stretch of blue overhead broken only by a bank of steel-grey clouds on the horizon.

With a sigh she raised her face and hands to the sky,

stretching her fingers as though to absorb the new day's offerings. Her sleep-tousled hair tumbled down her back, and her dressing gown fell open, exposing the silk chemise beneath.

Unaware the morning sun's rays bestowed on her an ethereal glow, or that the man working in the stretch of garden to the left of the building had stopped to stare, she continued paying homage to the beauty surrounding her, until growls from her stomach forced her to move.

Her admirer watched until she disappeared inside, before returning to the task of gathering the chef's precious rocket and fresh parsley from the well-tended herb garden.

Harvesting garnishes wasn't really his job, he was just doing it to appease chef Carl, who tended to make a song-and-dance when informed, even in advance, that he was to both cook *and* serve dinner in the castle. Well, Carl would just have to get over it, and it wouldn't hurt Emma to pitch in either.

Even butlers deserve an occasional night off.

As she emerged from breakfast in the Lodge's common room, Madeleine noticed the bank of clouds she'd glimpsed earlier moving in to hover overhead. Even as she gazed upward, ominous drops fell on her bare arms. How did the locals describe the peninsula's weather? Inclement. That was it.

Maybe the wildlife tour she'd planned to take would be more enjoyable on another day. Besides, she was yet to fully explore the castle and the nearby town of Le Froid, both good rainy day sightseeing options.

Back in her room, she tied a cardigan around her polo-shirted shoulders and set off to the castle, jogging through the spits of rain. No longer shrouded in night's gloom, the aged building felt more welcoming, if a little more damp in the drizzle.

Making her way inside, she began an exploration of its inner sanctums, touching doorknobs turned by past hands, inhaling air containing memories of past breaths, and picturing the daily lives of the building's past inhabitants. She struck pockets of warmth from internal heating but also a stony chill from the unheated hallways and dark, unused rooms, making her glad of the cardigan's warmth.

After soaking in the atmospheres of the top and middle floors—the aura of whimsy about the lady's bay-windowed drawing room, the genteel solemnity of the gentleman's room, the strong sense of duty to kin and country in the master bedroom—she made for the staircase leading to the castle's lower level.

Taking care not to slip on the worn-smooth stone steps, she descended into the dank gloom of the ground floor.

Once her eyes adjusted to the dimness she headed along the corridor, her footfalls whispering over the flagstones as she passed each doorway. Two stood open, revealing chambers empty of all but tourist posters and stands of wilting brochures, while the other doors were firmly shut. Then, at the end of a short passageway on the left, a single, closed door with a STAFF ONLY sign above the frame snagged her gaze.

It wasn't the sign that set her spine tingling. It was Gran's words, 'See if you can find a room marked with a musical symbol,' replaying in her head, and the decorative carving in the door's ancient timber.

After a furtive glance around, she sidled up to trace a finger over the cobweb-strewn carving.

A treble clef.

She tried the tarnished bronze door knob, and the aged metal parts grated promisingly only to seize an instant later, still in the locked position. Taking a step back she stood frowning at the door, until her ears caught the thump of footfalls on the floor above, heading for the staircase.

Time to go.

About to retrace her steps, she paused to whisper into the thick, unyielding silence outside the locked room, 'I'll be back.'

4

Emma looked up with a smile. 'Afternoon, Miss Brande.' She eyed Madeleine's sizeable shopping bag. 'Heading into Le Froid?'

'Yes. I explored the castle this morning, and thought I'd do a tour of the town this afternoon. The shuttle should be here soon to collect me.'

'Excellent choice for a rainy day. Now, how can I help you?'

'Can I take one of these?' and Madeleine indicated the pile of castle information brochures at the wall end of the counter. 'Meant to grab one when I checked in, but forgot.'

'Of course, help yourself.' When the phone behind her chimed Emma gave a distracted, 'Enjoy the tour,' as she turned to answer the call.

Nodding her thanks, Madeleine flicked open the brochure as she headed for the door.

Ooh ... a history of the castle. Promising.

It was rare for her to hope her transportation might be delayed, but it *would* give her time for a read before the shuttle arrived.

As she closed the brochure and went to tuck it in her bag, something slipped out and fluttered to the floor at her feet.

A postcard.

Bending, she scooped it up and eyed the picture on the front. It was a scaled-down copy of the painting gracing the wall beside her.

The painting of the *Polly Brown*.

Behind the reception desk, Emma ended the call and hung up. Seeing Madeleine standing staring at a postcard in her hand, she called, 'Don't tell me, you were expecting a pretty shot of the castle or grounds, right?' She gave a disdainful sniff. 'Well, it wasn't *my* idea to feature the castle's artworks on postcards, and have a gazillion of the damn things printed.' Lowering her voice, she added sourly, 'And end up having to *give* them away just to be rid of them.'

Flashing her a token smile, Madeleine slipped the postcard into her bag and made her way outside, where she paused on the stone staircase to bask in the shaft of sunlight that broke through the clouds. The light glinted off a bench seat situated beneath a blossom-filled arbour in the circular front garden.

The perfect spot to sit and wait ... and read the brochure.

She skipped down the stairs and across the drive to the bench, where she settled herself with a contented sigh beneath the twisted boughs of wisteria dripping with aromatic lilac blooms. From the shopping bag at her feet she extracted the brochure, and began to read.

Lorienne Castle has presided over the peninsula since the 1880s, when titled gentleman Richard Lorienne chose the site to build his family home, a literal castle. A well-to-do timber merchant, Lorienne chose to position the castle where he could watch the ships that ferried his lumber from east and west entering the harbour port. In the search for the best site, he and his young son rode the peninsula for months, often climbing trees to sample the view.

Once the location was secured, Lorienne sourced local timbers: Tasmanian blackwood, myrtle, blackheart sassafras, and Tasmanian oak for the castle's flooring and panelling. Other materials including Italian marble, Welsh slate, Venetian glass, and French tiles were shipped to the port and carted to the building site by dray.

Sadly, Lorienne did not live to see his castle completed, nor to enjoy the views he had so doggedly sought, but his dream was kept alive and realised by his son, Edward.

It took many years for the workforce of craftsmen to complete the construction, with Edward sparing no expense in making his father's vision a reality. The workmen lived on the grounds, even after the Loriennes took up residence, finishing the fine wood carvings and fretwork you see today.

Edward and family enjoyed many happy years at the castle, until a series of mishaps spelled an end to their idyll. Firstly, a dray carrying marble intended for the ballroom extension overturned, spilling its precious load and crushing the unfortunate driver to death.

Shortly after this misfortune, unmarried castle maid Molly Dillon was found to be "in the family way", and ordered to leave the estate in disgrace. She obeyed by climbing to the parapet and throwing herself from the battlements. In a scribbled note left in her cramped maid's room, she wrote of being alone in the world, with nowhere to go and no one to turn to; of there being only one course of action open to her.

It was later discovered that the dray driver killed in the accident had in his possession a ring sporting a tiny diamond chip. An unspectacular piece of jewellery by today's standards, it was worth possibly as much as a year's wages to the dray man. Could he have been the father of Molly Dillon's child, on his way to propose to the unfortunate girl? Either way, theirs were sad tales indeed.

And there was more grief awaiting those at the castle.

A family scandal preceded Edward's tragic death, sustained in the 1902 shipwreck of the Polly Brown. *Soon after, he was followed to the grave by his wife, Elizabeth, for whom he had built the ballroom as a wedding gift.*

Madeleine lifted her head and nodded, a faraway look in her eyes.

There it was, in black and white, the family scandal Gran had always fretted over, believing it was based on a false accusation.

Madeleine lowered her gaze to continue reading.

It's hard to imagine the magnificent ballroom, with its multiple fireplaces, stained-glass windows, chandeliers, and highly polished timber floors, being used as a barn to house sheep, but that did happen after the property was abandoned.

If you stand in the central doorway you'll see two entwined Es in polished brass above your head, testimony of Edward's love for his wife. And if you pause and listen under one of the chandeliers, you just might catch the faint echo of a ball in progress. The hum of genteel conversations, clinking of crystal glasses, and the swish of silken gowns....

Goosebumps sprouted on Madeleine's arms.

.   .   .

Dark days were ahead for the family, however. The spate of tragedies, in particular the deaths of Edward and Elizabeth, childless and under a scandalous cloud, followed by the subsequent legal battles over the estate's ownership, tore the remaining Loriennes apart. They quit the castle, abandoning it to the whims of the windswept peninsula.

Thus forsaken, the property deteriorated to such a degree, it took years of dedicated effort by the current owners, the McAlister family, to restore its original splendour. There are sections of the castle still awaiting restoration to this day, and not open to visitors for that reason.

'Well isn't this a pretty picture.' When she gave a start and clutched her chest, the intruder raised a hand. 'Oh, sorry, didn't mean to startle you.'

She sucked in a breath and glanced up at him. 'I thought I was alone out here ... Byron, isn't it?'

'At your service.' He bowed low and on straightening, fixed her with an admiring gaze. 'Once again, sorry for the intrusion. I was on my way to the ballroom and saw you sitting here. As your resident butler, I wondered if I might bring you something, a hot beverage perhaps?' His voice trailed off and for an instant, his expression conveyed a touching uncertainty.

Seeing that, Madeleine graced him with a warm smile. 'Thank you for the kind offer, but I'm waiting for the shuttle, which should arrive any minute.'

'Right. Well in that case I'll leave you to your reading,' and he tilted his darkly stubbled chin at the brochure she'd dropped in her lap. 'Interesting history, isn't it?' At her nod, he added, 'And what's in there only scratches the surface.'

'Really?' She arched an eyebrow. 'Of course, as part-owner I'm sure you have lots of "inside info" not available to the general public.'

He fingered his chin. 'Some.'

When he smiled into her eyes, she couldn't help smiling back. They gazed at each other and then, with a dip of his head, he wished her a good day and strode off. She watched him go, taking in his manly physique and firm stride, before blinking and returning her gaze to the brochure.

Before being rescued by the McAlisters, the abandoned castle sheltered many souls beneath its roof. Soldiers were billeted here during the war, with officers housed in Edward's and Elizabeth's grander quarters. The lower ranks shared the smaller children's and maids' rooms on the upper floors. Some 'grunts' left messages on the walls in what they obviously found to be cold, cramped, and often airless rooms.

Other inhabitants also left their marks, after the castle was commandeered by the government of the day for use as an insane asylum. One notable etching reads, 'You'll never know', signed, 'the Oyster'. Infamous thief Fred Chalmers, known as 'The Oyster', spent the last days of his life in the asylum. And he was right, no-one knows for sure what he meant by that cryptic note carved in an age-softened window surround.

There may be a clue however, in the newspaper article you will find on display in that room. An account under the headline, 'Oyster Holes up in Deserted Castle', reports that Chalmers took refuge in the then vacant castle, while being pursued for the theft of The Bedazzler, a priceless pearl and diamond necklace brazenly snatched from the throat of a visiting dignitary's wife.

Another newspaper article, dated some eighteen months later, reported that Chalmers had been found and apprehended, but that the necklace was never recovered. After being pronounced clinically insane Chalmers was committed, in a strange twist, to his old bolt-hole, Lorienne Castle. Not long after being consigned here, he took the secret of the Bedazzler's whereabouts to his grave.

These are just a few stories the aged building has deigned to share from its store of tales. And what would a castle be without secrets swirling wraith-like in its shadowy corners?

One thing's for sure, Richard Lorienne could not have imagined the trysts, tribulations, and tragedies his castle would witness over the years, nor the war-weary, ill-fated, and troubled individuals its ramparts would shelter from the wilds of the windswept peninsula.

Snapping the brochure shut, Madeleine sat staring into space.

There might be one less secret 'swirling wraith-like'

within the castle if she could make good on her promise. Gran had spoken bitterly of Elizabeth's 'fall from grace' and its consequences, including the tarnishing of the de Brande Barlow name, which was subsequently shortened in the hope of distancing the family from gossip.

The crunch of tyres on gravel brought her back to the present.

5

As the shuttle lumbered onto the circular drive, a dozen pairs of eyes gazed out through the vehicle's antiglare windows and were met with a smile from the waiting woman. The door slid open as the bus stopped beside her, and the sandy-haired driver flashed a boyish grin.

'Well hello there, Miss. I have one final passenger to collect for a tour of the fascinating local metropolis. I'm hoping that might be you?'

Madeleine's smile widened. 'Who am I to refuse such a tempting offer?'

'Excellent, come aboard.' After she'd settled into a seat, close to the front he noted with pleasure, the driver put the shuttle into gear with a metallic crunch and bounced it into motion.

Swinging the dash-mounted mic close to his mouth he announced, 'Right-o ladies and gents, let's get this show on the road. First let me introduce myself. I'm Jeff, your driver and tour guide today. Right now we're on our way to the town centre, our first stop, and from there to Le Froid's historic railway station.'

As they bumped along the castle's access road and through its impressive wrought iron gates, he changed up a gear. 'So you might want to have your cameras ready, folks. Lots of happy snapping coming up.'

'If you're looking for somewhere to grab a tasty counter meal,' Jeff announced as they trundled away from the last stop on the tour, 'I can recommend an eatery frequented by us locals, one that'll fill your tummies without emptying your wallets.' He indicated a brick building on a corner to their right.

A sign, hung amid its ornate cemented facades, read *The Cloak and Dagger*.

'This hotel was built in the 1880s,' he went on in tour guide mode, 'in the revived Italian Renaissance style. And if you go inside, you'll swear you're in a quaint British pub.'

Only half listening to his well-rehearsed banter, Madeleine gazed idly at the building through the rivulets of rain on her window, until his words filtered through.

'It has a great atmosphere and the food's beaut too. I can never resist the house speciality, bangers-'n-mash.'

That evening she once more stood on the castle's circular drive, this time waiting for a taxi. After another check of her watch, Madeleine tugged down her tailored battle jacket and ran a hand over her cream shift. She liked the way its silky knitted fabric skimmed her curves, the hem brushing the tops of her favourite tan leather boots. When she reached up to check the clasp in her hair, the movement sent shiny wisps drifting around her temples, cheeks, and neck.

'Ah, but you look *wery* nice, yah?' Beside her, tall, blonde Thomas Meier gave a broad smile, and waved a hand to include his wife, Selena. 'Both.'

'Why, thank you, Thomas.' Madeleine's grin encompassed the young couple. She was glad they'd accepted the spur-of-the-moment invitation to join her for dinner in town. Dining out alone was always less fun.

When their cab arrived a few minutes later, she spotted a familiar face behind the wheel. As she climbed into the back seat, she smiled into the admiring eyes in the rear-view mirror. 'Doing a spot of moonlighting, Jeff?'

His grin widened as he accelerated away from the kerb. 'You know how it is. A man's gotta do what he can to make a quid these days, even if it means being at the beck 'n call of you ten-dollar-tourist types.'

She chuckled and glanced at Thomas and Selena, who looked fazed by their driver's rapid speech. When they shrugged at each other and turned to gaze out the windows, she caught Jeff's eye in the mirror again.

'So, where to?' he asked.

'We're taking you up on your suggestion to dine at the Cloak and Dagger.'

He grinned. 'And you won't regret it.'

'Say, I think you mentioned being a local boy, Jeff?'

'Born and bred.'

'And you'd hear a lot of talk while driving people around?'

'I've been described as a good listener ... among other things.'

At his roguish wink she arched an eyebrow and plunged on. 'So a little bird told me the McAlisters might be considering selling the castle. Do you know if that's true?'

His chin crinkled as he pondered the question, his gaze on the road ahead. 'Well now, that's a sad story. You see,' and he fell back into tour guide mode, 'the whole family went into the venture with big plans, intending to restore the castle to its original splendour. Then the scale of the task became apparent, and more than a little overwhelming.

'Didn't help that Kathryn McAlister's obsession with

restoring the place didn't diminish at the same rate the money did. Word has it her husband tried to tell her to go easy on the spending but she wouldn't hear of it, had to have things just *so* for the castle, no matter the cost. And to be fair it *was* her money, inherited from a wealthy relative. Anyway, in the end hubby issued an ultimatum, "me or the castle", and the castle won.'

Madeleine gave a breathy whistle. 'Ouch.'

'Yeah, and the family's bank balance took a hit as well. McAlister was entitled to a fourth share in the place when they parted ways, a substantial sum as you can probably imagine. The remaining three have been struggling on ever since, financially speaking. Unable to continue with the restorations after the first stage was finished, so the story goes.'

'I guess it would make sense for them to sell up, even if it'd be a wrench.'

'Maybe not a wrench for all of 'em.' He flicked Madeleine a glance in the mirror. 'There are whispers the daughter might not be averse to cutting their losses and quitting the castle.' He returned his gaze ahead. 'The other two are still committed to the place, so I'm told, but having to pay out another third share would probably ruin them.'

'I see.'

As he nosed the cab around a corner, Jeff's tone lightened. 'Here we are, folks,' and he brought the cab to a stop outside the cosily lit Cloak 'n Dagger.

In the passenger seat Thomas took out his wallet—

paying their fare, he'd informed Madeleine earlier, was his non-negotiable right as their 'accompanying man'. So she opened her door to take in the town's sights, sounds, and the potpourri of grilling steak, cigarette smoke, and exhaust fumes.

Before climbing out, she caught Jeff's eye and smiled. 'Thanks for the ride, and the local info.'

'You're most welcome, any time.' He didn't bother to hide the invitation in his eyes. 'Any time at all.'

The moment she entered the Cloak and Dagger, Madeleine sent him silent thanks. Resisting the impulse to announce in a bad British accent, 'Well, isn't this pub simply tickety-boo,' she made her smiling way to the dining room.

Bathed in soft yellow light from coach lamps and with tavern-esque music playing in the background, the room was furnished with chunky wooden booths, and sported polished floorboards, and wainscoted walls lined with soccer jumpers and pennants. At the intricately carved timber bar, gleaming brass beer taps offered English lager and stout according to the labels on their ice-encrusted shanks.

A smattering of early diners in the room chatted quietly over bangers and mash, roast beef and Yorkshire pudding, steak and kidney pie 'n peas, and for the fast eaters, dessert of jam roly-poly and custard.

Madeleine led the way to one of the booths near the

front windows, and the three sat to peruse the menu. When German voices boomed from a nearby table, she noticed the Meiers prick their ears, so she asked, 'Would you like to go meet them?'

At their enthusiastic nods she slipped from the booth to let Selena out. While waiting for her to clamber past, Madeleine spotted a group of diners smiling at her from a nearby booth.

From: Madeleine.Brande
To: Connie.Brande
Re: Travelogue, day 3

I hope you're doing what the 'damn doctor' tells you without argument, Mum (that's it for the nagging so now you can relax * winky face *).

Thanks for the news from home, and for sending one of your minions to the spelling stable to check on Razoo. I'm sure you think I'm fussing, but Razzy *is* an Anglo Arab, not a run-of-the-mill horse, so I need to know he's being properly cared for.

And now for a round-up of what your 'ten dollar tourist' daughter has been up to.

Well, so much for the harbour cruise we'd earmarked in the brochure. The morning came over rainy so I opted instead for a daytime exploration of the castle ... and it won't be the last for a few reasons.

After lunch I took a bus tour of Le Froid's highlights, including the historic railway station you were keen to visit. I grabbed a brochure while we were there so you can read more about it, and I have photos to show you when I get home.

By the time I returned to the castle the day visitors had all gone, so I could wander the grounds freely. The property is really something, Mum. Whoever does the gardening really knows their stuff. I also took in the view from the castle's parapet, something I'd missed doing this morning as there was a queue waiting to climb the narrow staircase.

First called 'Lorienne's Look' and later 'Edward's Folly', the parapet was specially built so the Loriennes could watch their timber ships sail into the harbour. I guess back then Richard and Edward climbed those steep stone stairs a lot, but I'd hate to negotiate them in the dark. And although there were no day trippers hogging the staircase, I still ran into someone mid-flight.

And not just anyone.

It was Byron McAlister, one of the castle's current owners. He also buttles—rather well I must say—at dinner, and is something of a dish himself. So it wasn't too awful having to squeeze past him on the stairs. * winky face * And speaking of food, I had dinner in town last night at a delightful British-styled pub, where I met three other Aussies also on holiday.

Hey, you know the cat I told you about? He's officially claimed me as his BFF, so I've decided to name him Topaz, which is friendlier than calling him 'the cat'.

Oh, and before I forget ... remember I told you on the phone about the dream I had on my first night here? Well I had another vivid one last night. It was about a shipwreck, probably inspired by a painting in the castle of the ship that sank with Edward Lorienne on board.

And on the subject of Edward, I read in the castle brochure that he added the ballroom wing as a gift for his wife. What a cool guy. It's a shame he died without leaving a son to carry on the fine, gentlemanly tradition.

Until next time....

Luv,

Maddie xxx

6

'Morning, Madeleine.' A smiling Alan Jenkins made room for her at the breakfast table as the others nodded their greetings.

Jill Fox looked up from her honey-drizzled porridge to ask, 'Did you sleep well?'

'No ghostly visitations I hope?' Alan cut in, arching a teasing eyebrow.

Madeleine grinned and pulled out a chair. 'No visitations at all ... unless you count Topaz.'

'Topaz?'

'My feline roommate. He was in the room when I checked in, and doesn't appear to see any reason why he should leave. Not that I really want him to; I like having a roomie.'

'Oh, I would too.' Jill gave a wistful sigh. 'I *adore* cats but Peter won't let me have one.'

'I would,' her husband muttered from beside her, 'if I enjoyed sneezing out cat hair.' Ignoring his wife's glare, he shovelled another forkful of bacon and eggs into his mouth.

'Good morning, Madam.' The deep voice behind Madeleine ran featherlike fingers along her spine. 'What can I get for you?' Byron gazed down at her, butler persona firmly in place.

When she merely stared at him, he prompted, 'A hot drink to start, perhaps?'

'Oh ... ah ... yes. Um ... English Breakfast tea, please? White, and strong.'

'Right you are.' With a dip of his head, he strode to the buffet and took an elegant porcelain teapot from under a woollen cosy decorated with a coat of arms.

As she watched him pour steaming amber liquid into a fine china cup, Madeleine ran her eyes over his informal dress of cream chinos and white shirt. His hair, no longer slicked back in severe butler style, wasn't as dark as she had first thought. More brown than black....

'If I were your age and single,' Jill murmured close by her ear, making her jump, 'I'd quite like the cut of our butler's jib.' She indicated Byron with a lift of her chin, gave another wistful sigh, and leaned back to spoon sugar into her coffee.

Bemused, Madeleine hastened to change the subject. 'So, what are your plans for today?'

'Exploring the castle and grounds in more detail.' It was obvious the prospect pleased Jill more than her greasy-chinned husband.

Noting his down-turned mouth, Madeleine said brightly, 'You're in for a treat. The quality of workmanship is astounding, especially in the famous "hanging" timber staircase.'

'Yes, well, I've already seen examples of the woodwork.' Peter gave a patronising sniff. 'It's okay.'

Madeleine couldn't hold back a disbelieving frown. 'We mustn't be talking about the same thing. Nobody could describe the expert craftsmanship on display in the castle as simply "okay".'

'Well, you see, I'm more fussy than your average person.' He puffed out his chest. 'And something of a handyman myself—'

'So says the "handyman" who built the "stairs of death" at our place.' Glancing at a wide-eyed Madeleine, Jill explained, 'That's what the family christened the steps he constructed.' She caught her husband's indignant frown and her expression grew mulish. 'And rightly so. I've nearly come a cropper more than once on those damn stairs.'

To forestall the imminent quarrel, Alan gave the stony-faced Peter a good-natured thump on the shoulder. 'Women, hey old man? No livin' with 'em, but no livin' without 'em either.'

'You've got that right,' Peter said dourly.

Swallowing a grin, Madeleine turned to find a steaming teacup by her elbow, placed there by the ever-discreet Byron. Silently applauding his unobtrusive waiter skills, she sipped her tea and let the table conversations wash over her, before rising to grab a bowl of fresh fruit and yoghurt from the buffet. This she followed with sourdough toast, spread with a tangy marmalade made, the label proudly declared, from fruit grown on the castle grounds.

Humming as she strolled back to her room a while later, the sky overhead a clear blue and the sun's rays warming her face and shoulders, Madeleine decided this was not a day to spend indoors. She did need to check her emails, but that too could be done outside. She might even place an order for a picnic lunch from the castle's kitchen....

After hanging up the phone, she went into the bathroom to freshen up. Peering into the mirror, she applied daytime moisturiser to her face, then a touch of coral lipstick and a flick of eyeliner. Once she'd gathered her hair into a loose knot, she gave a satisfied nod at her reflection.

Now for the wardrobe.

Was it overly optimistic to assume the weather would remain sunny and warm? Her skirt and tee were fine now, but she'd been grateful for her cardigan the previous day....

With a shrug she slipped it off the hanger and tied it

around her shoulders. Next she slid her feet into white sandals, put her laptop into the trusty shopping bag amid the growing collection of tourist brochures and headed outside, swinging the bag in time with the tune in her head.

After meandering through the garden, admiring its meticulous layout and extensive collection of exotic plants, she found a park bench tucked away behind the coach house.

Perfect.

Seating herself in the dappled shade with a contented sigh, she plonked the bag beside her, tugged out the laptop, and began scanning the growing list of emails in her inbox.

As the shade grew sparse, allowing the late morning sun's rays to bring beads of moisture to her cheeks and neck, she yawned ... for the third time. Work-related messages didn't make the most scintillating reading, that was for sure.

Time for a break.

Snapping the laptop shut she stretched, and slid along the bench to the shadier end, where she propped herself sideways and stretched her legs along its length.

What harm could it do to close her eyes for a minute? She was on holiday, and no-one would see her tucked away there.

· · ·

Picnic basket in hand, Byron slowed to admire the pretty picture, framed by the garden's leafy greenery and back-lit by dappled sunlight. With her right arm supporting her head, Madeleine's left hand—free of wedding band or even a tell-tale pale mark, he noted—sat loosely on the laptop precariously balanced on her lap.

Stopping a few feet away, he let his eyes rove over her sun-pinked face, taking in the wisps of hair clinging to her cheeks in places, and the smattering of freckles across her nose. Without the intrusion of those striking, inquisitive eyes, and with a mouth made for smiling—among other things—she looked, he decided, like the quintessential girl next-door.

He was still staring when her skin prickled and she jerked upright.

The sudden movement sent the computer sliding off her lap. With a gasp she made a clumsy lunge for it, just as Byron leapt forward to catch it one-handed mere centimetres above the paving, somehow managing to keep hold of the picnic basket in the process.

The manoeuvre brought his face very close to hers she realised, after blinking away the remnants of drowsiness. Hastily drawing back, she dropped her feet to the ground and smoothed her skirt with unsteady hands.

What was she thinking, going to sleep on a park bench like some hobo?

'I believe this is yours.' Appearing maddeningly unaffected, he gave a lazy grin and handed her the laptop.

'Yes, um, thanks.' Summoning a grateful smile, she set the laptop on the bench beside her, making sure to wedge it against the backrest, and then glanced at the picnic basket. 'Is it that time already?'

'Midday delivery, as requested.' He passed it to her. *'Bon appétit.'*

'Thanks. Say, that was a brilliant save, one-handed and all.'

'Don't mention it. All part of the service. And you've picked a pleasant spot to ... shall we call it work?' His smiling, chocolate-brown eyes held a definite twinkle as he gazed down at her.

'Yes, well ... I *am* on holiday, after all.' She sat straighter and lifted her chin.

Still he lingered, and indicated the bench. 'May I?'

'Oh. Um. Yes ... yes, of course.' She slid along to make room. 'Fancy falling asleep like that, and so early in the day too. I'm not normally one for "nana-naps".'

'If you say so, m'lady.' With a smiling wink he settled himself beside her, stretching out his long legs, linking his hands behind his head, and squinting at the sky. 'Though you don't need to feel embarrassed about taking a nap.' No butler-ish mouth plum this time. 'Like you said, you're on holiday and free to sleep whenever and wherever you like.'

'I guess so....'

He lowered his gaze to her laptop. 'Although it appears you've been working.'

'Just checking emails, in case there was something important.'

'And was there?'

'A few.'

Not that it was any of his business. Though ... she did have him to thank for her undamaged computer.

She cleared the frown from her brow. 'I didn't get to read through them all before....'

'Mr Sandman came calling?' At her sheepish nod, he fixed her with a teasing gaze. 'So it was really *his* fault you fell asleep.'

They shared a laugh.

Sobering, she said, 'I *was* feeling tired, though. Haven't had the most restful of sleeps since arriving here.'

He sat straighter. 'Something wrong with your room?'

'No, it's perfectly fine. I've just been having some ... vivid ... dreams, which isn't all that unusual for me I guess. Mum says they're a product of my overactive imagination.'

'Dreams? What about?'

'Oh you know, ghostly apparitions, a shipwreck....'

'Yeah? Definitely not the cheeriest things to dream about.'

'As the ship went down,' she said, her tone sombre, 'I could hear the passengers screaming. It was really quite awful.'

Byron tapped his chin. 'There was this one tale about a

seafaring disaster ... now, how did it go?' He clicked his fingers. 'Oh yeah.' Rising, he struck a pose, one hand on his heart and the other stretched out front with the palm upright, fingers pinched together. Assuming a solemn expression, he recited in baritone, 'The boy stood on the burning deck, his pocket full of crackers....'

Madeleine gave a loud groan and slumped against the backrest.

'One fell down between his legs and blew off both his—'

'Enough!' Spluttering with laughter she threw up a hand and shook her head at him. 'You cad. There I was, thinking you empathised with me.'

'Just thought you looked like you needed cheering up.'

Her lips twitched. 'I bet you got a distinction in "Larrikinism 101" at Be-A-Butler College.'

Grinning, he assumed a self-important expression. 'Well, much as I don't like to brag....' The plum was back in his mouth. 'There's no denying that what you see before you, madam, is an academically gifted butler.'

At her spluttered, 'Not that you like to brag,' he bowed and resumed his seat.

They chuckled together, her eyes taking in the laughter lines on his face until her gaze locked with his and she felt a jolt, like electricity arcing between them.

Hastily turning away and clearing her throat, she didn't see the corresponding change in his expression, from easy conversation to bewilderment.

'Thanks for delivering my lunch,' she said crisply, 'and for saving my laptop. I'd be lost without it.'

The crease still in his brow, Byron rose saying, 'My pleasure, Madam.' The butler was back. 'If there's nothing more, I'll wish you a pleasant day.'

She dipped her head at him. 'The same to you.'

As he strode away, she sat chewing her lip and reminding herself why she was here, at Lorienne Castle.

And it wasn't to find a new love interest.

Although....

7

From: Madeleine.Brande
To: Connie.Brande
Re: Travelogue, continued

I knew you'd read more into my casual mention of Byron than it was due, Mum. When are you going to accept that your daughter is a dyed-in-the-wool singleton who lacks the moral fibre to sustain a long term relationship? Something of which we are now all painfully aware. But let's not dwell on that subject.

On a side note, Byron appears to be involved with someone else. I was at dinner with the mainlanders I met at the British pub the other night, when who should come in with arm candy glued to his side but Byron. The girl clearly wanted him all to herself, whisking him away to a secluded corner as soon as she could.

Thus ends the trivia.

While I was in town I sent off a postcard for you, bearing a picture of the *Polly Brown,* the ship Edward Lorienne was travelling in when it sank. The original painting of the ship is on display in the castle's foyer. And speaking of pictures, I found an inscribed group photo hanging in the gallery I figured you'd find interesting ... considering.

I took down the inscription, which reads *1892 Family portrait taken at front of Lorienne Castle. In the foreground is Henry Montville de Brande Barlow and his infant son, Charles.*

How exciting is that? A photo of great-great-granddad Henry, and great-granddad Charles, right here, in the castle. You must tell Gran I found it. Hopefully this little snippet will lift her spirits.

Now I'd better get ready for the wine tour I'm doing today. Looking forward to trying a tasty tipple or two!

Luv,

Maddie xxx

She pressed SEND and shrugged.

She'd purposefully glossed over the details of the restaurant encounter with Byron. Mentioning his broad smile on spotting her there would've had her mother jumping to all sorts of conclusions. And the teasing comment from one of her dinner companions that, 'Mr Just-a-butler-at-the-castle seems rather taken with you,' would've thrown petrol on an already smouldering flame.

Those were minor details anyway. They meant nothing.

Turning off the highway, the tour bus bumped along a dirt road toward the first winery on the list. The sign at the entrance to The Jump vineyard, located near a sweeping chasm, proclaimed it to have a 'dazzling variety of red and white wines served by an open fire, with an expert sommelier in attendance'.

The crackling fireplace in the corner of the tasting area certainly took the chill off the stone cellar building. All the same, Madeleine accepted the sommelier's offer of a 'fortified wine, to fortify you' with a glad smile. It was the first of many samplings from a tasteful selection of wineries, interspersed by offerings of water and palate-cleansing crackers.

By the time the bus set off on the return journey it was a battle to stay awake, with the outer and inner warmth dulling her mind and making her eyelids droop. Then she realised the bus was full of nodding heads and soft snores, so why fight it?

Pushing her folded cardigan against the window, Madeleine rested her head and gave in to sleep's unwavering summons....

. . .

In the dream, she sat at a dressing table in what was obviously a lady's bed chamber, brushing her hair. With every stroke, the embossed Gainsborough angel pattern of the Edwardian hairbrush glinted under the candlelight, reflected in the mirror.

Behind her, the satin coverlet of a generously cushioned Queen Anne bed also caught the light flickering from the candle holders. And in the background, dark burgundy drapes had been pulled back to reveal white lace curtains over a patterned glass window.

Then her eyes picked up movement close by.

An elderly woman very like Gran, or at least Gran before age and ill health diminished her, materialised to rest both hands on her shoulders.

Leaning in, the woman whispered, 'You're in Elizabeth's bedroom. It's just like we imagined, isn't it?' With a pleased smile, she withdrew her hands and stepped away from the light, to once more merge with the dimness.

In the dream, Madeleine whipped her head around, searching for the woman. Finding nothing but empty air and dark corners, she returned her focus to the ornate mirror, eyes widening as her reflection began to pixelate until her features were no longer discernible.

The shapely arm holding the hairbrush paused mid-stroke as a pair of bright, inquisitive eyes emerged from the hazy image, only to vanish again. Then came a pale face scrubbed of any traces of powder, fading away under a tumble of glossy, recently brushed hair.

The glossy locks fell almost to the wide neckline of an embroidered nightgown, which also began to pixelate.

Then, at the sudden rasp of a raised voice right behind her, Madeleine gave a start and dropped the hairbrush. It clattered to the dressing table as fear gripped her, robbing her of movement. Frozen to the chair, she could only claw at the stool's embroidered cushioning—

'Right folks, wakey, wakey! Time to get off the bus.'

Dinner in the castle that night was a little more sedate which suited Madeleine just fine, lost in her thoughts as she was.

'Ah, prawns and camembert with avocado cream,' the voice beside her announced, jolting her into the present. 'Quite the classic dish, you know.' Mandeep swept an enthusiastic glance around the other diners at the table. 'I am quite impressed.'

He was nothing if not a dedicated foodie.

Madeleine swallowed a grin.

When Byron arrived to collect their entrée dishes, he caught her eye and indicated the barely touched plate in front of her with raised, enquiring eyebrows.

'Oh. Um … yes … um … please tell the chef there's

nothing wrong with the dish. It's not the food, it's ... well ... it's me.'

His expression grew concerned. 'Is everything alright, Madel ... er ... Madam?'

'Of course.' She flashed a bright smile. 'I'm just ... not all that hungry tonight.'

'I see.'

With a measured glance he moved on, but after catching him looking her way more than once, she realised there'd be more questions if she didn't do justice to the next course.

What could she say about her lack of appetite that wouldn't make her sound crazy? *If I seem distracted it's because I'm attempting to solve a centuries-old family mystery about an ancestor who used to live here, in the castle, and was blamed—wrongly so, according to my grandmother—for the downfall of her husband's family.'*

Oh no, that wouldn't sound crazy at *all.*...

Despite a twitchy stomach she all but finished the main course of trout amandine, showcasing fish caught in the estate's own lake and served with duchesse potatoes. This earned her Byron's approving nod when he came to once more clear the dishes and deliver dessert. Thankfully the servings of meringue-topped queen pudding and freshly poached apricots were on the petite side.

While she savoured the creamy pudding, Madeleine's thoughts returned to her latest dream.

The bed chamber, the indistinct face. Had she dreamed

of Elizabeth? And what about the raised voice ... was it Edward's?

She gave a shiver.

From: Madeleine.Brande
To: Connie.Brande
Re: More Travelogue ... kind of

I wish Gran had given me some idea what the 'something to prove Elizabeth's innocence' might be. I've scanned every picture on the castle's accessible walls, studied the backs of paintings, searched for secret maps or clues, and peeked into 'off limit' areas through gaps and cobwebbed windows, hoping to find more about the Edward-Elizabeth story. And what did it get me? Nothing, except strange looks when people caught me doing it.

Scouring the local library's database has revealed more info on the castle's construction and Edward's business ventures though, and there was a brief account of the family's downfall and subsequent abandonment of the castle. That made me hope I was onto something, but while mention was made of the scandal that led to the downfall, there were no specific details.

So I'm no better informed as to what Elizabeth could have done that was so terrible. Surely not an affair? From what Gran has said and the pictures I've seen of the couple, they were very much in love, so what could have caused Elizabeth to stray?

I can't help wondering if her death so soon after Edward's is proof of innocence or guilt....

Anyway, that's enough intrigue for one day. I'm off to bed.

Luv,

Maddie x

8

The figure in the dream floated in and out of focus, tendrils of mist flowing around the body like a shawl spun from cobwebs. When it raised a diaphanous hand to cup Madeleine's face, the touch was like a gentle waft of cool air, holding no warmth or substance yet strangely comforting.

The figure bent her head to gaze into Madeleine's eyes. 'I see our family legacy, shining out at me.' The mellifluous words emanated from an indiscernible mouth in an indiscernible face, as if woven from the surrounding air.

'Elizabeth?' In the dream Madeleine's voice echoed thinly, sounding not at all like her own.

'Yes.' Drifting back a pace, the figure clasped her hands. 'How weary I have grown of the pain that fills my every moment, the eternal weeping from which my heart will not free me until I make my peace ... with him.'

'Him? You mean Edward?'

At the mention of her husband's name, Elizabeth's form trembled. 'Oh, to hear my beloved's name spoken with the warm throb of life in every syllable. What joy it brings in my sadness.' The fine thread of her voice was interwoven with tenderness and sorrow.

The comforting hand Madeleine extended met only cool, empty air.

'Would that I could feel your comfort, dear one,' Elizabeth said gently, 'but it is beyond my reach as are all good things. As is my one true love, who thought ill of me when forever taken from this life, and from me. The love we shared was crushed from his heart, with only the bitterness of betrayal to fill the void. It flowed into his veins like the cold waters of the ocean that claimed his earthly form.'

She bowed her head. 'How can a heart bear such pain? Knowing the one I love more than life perished, believing I had betrayed him and brought shame upon his family name. How can I declare my innocence when his face, that which I hold most dear, is turned from me forever?'

After composing herself, she went on in a flat, emotionless voice. 'Speaking of this brings only more anguish. Anguish upon anguish, ever growing, never diminishing. I must find the fortitude or forever languish in the torment of my besmirched virtue. This disgrace has been improperly thrust upon me and my family, and taints the memory of my existence.'

She took Madeleine's hands in a featherlike grasp. 'Please, help us regain our honour.' Her sigh at Madeleine's nod sent eddies of mist swirling around her. 'There is something hidden that must be found.'

'Yes, but what sort of thing?'

'Find the truth, prove the innocence of your stricken ancestor.' As she uttered the words, Elizabeth's image dimmed. The mist enveloping her lower body and face crept in to devour the rest of her image.

'Wait! Elizabeth. What am I looking for and where will I find it?'

'My strength wains....' The whispered words evaporated into the still air, as Elizabeth's countenance softened and her features blurred.

'Don't go, please. I have so many questions.'

The outstretched hand was barely more than a fragile wisp trailing from the enveloping fog. Before they too melted away, her translucent fingers brushed the tips of Madeleine's, and then she was gone.

From: Madeleine.Brande
To: Connie.Brande
Re: Travelogue

I had another dream, Mum, and in this one Elizabeth spoke directly to me. Not that she told me anything I didn't already know, of course. How could she, being only the product of my imagination?

Anyway, I'm at a loss how to proceed from here. I might take your advice and talk to Gran again. Could be there's something she hasn't thought to tell me before this, or only just remembered. Worth a try.

Wish you were here, sharing the ups and downs of this adventure with me.

Maddie xxx

At a quiet knock at the door Madeleine pressed the SEND button on her email, and rose to find an unexpected visitor standing on the doormat.

'Byron?' She gave a quizzical frown.

'Sorry to disturb you, Madeleine. I'm just trying to find the owner of these, left in one of the castle's downstairs rooms,' and he held up a pair of stylish cat-eye sunglasses. 'Something told me they might be yours.'

'Oh, super, thank you. I thought I'd lost them.' Smiling, she took them from him. 'Must stop wearing them on top of my head. I've lost a few favourites like that.'

His grin lit up his face. 'Glad I've reunited you. By the way, the room they were found in is empty, unused, so we leave the door closed and lights off to discourage tourists from entering. I'm curious as to why you were in there.'

Sprung.

'Just ... nosey I guess.' She twitched a mischievous eyebrow at him. 'And fascinated with the castle.'

As if on cue, the kettle sang in the kitchenette.

'I'd better get that.' When he made no move to leave she felt compelled to ask, 'Like to join me?'

'Thanks.' From the swiftness of his response it was obvious he'd been hoping for an invitation. As he stepped inside and closed the door behind him, the room immediately felt smaller.

While not an overly large man, Byron McAlister had a big presence.

Moving to the French doors Madeleine swept aside the drapes, allowing the vista to flood in accompanied by the sun's golden glow.

When Byron sauntered to the window to admire the view she tried not to ogle his wide-shouldered, slim-hipped physique in the chest-hugging polo shirt and butt-hugging blue jeans.

'Having someone else make the tea will be a pleasant change,' he said over his shoulder. 'By the way,' and he turned to look at her, 'you didn't answer my question.'

'Hmm?' At the sink, she pre-warmed the teapot with water from the kettle.

'You were in the closed room in the castle?' When instead of replying she began spooning fragrant English Breakfast tea leaves into the pot, he raised a hand. 'You're not in trouble or anything. I'm just curious why you'd bother going into a dark, empty room when others in the castle are way more appealing.'

'Well....'

It wouldn't be wise to let on what she'd been up to, but an abridged version might suffice.

'I'm attracted to intriguing places, being something of a mystery buff. And the castle is nothing if not intriguing.'

'An amateur sleuth, hey?' One of his dark eyebrows twitched. 'What sort of mysteries get your inquisitive nose twitching?'

'Well, right now I'm trying to solve a ... "cold case" I guess you could call it.'

'Involving the castle?'

His obvious intrigue left her certain she wasn't the only snoop ... er ... sleuth in the room.

Taking care to keep her expression neutral she asked, 'Wanna sit?' and indicated the table by the French doors. After bending to rattle around in the cupboards and extract two porcelain cups, a matching milk jug and sugar bowl, she eyed the pretty designs on the fine china and flicked Byron an approving glance. 'You guys certainly know how to do things around here. There isn't a dusty tea bag or mismatched mug to be found anywhere.'

'We aim to please.' From where he now sat at the table, Byron's deep voice settled on her like a warm caress. 'I take it you like it here, in our castle?'

'Oh yes.' Her words drifted from the depths of the compact fridge. Straightening with a milk carton in one hand and pack of spice-n-ginger biscuits in the other, she scanned the packet for the biscuits' use-by date.

Not out of Tutankhamun's tomb or the ark's pantry, scoring the establishment another mental tick.

Realising Byron was watching, she said quickly, 'I don't *like* your castle, I *love* it. It must be wonderful to own it, and to live and work here.'

'It is. At least,' and a crease formed between his dark brows, 'for Mum and me.'

No mention of co-owner Emma....

At a whistle from the kettle, Madeleine hastened to fill the teapot and open the biscuits. When she glanced up again and caught the look in Byron's eyes, her heart hammered in her chest and her fingers fumbled so much she tore the packet, almost ejecting the contents.

Byron chuckled. 'Glad to see it's not only me that does that.'

'You? I can't imagine you having any food-packaging malfunctions, Mr "Just-Right" Jeeves.'

'Thanks ... I think.'

They shared a grin.

'And this "Jeeves" is in the final year of an MBA, so I'll be—' Seeing her lift the laden tray he leapt up, hands outstretched. 'Here, let me.'

When his fingers brushed hers, something like voltage zapped between them and she sucked in a startled breath. The warm, tingling sensation went all the way up her arm and into her face, deepening the colour in her cheeks.

Byron stood motionless, incomprehension written across his features.

Had he felt it too ... whatever 'it' was?

She cleared her throat. 'I guess we should—'

'Would you like me to—'

They stopped, eyed each other, and burst into nervous laughter.

'What I was trying to say,' Madeleine said, lowering her gaze to the tray in his hands, 'is that we should have our tea before it gets cold.'

'And I was about to ask if you'd like me to pour.' The intimacy in his smile did nothing to lower her heart rate.

'Let me do the honours. Gotta be my turn, surely.'

'As you wish.' With a dip of his head Byron set the tray on the table, took the nearest chair, and watched her bend over the teapot to pour the tea.

Her hair, loose but for a headband keeping it back from her face, tumbled in glossy waves around her neck and shoulders.

Realising he was staring he cleared his throat, crossed his arms and said, 'Tell me about this cold case you're working on. I'm a sucker for a good mystery.' After a peek at his watch he added, 'Can't linger though. Duty will be calling soon.'

. . .

She flicked him an impish glance and parroted, 'As you wish.' Returning to the job of pouring the teas, she cast about for what she hoped would be a response that didn't reveal too much. Finally she said, 'I'm hoping to prove the innocence of an ancestor of ours, who we believe was falsely accused of wrongdoing.'

After taking the steaming teacup she handed him, he fixed her with an interrogatory gaze. 'And it has something to do with the castle?'

Damn, she should've seen that coming. Now what could she say that was both honest and non-committal?

She had to think, think, think. And stall.

Her eyes fell on the sugar bowl and she reached for it. 'Do you take sugar?'

'Nah. Sweet enough, or so I'm told.' He flashed a wink and took a sip. 'You make a good brew.'

'Why thank you, kind sir. Coming from you that's high praise indeed.'

'It's true I've made a few hot drinks in my time. Make that a few thousand.' He grinned at her from across the table. 'So, tell me, how are you going to prove this ancestor's innocence after all these years?'

Madeleine bent her head and stirred her tea, relieved he'd moved on from the earlier, trickier enquiry. 'That's the million dollar question, one I haven't found an answer to yet.' Raising her eyes, she was at first glad to find no incredulity in his expression, and then unsettled by the warm intimacy in his gaze....

'Perhaps I can help solve the case? Mystery *is* my middle name, after all.'

'Hmm ... Byron Mystery McAlister.' She pressed smiling lips together. 'Has a nice ring to it.'

'So does Madame Madeleine Clandestine Brande,' he said in his best butler voice.

'*Mistress* Madeleine Clandestine Brande, if you please.'

They laughed together until Byron took another hasty check of his watch. 'Oh-oh, the scullery calls.' He gulped the last of his tea. 'Others may work from sun to sun, but a butler's work is never done.' Rising, he paused to smile down at her. 'I've enjoyed sharing tea and mystery with you, Madeleine. We must do it again, soon.'

'Yes.' A thought occurred as she rose to see him out. 'Maybe you could give me the inside story about the Loriennes some time? I'm assuming there's more to their tale than what's in the brochure.'

'One or two tiny details, possibly.' He fixed her with a penetrating gaze. 'What say we discuss it over dinner one night? I have another off-duty coming up soon.'

The swiftness of his invitation startled her.

Would spending time with him create an obstacle in her investigations?

With what she hoped was a non-committal nod, she held the door open for him.

As he stepped out, leaving a fresh, woodsy man-scent in his wake, Byron bowed and wished her a 'pleasant morning' in his butler voice, before striding away.

She watched him go, through a gap in the doorway, thinking it had been an altogether unsettling encounter.

Much as she'd like to share the full story with him, it wouldn't be prudent. Byron McAlister was a part-owner of the castle after all, and might not approve of some of her investigative methods. Anyway, what did she know about him? Hardly anything, despite her heart carrying on as if they had some sort of connection....

Slowly pushing the door closed, she leaned against it. One thing was sure, she needed to make progress on the case, and fast.

Before a certain nosy butler could ask more tricky questions.

9

'It's Maddie here, Gran, calling from my room in Lorienne Castle.'

'Oh, how delightful, dear.' Antoinette's wistful sigh whooshed across the phone connection. 'A Brande in Lorienne Castle again, that brings back memories.'

Her elderly voice, once so firm and melodic, had grown weak and breathy over the years. Madeleine swallowed and blinked hard. Gran's time on earth was, as she'd taken to telling family members, 'drawing to a close'. Some good news about Elizabeth might give her a renewed lease on life ... if only Madeleine could come up with the goods.

'Did I tell you your great-great-grandmother, Constance, stayed in the castle for a while?' Antoinette went on. 'It was when her son, your great grandfather, Charles, first started school.'

'And did Mum tell you I saw a photo here,' Madeleine prompted, 'of great grandad Charles and his dad, Henry?'

'She did.'

The smile in Gran's voice had Madeleine smiling too. 'I've only scratched the surface with my snooping, though.'

Antoinette sniffed. 'I'd prefer another word to "snooping", but you young ones don't worry about things like that.'

Madeleine gave a fond chuckle. 'So, when was Constance here at the castle?'

'I don't recall exactly. Henry's business ventures had them moving around a lot in the early years. I do remember her splendid descriptions of castle life, though.'

'Made you wish you lived here?'

'As a child, yes. While I found Henry to be a little ... aloof ... I loved Constance. She used to say I was like the daughter she never had. You know I named your mother after her.'

Madeleine grinned to herself. Gran was off and running, reliving the past as she'd taken to doing more and more lately....

'Her only child, Charles, never married, though he had a son out of wedlock, to a woman Constance described as being from "unfortunate circumstances".' Antoinette's voice took on a dreamy quality. 'When the child's mother died and he came to live with his father, Constance became a grandmother ... of sorts. She wrote to me of meeting the boy, admitting she'd held doubts about his parentage.'

When Antoinette paused to cough and then swallow, worry for her gnawed at Madeleine's insides. Was Gran coming down with something? At her age, a cold could be deadly....

'Thankfully she never shared those doubts with Charles,' Antoinette continued, 'for they were dispelled by one look at the boy's topaz eyes.'

'Our family legacy.'

'One of them.' Antoinette sniffed. 'Anyway, Constance helped Charles raise James, and he became like another son to her. She never looked down on him for the unfortunate nature of his birth, nor would she allow others to do so. That boy, as you've probably guessed, was your Grandad, James, my darling husband.' Antoinette gave a tinkling laugh that turned into another cough. 'She gave me such an interrogation when James first took me to meet her.'

'You obviously passed muster.'

'Yes, although she took some convincing. Very protective of James and the family name, Constance was.'

'On that, how did she feel about the change of surname to plain old Brande?'

'What do you mean, *plain*? Brande is a fine name.'

'Sorry, Gran, I didn't mean it like that. I'm proud to be a Brande, just ... trying to fit all the pieces together. And right now I'm here, at Lorienne Castle, snoop— er ... searching for more pieces.' When the only response was another sniff, Madeleine said softly, 'I know you don't like going into details about family "skeletons", but it's time to tell me everything you know about what happened here. Please, Gran.'

'Well....' Antoinette cleared her throat. 'I suppose you're right. Who in the family will know what happened if I take the history with me when I go?'

Her voice firmed. 'When it first happened, Constance told me she was glad Henry shortened their surname from de Brande Barlow to Brande, as she'd never wanted triplets. She was such a card.'

In Gran's soft chuckle Madeleine heard echoes of her own, and smiled fondly at the precious family connection. 'You obviously enjoyed a close relationship.'

'We did.'

'Go on.'

'I recall her later complaining that the change of name caused problems in their business dealings. Said the disadvantage stemmed from ... what was it? Oh yes, "alleged youthful wickedness" is how she described it.'

'Alleged?'

'That's right. While unhappy about the consequences to the family, she never fully believed Elizabeth guilty of any wrongdoing.'

'Did she say what was behind this "youthful wickedness"? What actions led to Elizabeth's downfall?'

'Nothing specific, although I got the impression it was some sort of serious impropriety. In those days, it was easy for a young woman to fall foul of society's expectations.'

Madeleine thought back to her reading of the brochure. 'There's an account of another young woman here, a castle maid, falling into disgrace when evidence of her "impropriety" became obvious. She died too, but by her own hand.'

'Yes, that happened more than was made known in those days. A woman was often left "holding the baby"—literally in many cases—with indiscretions of this kind rarely considered to be the man's fault.'

Madeleine could imagine Gran shaking her head in disgust.

'Speaking of men and their faults,' Antoinette went on after once more clearing her throat, 'one of the few times I heard Constance criticise Henry was in regard to her sister-in-law's demise. You see, Constance believed he had failed Elizabeth badly, at the end of her life.'

'Failed his sister? How?'

'Apparently the siblings became estranged after Elizabeth's very public fall from grace. On hearing she was near death, however, Henry relented and rushed to his sister's bedside. He later reported to Constance that in her final moments, Elizabeth begged him to locate "from within the castle" what she said would "reveal the truth and lead to the deliverance of his stricken sister".'

At the other end of the call Madeleine sucked in a breath.

'According to Henry's account, she died before saying anything more.'

'No specific details about the proof she wanted him to find, or its location in the castle?'

'Sadly, no.'

'Henry still searched for it though?'

'He did not, and therein lies the source of Constance's criticism.' Antoinette's chesty exhale crackled over the phone connection. 'I don't think Henry believed Elizabeth, and to be fair, she *was* in the grip of death. It's possible he assumed they were simply the ravings of a dying woman and therefore not to be taken seriously.'

'So instead of doing what he could to fulfil her dying wish,' Madeleine muttered, 'my great, great grandad simply changed the family surname to avoid being connected to the scandal?'

'As I said, this was Constance's view of events. And keep in mind that in those days, a man's family honour meant everything. Unlike today....'

As Antoinette launched into one of her favourite gripes about the moral decay of contemporary society, Madeleine's mind wandered until the words, 'I never got to see the castle for myself, as you know,' brought her back to the present.

'I'm looking forward to seeing your photos,' Antoinette went on, 'so take plenty, of the interior, exterior, gardens and all.'

'Of course, Gran. Love you.'

After signing off, Madeleine sat staring out the window

as obligation and a fear of failure joined the apprehension tugging at her insides.

Would photos be all her grandmother ever got to see of the castle following the lopping of the 'blighted' de Brande Barlow branch from the Lorienne family tree?

Had things been different, had life-ending misfortunes not befallen Edward and Elizabeth, would her extended family and their ancestors have been welcome regular guests of the Loriennes? Most likely yes. And when the time came, Elizabeth's descendants may even have inherited a share in the castle, likely saving it from years of abandonment and desolation....

From: Madeleine.Brande
To: Connie.Brande
Re: More Travelogue

Firstly, I've spoken with Gran. More about that later. Now for some overdue reporting on my travels.

I finally got to do the harbour cruise and it lived up to the advertising blurb. We had calm weather so the well-informed captain took us cruising around the edge and pointed out the different birds, animals and landmarks on the way. We saw silver gulls, little penguins, flocks of short-tailed shearwaters and Australasian gannets. Also fur seals sunbaking on the rocks, expressions of pure bliss on their whiskered faces. :)

As for the shy albatross (also known as the shy mollymawk), they're medium-sized compared to their Wandering cousins, and are Australia's only endemic albatross. They breed on three remote islands off Tassie and are sadly classed as endangered. It was a real privilege to see some in the skies above us, living their seafaring lives.

While that was all delightful, what I found most interesting on the cruise was seeing the port where Edward Lorienne's timber ships docked all those years ago. I could visualise him standing on the dock, watching intently as his cargo was unloaded from the hold of a tall ship. * indulgent sigh *

But back to the cruise....

We were served champers on the return trip and sat sipping, enjoying the sunset, and listening to the slap of water against the hull while puttering to the jetty. I reckon you would've loved the cruise, Mum, and I'll be happy to do it again with you next time.

I'm dining in the castle again tonight, where there'll no doubt be more ghost stories. You talk about *my* overactive imagination! It's hard not to scoff at the reports of 'unexplainable sights, sounds, and smells' from the other guests, who are doing a bang-up job of talking themselves into believing all this spooky guff.

Now, getting back to my chat with Gran, she went into a little more detail but could only reiterate that Elizabeth left 'something' hidden in the castle somewhere; something she believed would prove her innocence. I've had a snoop around and am starting to think the 'something' has already been discovered and taken. Or is hidden somewhere I haven't been able to investigate yet, like in the off-limit rooms downstairs.

And speaking of off-limit places, I think Elizabeth's music room, the one Gran suggested I find, might be on the ground floor, locked like others in that area. Of course the fact they're locked makes me even more curious to discover what secrets they might hold....

Luv,

Maddie xxx

From: Connie.Brande

To: Madeleine.Brande

Re: 'Mainland' news

Thanks for the update, love.

As for my news, I don't want you to fly off and book the next flight home. Rest assured everything's okay here, but I thought you should know that Gran's health took a bad turn last night and she's been admitted to hospital.

And before you ask, it was the same old complaint, nothing at all to do with your phone call to her. She loves hearing about the castle and what you're up to down there, and is always asking me to read your latest email to her.

She gave us all a fright but is hanging in there. The

doctors are confident she'll recover and be able to return to the nursing home in the next few days.

Now, the last thing Gran would want is for this to spoil your holiday, so don't let it. I've been reading her your emails so keep them coming. And try not to worry, love. Just keep doing what you're doing.

Much love from me and your Gran,

Mum xoxo

As her distress diminished to a low burn Madeleine re-read the words, '... hanging in there,' and, '... keep doing what you're doing.' The subtext was, of course, 'We're counting on you to give Gran a reason to *keep* hanging in there.'

It was time to pull out all the stops.

Additional dinner guests arrived by shuttle that evening. They were greeted by a smiling Kathryn wearing a black and gold striped Victorian gown with cinched drop waist, black velvet jacket, and full skirt complete with bustle.

Byron too was in full butler mode during the dinner service, unobtrusively delivering the fragrant beef consommé and crusty French bread entrée, braised spatchcocks with steamed vegetables, and charlotte russe dessert. He only dropped the best-butler-ever act once, on catching Madeleine watching him. He flashed her a wink, after first making sure none of the other guests would notice.

In pride of place at the head of the table, Kathryn enthralled her audience with tales of the castle's heyday. 'The Victorian hostess's main goal was to flaunt her status and impress her guests. Much care was taken in her choice of menus, and in dressing both herself and her dining room for the occasion. Tables were ornately decorated, usually with a centrepiece of flowers or a fruit pyramid like this one,' and she indicated the tower of fruit presiding over the table's centre. 'All local produce, of course.'

When Kathryn paused to allow the diners to take in the centrepiece, Madeleine peered around the sizeable pillar of apples, strawberries, fuzzy kiwi fruit, and plump grapes. She saw Emma seated opposite, arms crossed, staring at the ceiling.

Had she been made to sit through this performance too many times?

'Guests were given menus,' Kathryn continued, 'often written in French. And meals were served in one of two ways. *A la Francaise*, where food was carved at the table and passed around, and *a la Russe*, as we do here, where food was ready to be served when brought to the table.'

A gloved hand appeared in Madeleine's side vision and a voice close by her ear murmured, 'I'm off-duty tomorrow,' as the hand whisked away her empty dessert bowl.

'Oh? How nice for you.' Heat crept up her neck.

Bending to add the bowl to the growing stack on the trolley, Byron murmured, 'So, are you free for that dinner we talked about?'

To hide her rising colour she bent her head and smoothed the linen napkin on her lap. Then a thought occurred. Flicking him a mischievous glance from under her lashes, she asked in a tone heavy with sugar, 'Will your pretty friend from the other night be joining us?'

This earned her a narrow-eyed, I-know-you're-teasing glance and a curt, 'No,' as he moved on to clear the next place.

When Kathryn rose from the table to invite her guests to the drawing room for post-prandial port and coffee, Madeleine politely declined and left the dining room. Once alone in the corridor she paused to listen before hastening on quiet feet to the butler's pantry. Cleared of dinner dishes, it was once again in scrupulous order. After slipping inside, she pressed herself against the nearest wall and listened.

The only sound was the hum of voices from the port-and-coffee set in the drawing room.

She blinked, and when her gaze fell on the ancient keys hanging from their spot on the wall, blew a breath through pursed lips.

So far, so good.

Hoping her hunch was right, she grasped the heavy

brass ring and lifted it down, taking care not to let the keys jangle. After wrapping them in a wad of tissues to muffle any noise they might make, she tucked the keys into her pocket and poked her head around the door.

All clear.

Slipping into the corridor, she crept to the lady's drawing room and made straight for the bay window. Once in the recess she drew the heavy damask drapes across, to shield herself from anyone entering the room.

Now she just had to wait for the castle to empty of people.

She settled herself on the cushioned window seat as the minutes ticked slowly past. In the silence her mind wandered to another night....

Banks of blinking, beeping machines surrounded a figure lying motionless on a hospital bed. Sanitised white sheets covered the patient's body, but his bruised and swollen face was clearly visible.

Visible, though unrecognisable.

And whose fault was that?

Squeezing her eyes shut, Madeleine fought to dislodge the recollection, only to have another memory lunge at her.

Local MD's reckless driving ends in tragedy the newspaper headline read, above an article reporting on a colleague's description of the incident....

'Speeding out of an intersection in his flashy sports car,

straight into on-coming traffic. It's no wonder he sustained life-threatening head injuries. If you ask me, he's lucky to be alive. Though I don't understand how this happened. I wouldn't have picked Dr de Voss as the reckless type.'

10

A creak of aged timber floorboards jerked Madeleine back to the present, and she held her breath as the rhythmic clicks drew closer.

Kathryn's Victorian heeled slippers would make that sort of clicking sound. Was she closing up for the night?

Then Madeleine's straining ears caught another set of footsteps, approaching with a light but determined tread.

'Mum?' a young woman's voice called.

The clicking footsteps stopped, right outside the door to the lady's drawing room.

From in her hiding place Madeleine froze.

'Yes, Emma.'

Yep, definitely Kathryn.

'I've been trying to talk to you all night but you've been too busy performing ... and finding other ways to avoid me.'

The pout was clear in Emma's voice, and she slurred some of her words.

After a pregnant pause her mother asked, 'How much wine did you have this evening?'

'Don't try to change the subject.'

Kathryn blew a long sigh. 'I wasn't avoiding you, Emma. And you know it's important for our guests to be entertained at dinner.'

'It's clearly important to you.'

Kathryn sighed again. 'So what is it you want to talk to me about?'

'I think you know.'

'Not this again....' An edge crept into her voice. 'We've been through this before, Emma. I don't want to sell the castle, and neither does Byron.'

'And I don't think you realise, mother, the difference between want and need,' Emma snapped. 'You and Byron may not *want* to sell the castle, but surely you both realise we *need* to. Make that *have* to. This damn place,' and her voice wobbled as if she were waving her arms around, 'is leaching money from our very bones.'

The edge in Kathryn's voice hardened into ice. 'No need to exaggerate.'

'You think I'm *exaggerating?*' Emma's voice rose. 'And is that what our bank manager, financial advisor, accountant, even our operational bottom line, are doing too? Simply *exaggerating* how dire our situation is?'

A fraught silence followed. Trapped into eavesdropping, Madeleine quelled the impulse to squirm.

'Mum, you can't keep avoiding this,' Emma muttered into the silence. 'The castle is ruining us. And I know you don't want to hear this, but Dad was right. Buying the castle was a bad idea.'

'Is that so?' It was Kathryn's turn to raise her voice. 'So you think your father was right about the castle. Right about how he treated Byron. Right to walk out on us all—' A choked gasp swallowed the rest of her words.

Another tense pause followed until Emma finally said, 'Sorry, Mum. I didn't mean—'

'So say what you *do* mean.' Kathryn's words swelled with unshed tears.

'Just that....'

Madeleine heard a fretful scuffing of the floorboards.

'We have to face facts, Mum. The castle's not paying for itself, it's not viable. And if we don't sell up soon, we'll go to the wall.'

'But, Emma,' Kathryn murmured, sounding tired now, 'the castle is our life.'

'Yours maybe, and Byron's, although I think his commitment is more from obligation than anything else. Because of what happened between him and Dad.'

'Let's not talk about that,' Kathryn snapped.

'No, let's sweep it under the carpet with the rest of our family dramas.'

'That's enough, Emma. I don't want to discuss this any further now.'

'So when will we discuss it? After the bankruptcy administrators come to oversee division of our assets?'

The only reply was an indignant click of heels as Kathryn made for the family's living quarters.

With a whispered, 'Damn,' Emma trudged after her, audibly switching off the lights as she went and leaving the castle in darkness.

At the heavy thump of the last door being shut, Madeleine released a long breath and frowned. Eavesdropping wasn't something to be proud of, but that certainly was an interesting conversation to overhear.

After reaching under her jacket for the compact torch she'd brought along for just such a purpose, she stood and opened the concealing drapes a crack, and shone the beam around the drawing room.

Empty.

All the same, she took care to switch off the torch and move quietly as she opened the drapes wider and slipped out, all the while pondering Kathryn's situation.

What did the future hold for her beloved castle, not to mention her at-odds family? And what was the skinny on Byron and his father?

It seemed the castle's closets contained more than one skeleton—

Wait, what was that? A shadow? Coming toward her?

Pressing a hand to her chest Madeleine froze, watching

wide-eyed as the shadow slinked across the floor from the dimness of the gentleman's drawing room. It drew closer, and just as she was about to make a run for it, the shadow morphed into a cat and proceeded to wind itself around her legs.

With a roll of eyes she rasped, 'Don't scare me like that, Topaz,' and dropped her hand to her side. As her heart rate returned to normal she whispered, 'Come on then, Mr Curiosity. People are relying on us and we've got rooms to explore, and secrets to uncover.'

She tried the ancient handle, grinning when it turned and the heavy timber door creaked open. In the eerie bluish moonlight spilling from the stairwell's bay window, Madeleine could see the room was piled high with broken and, judging by the odour and ominous rustles amid the debris, rodent-infested furniture.

Eeeooo.

When Topaz gave a predatory flick of his tail she hastily scooped him up and backed out of the doorway. After a final glance around, holding Topaz close to her chest, she eased the door shut behind them and moved on.

Unlike the first, cluttered room, the next two were empty, but with similar sagging brickwork and bare, boarded-up windows. In the last room, shards of crystal littered the floor from what appeared to have been a vintage chandelier, recognisable only by what remained of a metal leaf-embossed frame lying amid the debris.

Pausing to shine the torch around and finding nothing of interest, she backed out, mentally thanking her thick-soled sneakers for keeping her feet safe and her footsteps noiseless.

Now to the locked room she most wanted to investigate, the one she hoped might be Elizabeth's music room.

Could she be so lucky as to have the key for that very room in her pocket? Or was that asking way too much? Then again, here she was at midnight, snooping in a restricted area of a supposedly haunted neo-Gothic castle with a cat in her arms.

So anything was possible.

After setting Topaz at her feet, she took out the swaddled key ring and, with hope swelling in her breast, unwrapped it. When the big brass key slipped easily into the lock she blew softly through pursed lips, only to wince when grinding, metal-on-metal sounds resulted from a careful turning of the key. Still she kept turning, hoping the castle's stone walls would trap the sounds, and was rewarded with a rusty metallic click as the lock finally released.

The door opened quietly enough, with a puff of musty, ancient air. As the combination of moonlight through the window and torch light spilled into what was a sizeable room, Madeleine glimpsed ornately carved pillars keeping faithful sentry, a chandelier dripping cobwebs and dangling from the ceiling on only two of its three metal chains, and in one corner, a cold and lifeless fireplace with lumps of coal from its final blaze still littering the grate.

On the sculpted mantelpiece above the fireplace, a pair of once shiny, now tarnished, silver candelabras glimmered faintly. The nearest lay face-down where it had fallen, or been tipped. One of its three wax-dripped candles rested nearby, the partly burned wick crumbling into the dust.

When the torch light bounced back at her from the milky glass of an oval mirror hanging amid the once beautiful but now peeling wallpaper, Madeleine hastily moved the beam along the wall. It passed over a precariously listing suit of armour and a parlour chair with stained and torn upholstery, then fell on a painting, whose cobwebbed frame held the canine image of a King Charles Spaniel, depicted in oils on a canvas now faded and blemished by the passage of time.

Next the beam lit up a grandfather clock standing resolute against the wall, the brassy face legible but tarnished with age, the graceful wrought iron hands frozen in time, the clock mechanism left unwound and morosely silent.

Beside the clock a pile of ruined antiques was heaped against the wall, in front of an indiscernible bundle on the floor covered by a dust cloth. Creeping closer, she lifted a corner of the cloth, hoping nothing with eight legs, a winged carapace, or whiskers and a long tail would emerge.

Something glinted in the torch light.

A gilded picture frame, in three pieces, the canvas clinging to it in jagged strips.

With Topaz lurking nearby, eyes peeled for pounce-worthy prey, Madeleine dropped to her haunches amid the dust, cobwebs, and who-knows-what-else, to piece the canvas strips together on the floor. Once the final piece of the jigsaw was in place she sat back to take in the painting.

It was a portrait in oils, of a young woman in a Victorian evening gown of rich maroon velvet and lace, seated at a baby grand piano with a tabby cat, very like Topaz, at her feet. A double-strand diamond bracelet dangled from one satin-gloved wrist, while her other hand held a book with a ribbon page marker and an ink-tipped quill in the fold.

A diary perhaps?

As she peered at the book, Madeleine recalled Gran remarking that in Victorian times it was common for women to record their life events in elegant notebooks, like the one in the painting.

Was it possible Elizabeth too had kept a diary, a record of the events leading to her downfall? The facts in her own words? Her side of the story?

The distant rasping screech of a Tasmanian masked owl sent a shockwave of prickles along her spine.

Gran had never mentioned anything about a diary, but what an exciting possibility! If such an account of events did exist, it would take the fact-finding cake, or at least a generous slice of it. And even if it wasn't much help in the cold case, a personal record like that belonged with Elizabeth's own family, the Brandes. Especially as the Loriennes had pretty much wiped their hands of her.

Of course this was all assuming such a valuable resource existed, and if so, that Madeleine could locate it ... which could prove the most difficult task.

Her insides zinging at the prospect of another lead, she shone the torch on the woman's face.

And gasped at the eyes smiling back at her.

Brown-gold, green-flecked hazel eyes. Brande Topaz eyes.

In the early hours of the morning, on the dusty floor of an off-limits room in a Tasmanian castle, Madeleine Brande was staring at a portrait of her long dead and much maligned ancestor.

Elizabeth Lorienne, nee de Brande Barlow.

Still reeling from seeing her ancestor brought to life in dramatic swirls of oils on canvas, Madeleine eased the door shut with a disappointed sigh, having found nothing else of note in the room. Once she'd carefully re-locked the door with the brass key and slipped the wad of tissue-wrapped keys back into her pocket, she made for the staircase on whisper-quiet feet. Pausing at the base she gazed upward, ears alert and eyes peeled for movement, human or otherwise.

The castle had a different vibe at night, a sort of restless despondency as if the building and its inhabitants—seen and unseen—all suffered from troubled slumber. Iciness oozed from the stone walls, chilling her as she crept along corridors that were hollow, empty of life, loveless.

With a shiver she glanced at Topaz trailing behind her and whispered, 'Thanks for keeping me company, buddy.'

He responded with a feline smile and jaunty flick of his tail.

'C'mon then,' she murmured, scooping his comforting warmth into her arms. 'It's time we were gone.'

Once outside the butler's pantry she set him down and took the keys from her pocket. After carefully unwrapping them she gripped the bunch firmly to stop them jangling, stepped into the compact space, and slipped the brass ring onto the hook, keeping hold until all the keys were motionless. Then she stood staring at them, a furrow forming in her brow.

If the castle's external doors were all key-locked she might have to retrieve the bunch again, to let herself out.

And if none of them fit?

She winced.

Being found inside the castle in the morning would be awkward in the extreme.

After bending to collect Topaz, who'd sat to clean his whiskers, she held him close and stepped into the corridor. Still watching her step to avoid any sneaker-squeak, especially on tiled sections of floor, she crept to the back door and used her free hand to grasp the ancient brass handle.

And gave it a tentative turn.

Its initial mulish inertia set her heart racing until, with an indignant creak, the heavy door swung inward, wide enough for her to slip through. Once outside she closed it quietly behind her and stood, blinking and panting with relief, before hurrying to the safety of her Lodge room.

11

The scream rent the night air, jarring Madeleine awake and sending her heart hammering in her chest. At another spine-tingling scream she lurched upright, and caught footsteps racing past her door as a man's voice barked, 'Room ten.'

Number ten? Wasn't that the Fox couple's room? Had something happened to one of them?

More feet raced past the door and another voice cried, 'What's wrong?'

Thrusting back the bedclothes, Madeleine jumped out and pulled on her robe, tying it firmly around her waist as she padded to the door and opened it a crack to peep outside.

Another man rushed past, tugging a crumpled tee shirt

over crookedly-donned track pants. On reaching room ten, he pushed through the people clustering around the doorway and disappeared inside.

A sleep-rumpled Alan Jenkins, along with Mandeep Singh-Samra and the Meiers, stood amid the cluster. When she leaned out further, Madeleine caught a woman's chilling wails coming from room ten.

Oh no.

Diving into the corridor, she let the door swing shut behind her as she dashed up to number ten, where she caught a woman's subsiding wails coming from inside. Peeking around the cluster of heads, she saw Byron standing at the bedside holding Jill's hand in both of his. Peter Fox, in 'Bob the Builder' pyjamas, stood on the other side of the bed, scowling down at his wife.

Scrunched hard up against the headboard with the bedclothes drawn tightly under her chin, Jill's eyes appeared enormous in her pale face. They flicked back and forth, scanning the room in a frenzy of fear.

'Now, Mrs Fox,' Byron soothed, 'can you tell us what happened?'

Madeleine nudged Alan. 'What's going on?'

'Don't know,' he murmured gravely. 'An intruder maybe? Whatever it was sure freaked her out.'

Still breathing heavily, Jill shuddered and dragged an unsteady hand over her face.

Byron kept hold of her other hand. 'Take your time.'

'I-it ... h-he ... came out of the b-bathroom.' She pointed a trembling finger. 'And was leaning o-over me....'

'Who was?'

'I was s-so f-frightened!'

'Understandably.' Bryon patted her hand. 'Can you tell us *who* was leaning over you?'

'A m-man.'

Byron frowned. 'A man came out of the bathroom and leaned over you?'

Jill twitched a nod.

'Did you know him, this man?'

'N-no.' She winced. 'Though it....'

'Yes?'

'Well ... it might've been....'

'Who?'

'You'll think I'm crazy.' She flicked a furtive glance at her florid-faced husband.

He gave a condescending sniff. 'What's a man supposed to think? Damn near gave me a heart attack with all that screeching.'

'I doubt your wife did this to frighten you, sir.' Byron's tone was even but held a hint of disdain.

'Oh, I wasn't frightened,' Peter blustered. 'Just rudely awoken for no apparent reason.' Whirling away, he marched stiff-backed into the bathroom.

Byron waited until the door closed behind him before asking again, 'Who might it have been, Mrs Fox?'

She sat gnawing on a fingernail.

'Mrs Fox?'

'Not who,' she finally murmured, 'what.'

'What?'

'Yes. A ghost.'

A pause, and then Byron said evenly, 'You believe you were attacked by a ghost?'

'I knew it! You think I'm crazy, don't you?'

'No, but—'

'He ... it ... was in old-fashioned dress,' Jill said, still indignant. 'So tell me, if it was a prowler, why bother to dress up before breaking into someone's room?'

Releasing her hand, Byron turned to eye the apartment door. 'There's no evidence of a break-in....'

'Exactly.'

Catching sight of Madeleine standing by the doorway, Byron beckoned her inside. On turning back to the 'patient', he noticed the paperback on Jill's bedside table. A ribbon bookmark trailed from midway through the book, whose glossy cover sported the misty image of a faceless man in old-fashioned dress, and the title *The Wraiths of Bixby Manor*.

Still staring fixedly ahead, Jill didn't notice his interest in her reading material. 'He ... it ... said something.'

Byron once more focused his gaze on her. 'To you?'

She gave a mute nod.

'What did he ... it ... say?'

'S-something about my presence sullying his castle, and to be ... no, wait, that's not right.' Jill gulped and squeezed her eyes shut. 'Um ... I think it was "Be gone." Yes, that's what it said. Snarled, actually. Then it d-disappeared.'

The bedclothes quivered as her whole body shuddered. 'Its breath was so cold, and smelled awful, like ... like the sea, or a marsh. And the eyes weren't eyes at all, just black holes in its face.' Her voice rose. 'Bottomless, evil black holes.' She clawed at the bed clothes, tugging them higher under her chin.

'It's alright, Mrs Fox,' Byron said, patting her hand. 'You're safe now.'

When she closed her eyes and leaned back against the headrest, Byron gestured for Madeleine to come closer and surreptitiously handed her Jill's paperback.

She scanned the cover image and read the title, then opened to the bookmarked page. The first lines of the chapter read:

The wraith slithered closer until she could feel its foul breath against her cheek. Terrified, she squeezed her eyes shut as the black hole of a mouth rasped, "Be gone, damnable creature! Sully my home no longer with your vomitus presence!"

Catching Byron's eye, she pointed to the paragraph and he read the lines.

They exchanged a knowing glance.

Rising, he said kindly, 'I'll make you some tea, Mrs Fox. That'll restore your spirits—' Wincing at the bad choice of words, he went on hastily, 'You'll feel better after a cuppa.' As he made for the door he whispered to Madeleine, 'She could probably use some female comfort.'

'Looked to me like you were doing just fine,' she murmured back, earning herself a grateful arm squeeze.

With a quiet, 'Won't be long,' he left.

As she took his place by Jill's side, Madeleine returned the paperback to the table. When Jill slowly peeled herself off the headboard, she flashed an encouraging smile. 'Been something of an eventful night for you. How are you feeling now?'

Jill took her time replying. 'I'll be alright.' The frenzied light had left her eyes, and she fixed Madeleine with a solemn gaze. 'They think I'm crazy, or stupid, or both. Don't they?'

'Why would you think that?'

'Because....' Jill paused and looked away. 'I said it might've been a ghost that scared me.'

'Hey, don't forget that everyone here,' and Madeleine swept an arm to indicate the dispelling group outside, 'is inhabiting what the owners themselves describe as a "haunted neo-Gothic castle". That means we can all relate, and anyone who says they can't, is fibbing.'

After a long, pensive moment Jill murmured, 'I guess you're right.' Appearing to claw back more inner fortitude she said, 'Anyway, it doesn't matter what others think or say. They weren't here when it happened. They didn't see the ghost ... but I *did*.'

At a loss for what to say in reply to that, Madeleine opted for an over-bright, 'Oh look, here's you tea,' when Byron showed up, tray in hand.

With a cheery, 'Here you go,' he handed Jill a steaming cup.

'Thank you.' Putting the cup to her lips, Jill took a sip. When Byron made to go, she snaked out a hand to grasp his. 'And for being so kind to me. When others...,' and she glowered at the bathroom door.

'I'm just glad to see you're feeling better.' When she released his hand, Byron gave her a reassuring smile, dipped his head at Madeleine, and left.

A short while later the bathroom door opened and Peter peered out.

Spying him, Madeleine gave Jill's hand a final pat. 'I'll leave you two to get some sleep.'

Keeping a tight hold on the restorative tea, Jill nodded her thanks and scrunched down further on the bed.

With a gentle, 'Sweet dreams,' and adding a silent *this time* as she moved away, Madeleine found her eyes straying to the book on the bedside table.

Jill's 'ghost' was sure to be a fictitious presence, not an actual one, inspired by too many ghost stories and too much scary, late-night reading.

Sally swept a glance over the others seated at the breakfast table. 'I'm glad it's not only me who looks the worse for wear after a broken night's sleep.' She gave a wry grin. 'Tonight, we'll probably all sleep like the dead—' Her eyes widened and she stammered, 'I mean we'll all ... um ... sleep well ... tonight.'

Alan dug her in the ribs and they spluttered into laughter.

Madeleine eyed the pair. Weren't they being a bit callous? Even if Jill had only been scared by a bad dream, it had shaken her up so much that she hadn't joined them for breakfast.

Thomas caught her eye and indicated the Jenkinses. 'I am glad someone is enjoying *zis.*'

Sobering, Alan blustered, 'Oh, we're not laughing at Jill's ... misfortune. We feel bad for her, we really do. But the possibility of a spectral visitation is one of the reasons we chose to holiday in a castle. And ... well....' He shrugged.

'So,' Thomas muttered tartly, 'you must be *wery* happy.'

'Not happy Jill had a huge fright, of course,' Sally blurted, just as a knife dropped onto a plate with a loud clatter, to gasps and flying of hands to chests.

At the end of the table Mandeep winced an apology for his clumsiness.

'A jumpy lot this morning, aren't we?' Madeleine said brightly, and then gave another start when a hand touched her shoulder.

'Sorry, didn't mean to startle you.' Byron cast an amused glance around the table. 'If you don't mind me saying, you all look like you've seen a—' He paused and grinned. 'You're freaking each other out by telling more ghost stories, right?'

Assuming their best casual expressions, the five at the table gave dissenting murmurs and vigorous head shakes while studiously avoiding his gaze.

When Madeleine flashed him a guilty grin, he said, 'Yep, thought as much,' and wagged a finger at them. 'Ghost-crazy, that's what you lot are. It's no wonder Mrs Fox had a nightmare.'

Mandeep's lips tightened and he rose to his feet. With a dip of his head he said stiffly, 'If you will excuse me, I must return to my wife's side.'

A crease formed in Madeleine's brow as she watched him go.

When the others at the table also rose, Byron waited for them to leave before asking her, 'Are we still on for tonight?'

'Oh, right, yes ... dinner tonight. Um—'

'Don't tell me you're going back on your promise?'

'No ... I.... Hey! I never *promised* anything.'

'Maybe not, but you also didn't say no. So I've made plans—'

'What sort of plans?' She arched an interrogative eyebrow.

'All above board, don't worry.' He raised his hands as if in surrender. 'I thought we could take in the sunset over Witchcliffe Bay. Have you been there yet?'

'Witchcliffe Bay? No.'

'After that we'll head into town for dinner. And before you ask,' he added with a wry twist of lips, 'it'll be just the two of us.' Undeterred by her continued silent scrutiny, he prompted, 'So, shall I pick you up around five?'

Was going on a date with Byron a bad idea?

She took her time replying, 'O...kay.'

'Great.' Grinning broadly he rose and dipped his head at her. 'See you at six then.'

She watched him stride away and pressed her lips together.

Just a little holiday flirtation, nothing serious. No need for the warning, like the one she'd given Kris.

Which hadn't worked anyway.

Old feelings of guilt washed over her at the memory of that particular conversation....

'I need to tell you something. Something ... important.'

He'd continued nibbling her ears.

With head back and eyes closing, she'd managed to rasp, 'Before you ... get in too deep.'

If she'd been thinking straight she would've realised Kris wasn't listening, was merely indulging her as she went on breathily, 'First I get excited, then I get comfortable, and then boredom sets in. After that it's only a matter of time before I get ... well ... going. I don't mean to hurt anyone, it's just the way I am, for now anyway. So be warned—'

She'd barely managed to get the last words out before he'd covered her mouth with his. With passion overriding her mind, she'd succumbed to his love making—

something he was awfully good at—reassured that her 'due diligence' was done.

And it had been, in a way.

But not in a way that made any difference to the disaster that followed.

12

At the approaching thrum of a motorbike engine Madeleine tripped lightly down the stairs to see a black sport bike nosing to a stop outside the Lodge. Unable to see a face beneath the dark visor of the full-face helmet, she paused until the tall rider in jeans and leather jacket switched off the engine and lifted the visor to look her way. When his lips parted in a slow, broad grin, her stomach fluttered in reply.

Byron remained on the bike, forearms resting casually on the dropped handlebars, watching her approach.

On drawing near she said, 'Hey,' in a voice breathy with admiration. 'Nice bike.'

'Thanks.' He flicked a gaze over her crimson blouse and fitted blue jeans. 'And nice ... you.'

The warmth in his smile and voice brought a bloom of pink to her cheeks.

He handed her a helmet and a stylish, if well worn, leather jacket. 'Here you go.'

As she slipped on the jacket she caught its masculine, leathery scent. Although the sleeves extended past her hands, the jacket too large overall, she was glad of Byron's thoughtfulness. Her blouse's fine, silken fabric and scooped neckline wouldn't provide much wind protection. At least she'd teamed it with bike-worthy jeans and boots.

'So,' she said, rolling up the jacket sleeves, 'you're a bike, not a car, man?'

'I have a clapped-out old Mazda as well as the Ducati, but I use the bike whenever I can. Hope you don't mind?'

'Not at all.' Shaking back her hair as she went to don the helmet, she said, 'I do some riding myself.'

'You have a bike?'

'Something much more challenging. A horse.'

'Oh, right.' He grinned. 'I prefer a motorised steed myself.'

As she settled behind him on the bike's wide seat, she noticed a chiller bag in the carrier.

Wine on ice? The bloke thought of everything. Did it come naturally, or was it just from his butler training?

When he patted his side with a hand indicating she should hold on, she wrapped her arms around him. He felt firm, strong, and smelled good. At his rumbled, 'Tighter,' she happily snuggled against his broad back.

'Okay, we ready?' Feeling her nod against his back, he flipped his visor closed and started the motor. It settled into a rumbling growl before the bike leapt into motion when he toed it into gear.

At the exhilarating surge of power, Madeleine gave a throaty laugh and tightened her grip around Byron's waist.

From where he'd stood watching them, Topaz gave a twitch of his tail and slipped into the deepening shadows.

The breeze off the ocean sent a cluster of clouds scudding across the darkening blue of the sky, as Madeleine settled herself on the rug Byron had spread on the ground beside the bike. Sipping bubbly while taking in the dusk light's golden hue, she leaned against the boulder at her back and looked for shapes in the clouds' brooding presence.

Byron too sat with his back against the boulder, one leg bent and the other stretched out in front. Shifting his gaze from the coastal panorama to the young woman at his side, he cleared his throat to break the companionable silence. 'So, Maddie, what do you think of the bay?'

His use of her shortened name, coated in the chocolate of his deep voice, carried an intimacy that brought warmth to her cheeks. 'Gorgeous.' She accompanied the word with a contented sigh.

'Thought you'd like it.'

'I *love* it. The way the sheep-dotted green hills roll down the peninsular to where the sand meets the white-tipped blue water....'

Byron quirked a smile. 'Sounds like you're composing a song.'

She reddened, but his eyes were kind.

'Can't blame you for getting all lyrical.' With some reluctance he returned his gaze to the view. 'Conquest Beach is a real picture when the wind drops and the ocean's calm. It's usually blustery as all heck.'

'Conquest Beach?'

He pointed at a strip of white sand bordering the bay. 'Longest beach on the peninsula.'

'Did some sort of conquest inspire the name?'

'The *SS Conquest* ran aground here in the late eighteen hundreds.' His darkly-lashed brown eyes gazed into her bright, interested ones. 'And the bay is named after another ship, the *Charles Witchcliffe*. She was loaded with convicts when she went down.'

Thinking of the *Polly Brown*, Madeleine murmured, 'Shipwrecks certainly featured a lot in Tassie's past, hey?' She didn't wait for a response. 'Say, speaking of convicts....'

'Mm?'

'What's the deal with Fred Chalmers?'

'The "Oyster"?'

'Yeah.'

Byron pursed his lips. 'Sticky-fingered Freddy stole a priceless necklace, right from a woman's throat apparently, then stowed himself away in the castle.'

'And the necklace?'

'Never recovered.'

'Do you think he might've stashed it somewhere in the castle?'

Byron's chuckle rumbled in his throat. 'The thought had crossed my mind.'

'So.' She sat up abruptly. 'Have you looked for it?'

'Of course. Byron *Mystery* McAlister, remember?'

'Oh yeah.' She gave a sheepish grin. 'And did you find anything?'

'No necklace, or anything of real value I'm afraid.'

'What about secret documents?' Lowering her gaze, she took a sip of wine. 'Old letters ... diaries ... that sort of thing?'

He shook his head. 'My only discovery was a stash of old tools, left by the castle's tradesmen I imagine. Some appear to have been handmade, and I have no idea what a couple of them even do.'

'Treasures indeed.' Keeping her gaze fixed on the ocean vista, she drained her glass and said crisply, 'Well, that's the wine gone. Now I'm hungry.'

Byron rose and held out a hand. 'Your chariot awaits, madam.'

A short distance along the narrow road running atop the peninsula's spine, Byron pulled the bike over at a look-out point and indicated dark columns of rock silhouetted against the sun-gilded ocean and sky.

Behind him, Madeleine put her chin on his shoulder to

take in the view, and when he rested a warm hand on her thigh, nestled beside his own, the intimate touch sent a thrill coursing through her.

The kind of thrill she hadn't felt for a long time.

Not since ... Kris.

Why did he have to spoil a good thing by dropping M bombs—marriage, mortgage, motherhood—into almost every conversation, and so soon after they got together? And worse still, referring to Madeleine as his 'soon-to-be fiancée' in public. Her protests had met with teasing grins and comments like, 'Just pulling your chain,' but it was obvious he hadn't taken the warning about her fickle nature to heart.

To be fair, capriciousness was all very well in a casual relationship, but ... marriage? That was a very different scenario.

And life as a doctor's wife with the formidable Mrs de Voss as mother-in-law?

Ouch.

Would the fourth M be for misery, and not just Madeleine's own?

Some of her married friends complained of hard falls to earth after the glitz of their auspicious nuptials faded and the roses-and-chocolates gift giving slowed to a trickle. And while most had morphed into years of 'regretting at leisure', more than one of those marriages had ended in acrimonious divorce.

Would the rosy start to her union with Kris also disintegrate into domestic tedium at best, domestic strife at worst? Then again, if they loved each other, wasn't marriage the natural next step for their relationship? So why the total lack of joy when, with a sense of reverence, he'd placed a jewellery box in her hand?

Why had the possible significance of his birthday gift not brought on the swell of joy one might expect to feel in those circumstances?

What about gratitude? Had she at least felt that?

No.

Delighted anticipation?

Also no.

Panic?

Yes.

Dismay?

Oh yeah.

It had taken all her courage just to open the box with reluctant fingers. What a relief when its contents proved to be a pretty set of earrings, made prettier still by not being the dreaded engagement ring.

It felt like she'd escaped a *really* close call, and that panicked reaction sent a powerful message, one she couldn't ignore.

While she cared deeply for Kris, she didn't love him. At

least not enough to withstand all that she envisioned their marriage would throw at her.

The only right thing to do, for both their sakes, was to end the relationship. And although she achieved that outcome, her fear of commitment came at a high price.

And it was Kris who paid it.

The bike slowed beneath her, jolting her back to the present.

She watched lights blinking on in town as Byron slowed further, searching for a parking space. When she glimpsed the flash of a scooter's indicator in a spot ahead, Madeleine pointed over his shoulder. 'There's one.'

She dismounted while he reversed the bike into the spot. Handing him the helmet and jacket, she shook out her hair and asked, 'So, where are we going for dinner?'

He tilted his chin over a shoulder. 'The Prima Donna—'

'Eh, Byron!'

At the call from behind he tensed before glancing around. 'Um ... hey, Ma.'

Madeleine turned from eyeing the Prima Donna's brightly lit frontage to see a motherly figure in a floury checked apron standing hands on hips, gazing at Byron.

The woman waved a chubby finger at him before striding up to cup his face in her hands. 'You bad-a boy,' she scolded in a broad Italian accent. 'You no come see us for a while.'

'It's not all that long since I saw you last. And I've been busy.'

'Ah! Busy. Always-a busy.' The woman threw dismissive hands in the air. Then her probing gaze fell on Madeleine. 'So, who is your pretty *amica*? You introduce us, *si?*'

Turning with a smiling eye-roll, Byron announced, 'Maddie, this is Signora Ada Capaldi. Ma, this is Madeleine Brande.'

'Nice-a to meet you, *cara*.' Beaming, Ada stepped in to take the younger woman's hands in both hers.

'And you.' As she returned the smile, Madeleine was pulled in for enthusiastic kisses on both cheeks. 'Ma' smelled like a motherly mix of garlic, warm pastry, and Sunlight soap.

'Ada and Gino own Gino's Café,' Byron explained, pointing a few doors up the street.

In comparison to the sparkling Prima Donna, the quaint bay-windowed café was softly lit, with wrought iron tables beneath a striped awning and fire-red geraniums overflowing from window boxes. At one of the outdoor tables, a not-so-young couple sat staring into each other's eyes over a wicker-encased wine bottle.

From inside the bay window a candle flickered cheerfully from a crimson glass holder at the centre of a table for two, laid with a red and white checked tablecloth.

'You eat-a with us tonight, eh,' Ada said, as though stating a fact.

'No, we ... um....'

Seeing Ada's face crumple, Madeleine put a hand on Byron's arm. 'I could really go some Italian food.'

He gazed at her and said hesitantly, 'Gino's carbonara *is* particularly good ... but I booked us a table at the Prima Donna, for seven o'clock.' He glanced at his watch. 'And it's almost seven now.'

'You could phone "Chez Swank" and cancel?' Flashing him an encouraging smile, she indicated the people milling around outside the Prima Donna. 'I doubt they'd have any trouble filling our spot. And I bet they don't have *authentic* carbonara on the menu.'

Ada's expression brightened.

'Well....' At Byron's uncertain frown, Madeleine squeezed his arm and smiled into his eyes.

With a clap of her hands and an exultant, 'Yes!' Ada slipped between them and took their hands in hers. 'You come-a with me. We give-a you the *best* carbonara you ever tasted!'

Ushering them into the café, she indicated the table for two in the bay window and pressed Madeleine's hand into Byron's. 'You sit while I get-a some menus.'

As she swept a gaze over the establishment's unpretentious decor, Madeleine's ears caught Frank Sinatra's velvety voice in the background, crooning a love song. Then her nose picked up the aromas of melting butter, frying garlic, and fragrant Romano cheese, and she closed her eyes in rapture.

'I hate it when people cancel on us at the last minute.'

At Byron's words her eyes snapped open.

Dropping into the chair opposite, he muttered, 'So I don't like doing it to other restaurants,' and shoved his mobile phone into a pocket in his jeans.

'I bet they've already found takers for our spot.'

'Here.' Ada bustled to their table carrying a dewy bottle of Lambrusco and basket of golden garlic bread. 'To have-a while you decide.' After setting the wine and bread on the table she handed them each a menu before bustling off again.

13

Madeleine licked garlic butter off her fingers and grinned at Byron. 'If the bread's any indication, the carbonara will be to-die-for. You must be glad we changed dinner venue?'

'I know how good the food is.' He returned the smile. 'And yes, I'm glad to be here.'

'You've been coming here a while I take it?'

'Ever since it first opened.'

'*Si,*' Ada chimed in, arriving with two bowls of mixed leaves, cherry tomatoes, crumbled fetta cheese, and plum-coloured Kalamata olives. 'And our Byron, he-a saved us when things they got-a bad.'

'Oh Ma—'

Flapping a hand at him, she turned to Madeleine. 'He's-a too modest. We would not be here, serving you tonight, if not-a for our boy.'

'Oh?'

'Yes, he—' She broke off, lifting her head to listen. 'Oh. Please excuse, Gino calls.'

As Ada hurried back to the kitchen, Madeleine arched an inquisitive eyebrow at Byron. 'I didn't realise I was dining with a local hero.'

'Hardly. Ma's just exaggerating, as usual.'

'So give me the real story.'

'It's not that interesting.'

'Let me be the judge of that.'

He blew a longsuffering sigh. 'Not long after the Capaldis chose to locate their café here, the Prima Donna changed hands and the new owners relocated the restaurant to its current spot, right across the street. Their high-profile, professionally run re-launch sadly took the shine off the café's opening.

'Gino and Ada had gone into debt to establish the café, and kept hoping business would improve, but with high establishment costs and dwindling custom, they were in danger of going under.'

He took a mouthful of wine before going on. 'I'd taken to eating here firstly because I felt sorry for them, and then because the food is so damn good. Then I overheard them talking about their money problems, and realised I could help.'

'Oh?' Madeleine sat straighter. 'How?'

'I've handled most of the marketing for the castle, so have an idea what works ... and what doesn't.'

At his rueful grin, Madeleine recalled hearing Emma complaining about the postcards, and swallowed a smile as he continued.

'For starters, I encouraged our guests to eat here on the nights they weren't dining in the castle. Then, to attract the attention of the local media, I managed to convince some trend-setting friends of mine to hold their engagement parties here.' He flashed Madeleine a wink. 'The whole world loves a romance, right?'

At her wry nod he carried on. 'In addition to the all-important online advertising, we arranged for printed fliers to be pinned up around town, and I even convinced the Capaldis to offer discount coupons and loyalty cards for repeat diners.'

'I take it the strategy worked?'

He nodded. 'Once we got the word out and put bums in seats, the quality of the food did the rest.' His eyes swept the room. 'Now this place is one of the most popular Italian eateries in town. It might not look it tonight, being mid-week, but on Fridays and Saturdays there are queues outside. You have to book early if you want a table.'

'Byron, *mio figlio,*' a voice boomed from behind them. 'You not-a come and see me in-a the kitchen?'

'Gino!' Rising to his feet, Byron was drawn into a bear hug by a large man in a sauce-splattered apron.

'Why you out-a here?' Then his reproachful gaze fell on

Madeleine and his face lit up. 'Ah ... you want to impress-a your *bella ragazza*, eh? Heh, heh, heh.' With each chuckle, Gino's aproned belly bounced up and down.

Smiling, Byron said with a note of pride, 'Maddie, this is, obviously, Gino Capaldi. Gino, may I introduce Madeleine Brande.'

'Please, call me Maddie.' When she made as if to rise, Gino waved her down.

'It's-a my pleasure to meet-a you, Maddie.' He took her hand and put it to his lips. 'And to have such a beautiful *rosa* in-a my café.'

Blushing, she turned to a grinning Byron who cautioned, 'Watch him, he's a silver-tongued devil.'

'Ah!' Gino thumped the younger man on the shoulder. 'You make-a the fun, *buonfiglio,* but I think this Maddie-rosa, you like her too, *si?*' He turned to Madeleine again. 'He no bring other *ragazze* here for a long-a time, and Mama, she start-a to worry. But now,' and with a flourish of outstretched hands indicating the two of them, he pronounced, 'this make-a her glad.'

With a wince at Madeleine, Byron mumbled, 'Now you know why I booked the Prima Donna.'

'That-a place?' Gino roared. 'Why you wanna go there?'

'I knew you'd embarrass me if I brought Maddie here.' Byron grinned at him. 'And you have.'

'*Disgraziato!*' Gino pretended to box his ears while Byron laughed and ducked. '*Ingrato figlio.*'

'*Inglese,* Gino, *Inglese,*' Ada chided, putting a restraining hand on her husband's arm. 'And-a the kitchen, she needs-a you.'

He threw his hands into the air in mock exasperation. '*La cucina*, always she wants me. Like-a my beautiful *cara*.' Grabbing his wife around her ample waist, he planted a noisy kiss on her floured cheek, before beaming at the young couple and hurrying back to the kitchen.

As both Capaldis bustled through the swinging doors, Madeleine turned to Byron. 'My Italian is ... well ... non-existent, so can you tell me what *ragazze* means?'

'Mine isn't all that great either. But I think it means ... um ... girlfriends.'

'Ah.' She gave a knowing smile and sipped her lambrusco. 'And what Gino called you? Filio or something?'

'*Figlio* is Italian for son.'

'So you must be special to them.'

'They say I'm like the son they never had.' He sobered. 'And Gino has been like a father to me since my own—'

The swinging doors banged once more as Ada bustled out, carrying two generously-sized pasta bowls. Steam curled tantalisingly from the creamy pasta with its golden bacon bits, sautéed mushrooms, and topping of freshly-shaven parmesan cheese.

Sniffing the fragrant vapour rising from the bowl Ada placed in front of her, Madeleine closed her eyes. 'Mm *mmm*.'

After a beaming Ada wished them a hearty, '*Buon*

appetito!' and left them to eat, Madeleine sat back to savour her first delicious mouthful.

'You were saying about your dad?' she finally said.

'Old news.' Sadness tinged with resentment flittered across his face. 'Don't want to bore you with it.'

'You won't bore me, I promise.'

Setting down his fork and dabbing his mouth with a linen napkin, he sat back to eye her. 'Back when we were considering buying the castle my father was against going ahead with the purchase. And it wasn't long after Mum ... well, the three of us ... went ahead and bought it anyway, that he spat the dummy and did a runner. Packed up and ran off to the mainland.'

In her mind Madeleine heard again Kathryn's words, 'So you think your father was right? Right about the castle, right about how he treated Byron, and right to walk out on us all—' Banishing the recollection, and the guilt from having overheard a private conversation, Madeleine cleared her throat and asked, 'What was he like?'

'Who?'

She rolled her eyes. 'Your dad of course.'

Byron frowned. 'Why are you so interested in my father?'

'Sorry if I seem nosy. I just ... like to hear about other people's dads.'

'Again, why?'

'Well ... I lost my own Dad when I was five. Was only beginning to know him and then ... he was gone.'

'Oh. I'm sorry, Maddie.' Byron reached over the table to cover her hand with his. 'Don't suppose he did a runner like my father did?'

'Kinda wish he had, 'cos then he might've come back to us.' She shook her head sadly. 'We lost him to cancer.' Shrugging off the sympathy in Byron's eyes, she went on crisply, 'Losing him so young makes the memories I have of Dad, and the stories Mum has told me about him, all the more precious.'

'I know what you mean.' Byron withdrew his hand and sat back. 'I try to focus on the good memories about my father, like the fact he's a natural born adventurer. He and Mum volunteered abroad 'til Emma and I came along, but even becoming a father didn't stop his globe-trotting. After settling the three of us in a cottage in town he sailed off to South Africa, to a job teaching English.

'He kept in contact with us through phone calls and the odd letter, and came home in between adventures. Never stayed long, though, was always off on another escapade. I reckon that's partly why Mum decided to embark on an adventure of her own, and bought the castle. I think she hoped that having a project to work on might keep Dad here....'

With a slow shake of his head, he reached for the wine bottle and topped up their glasses. 'In the end, it had the opposite result.'

Glimpsing the empathy in Madeleine's gaze, he gave a tight smile and said with an air of finality, 'I'm too much of a realist to give any credence to spells and jinxes, but maybe there *is* some element of truth in the curse of Lorienne Castle.'

The bike's headlight cut through the blackness as they left the well-lit town centre. Madeleine tightened her hold around Byron's waist and rested her helmeted head between his broad shoulders, admiring his confident handling of the powerful Ducati. With little to no other traffic on the road, they could've been the only two people on the planet.

The chill night air invaded her open-face helmet, brushing past her cheek like freedom's breath.

Wonderful.

Then the engine's note changed and the bike slowed as they passed through the castle's gates.

Here already? Damn....

Stopping outside the Lodge with the Ducati's motor running, Byron lifted his helmet's visor and turned to pat her on the knee. 'Home sweet home ... unless you'd like a nightcap at my place?' With his hand resting warmly on her thigh, he made no secret of the question beneath his question.

She raised her visor to arch an eyebrow at him. 'This'll be fine, thanks.'

'Can't blame a bloke for trying.'

He removed his helmet, and she caught his roguish

grin. And when he switched off the bike's ignition, silence, the thick, dark kind that follows nightfall, closed in around them, broken only by the ticking of the bike's warm engine as it began to cool.

Dismounting, Madeleine slipped off her helmet and ran fingers through her hair. After handing the helmet to Byron she went to shrug off the jacket, shivering when the night air brushed over her skin.

'You might need the jacket again, so hang onto it.' His eyes danced. 'I'm owed more time off.'

She smiled her gratitude and didn't move away when he put a hand to her face.

After stroking her cheek with a thumb he lifted her chin, gazed into her eyes, and bent his head.

And pressed his firm lips against hers.

A starburst radiated from her inner core to the outer edge of her aura—the latter not something she really believed in, but let's face it, lots of her convictions were being tested lately. With every cell in her body doing what felt like victory laps and yelling, 'OH WOW, OH WOW, OH WOW!' she remained rooted to the spot.

When he finally raised his head to gaze into her eyes again, she managed a husky, 'Thanks for a lovely evening, Byron,' while slowly extracting herself from his embrace. 'I'll ... um ... ahem ... see you at breakfast.'

'Goodnight, Maddie-*Rosa*,' he said softly, keeping hold of one of her hands until it slipped from his grasp.

Aware he was watching, she walked, less than steadily

to her dismay, to the Lodge's entrance, where she turned and gave him a wave.

Raising his hand in answer, he started the Ducati after slipping his helmet back on. Then, taking care not to over-rev the motor—in consideration of the castle's sleeping guests, she assumed—he throbbed slowly up the laneway and out of sight.

With a tremulous sigh, Madeleine stepped into the Lodge and quietly closed the door.

After parking the bike in the shed beside his old Mazda, Byron cut the motor and once more removed his helmet. He staying seated, reflecting on the evening's events, as silence once more settled around him.

There was something special about Madeleine. Something that made her stand out from the other women he'd dated.

But wasn't this simply a holiday fling? Wasn't she here today, gone tomorrow?

A crease formed in his brow.

So why was he letting her infiltrate his thoughts to such an extent?

With a shrug he dismounted and yanked the key from the ignition. After throwing a cover over the Ducati he strode to the quaint, if shabby, cottage nestled between the castle and the Lodge.

The place he called home ... for now.

14

'Diet be damned,' Jill announced, licking her lips. 'I'm having a full cooked breakfast this morning, to make up for yesterday.'

'Right you are ma'am, and the same for you, sir?' Byron smiled at Peter Fox, who nodded.

Making for the kitchen, with another quick check for more arrivals and one arrival in particular, Byron pushed through the swing doors and barked, 'Two fulls,' at Carl, the castle's talented, if tetchy, cook.

He received a menacing, narrow-eyed glare in response; the kind that often preceded one of Carl's famous walkouts. Make that stalkouts. Not that it mattered which - either would leave Byron on his own to both prepare and serve meals.

And that wasn't going to happen today, not if he could help it.

Assuming his best placatory tone he said, 'That's two full cooked breakfasts, thanks Carl.'

After a tense moment he received a curt nod, and the temperamental chef returned to the sizzling griddle plate. Behind his back Byron blew a relieved breath and began assembling the crockery and cutlery.

In the common room, Thomas called, *"Gudt morning,'* as he and Selena walked up to the Fox's table. 'May *ve* join you?'

'Of course,' a smiling Jill replied. 'We got this big table so everyone can share it.'

'Does that include me?' Without waiting for a reply Alan Jenkins pulled up a chair.

'Sure. Where's Sally?'

'She's ... ah ... still asleep.' A shadow crossed Alan's face. 'I was too hungry to wait.'

'Psht! It takes so long for *ze vives* to get ready, a man could starve, *yah?*' His comment earned Thomas a glare from Selena and guilty chuckles from the other men at the table.

Strolling up with a smile, Madeleine called, 'Morning all.'

'Good morning! Sit here beside me, Madeleine.' A beaming Jill gave her husband a shove. 'Move along one,

Peter.' When he reluctantly obliged, she patted the spot he'd just vacated.

As she settled in the chair, Madeleine's eyes swept the little group. Cheery nods greeted her from all except an unusually preoccupied Alan Jenkins.

She turned to Jill with a smile. 'Glad to have you breakfasting with us again.'

'Yes, I'm fine.' Glancing over the young woman's bright eyes and rosy glow, Jill added, 'Though I wish I looked as good as you do this morning.'

Waving away the compliment with a smile, Madeleine turned to Alan Jenkins. 'Sally not eating with us this morning?'

'She was still sleepin' when I ... um ... left.'

Madeleine eyed him, thinking it was unusual for Sally, with her up-and-at-'em approach to life, to still be sleeping at this hour.

'Morning all.'

Byron's deep voice from behind her had the breath catching in Madeleine's throat. She managed a husky, 'A-and a g-good morning to you.'

Their gazes caught and held for what seemed like a long, breathless moment, until both became aware Jill was watching.

With a hasty dip of his head Byron took Madeleine's order for a pot of tea, and moved on to the other new arrivals.

She watched from under her lashes as he strode to the

kitchen, and then turned to the others at the table without looking directly at Jill. 'Should we wait for Sally to join us before eating?' Frowning when Alan remained silent with eyes downcast, Madeleine prompted, 'Is Sally okay, Alan?'

'Not really,' he finally mumbled.

'Oh dear. What's wrong?'

'She ... um....' He raised his eyes to meet Madeleine's concerned gaze. 'She's had a ... scare.'

When the others at the table stopped talking to stare at him, Alan ran an agitated hand through his thinning hair and darted glances at them from beneath his eyebrows.

Madeleine put a hand on his arm. 'What's happened, Alan?'

'Well now, I....' He swallowed. 'Y'see I'm feelin' ... *we're* feelin' a mite foolish.'

'Foolish? Why?'

'There we were sayin' we was hopin' for some spooky entertainment....' He winced.

'And...?'

'Well, y'see,' and his chest rose as he took a deep breath, 'yesterday evenin' we ... that's me 'n Sal ... decided to go for a canoe paddle on the lake. I wanted to see if I could catch one of them so-called "ginormous" trouts.' His voice firmed with the telling. 'Was a good night for it, too, with a thick mist on the water. They say that's when you'll catch the big 'uns.'

No one spoke, just leaned in to hear better.

'Once we were out on the water,' Alan went on, 'Sally

got to sayin' somethin' about ... well,' and he gave a guilty chuckle, 'I didn't catch what she said, was busy plannin' my fishin' strategy. And my Sal gets talkative after a couple'a glasses of red. Anyways, turned out she was feelin' cold and damp from the mist.'

He flashed a contrite glance around the table. 'I thought she was bored, and would be okay once we'd thrown a line in, so I kept paddlin' out to the middle of the lake. Figured that was the best spot for catchin' something.'

After a pause to gather his thoughts, he rushed on. 'I'd only just cast a line when Sal let out a scream like I'd never heard 'er give before.' He blinked at the memory. 'The canoe rocked real violent like, and I had to drop my fishin' rod to grab onto the sides. Felt like I was on a buckin' bull ride. Next minute, the canoe flipped and we're both in the drink. Lost my rod 'n all.'

Audible gasps from around the table.

'Soon as I surfaced I looked for Sal, but couldn't see her anywhere. Had to go divin' to find her.'

At a BANG from the kitchen everyone at the table jumped, and Jill almost hit the ceiling. An instant later all attention was fixed on Alan again.

'I found 'er alright.' He paused, thoughtful. 'Never seen nobody scream under water before....'

Jill flinched and her hand flew to her mouth.

Beside her Madeleine blew a breath through pursed lips. 'Oh, Alan.'

'Yeah, was bad. Anyways, I managed to grab 'er and

brought 'er to the surface. She was still screamin' but no sound was coming out, just this awful ... kinda ... rasp. I managed to drag 'er to shore, and carried 'er, ringin' wet, to our room.'

Madeleine stared at him. 'What was it that frightened her so badly?'

'That's the embarrassin' bit.' He dragged a hand over his face. 'Sal thinks she saw a ... a ... figure in the water below the canoe, and—' He broke off.

It was Jill's turn to stare. 'A figure? Do you mean a person, or....' Eyes widening, she tightened her white-knuckled grip on the chair's armrests.

Madeleine put a comforting hand on her arm before prompting, 'Go on, Alan.'

'When she could finally speak, Sal described the ... thing ... to me. Said it was hard to see 'cos of the thick mist but it had a face, she was sure 'n certain 'bout that. A face with holes where the eyes 'n ears should've been, she said. My Sal ... well ... she's convinced she saw a ghost—'

'Oh no!' Jill leapt to her feet, face pale, hands pressed to her mouth.

Rising only a tad more sedately, Peter wrapped a comforting arm around his wife.

'Is Sally alright, Alan?' Madeleine asked. 'Does she need anything?'

'Reckon she'll be okay now. When we got back to the room I gave 'er a sleeping pill so she could get some rest. That, on top of the seasickness tablet she took before we went to the lake will have her out to it for quite a while.' His wry smile lacked any hint of amusement. 'Not a good sailor, my Sal. She'd get sick in a wobbly bathtub.'

Madeleine's eyes narrowed. 'She drank wine yesterday evening *and* took a seasick pill?' She gave a silent groan when Alan nodded.

Hadn't she believed the Jenkins too level-headed to be frightened by ghost stories? But it seemed they too had been affected by all the spooky talk. First Jill and now Sally. Who else would fall prey to fanciful imaginings? The collective imaginations of all in the group appeared to be working overtime.

Wait.

All in the group?

Some weren't here.

How long had it been since she'd laid eyes on the Singh-Samras? Had to be a couple of days at least....

She raised her voice to address the table. 'Has anyone seen the Singh-Samras today, or recently?'

Amid the head shakes Peter piped up. 'Mandeep was at breakfast yesterday, but I can't recall when we last saw ... whatshername ... you know, his wife.'

A pensive silence greeted Byron when he arrived at the table with a tray of steaming cups and mugs, a cosied teapot, tiny milk jug, and sugar bowl. Laying the last three items in front of Madeleine he remarked, 'You're all very quiet. Is something wrong?'

'We're a bit concerned about the Singh-Samras,'

Madeleine replied, fixing him with a troubled gaze. 'Nobody's seen them for a while.'

'Oh, right. Well, they might be ... you know ... spending some quiet time together.'

'Still....'

Gazing into her face and noting her concerned expression he said crisply, 'I see. Well then, we'd better check on them.'

It took a few tries before Byron's knock was answered. When Mandeep finally opened the door, pungent smoke curled around him from inside and billowed outward, as if to wrap itself around the visitors.

Taking an involuntary step back, Byron bumped against the group pressing in behind him. Alan, Thomas, Selena, Peter, and even Jill had insisted on coming along on what she called a 'welfare check' of their fellow guests.

Mandeep squinted at them through the smoky haze. 'Yes?'

'Sorry for disturbing you.' Byron stepped forward again. 'It's just ... we missed you and Randeep at breakfast. Thought we'd call and see if everything's alright.'

Mandeep's manner softened. 'Is okay.' He punctuated the words with a sigh.

As more smoke curled through the open doorway Byron gave a strangled cough.

Moving closer, Madeleine asked, 'So *is* everything okay,

Mandeep?' When he mumbled something under his breath, she asked, 'Pardon? I didn't catch that.'

'I said no, not really.' He ran an agitated hand over his already smooth black hair. 'Everything is *not* okay.'

'What's wrong?'

After a quick, uneasy glance inside the room he stepped out, closing the door behind him with a gentle click. 'It is Randeep,' he murmured. 'She will not come out. Stays locked inside, praying and burning *so* much incense! *Too* much.' He turned smoke-reddened eyes on Madeleine and then Byron. 'I do not know what to do with her.'

Byron put a hand on his shoulder. 'Perhaps we can help, if you tell us what's happened?'

With another glance at the door, Mandeep indicated for them to follow. 'I do not want to upset my wife further....'

Byron nodded, and all seven trooped along the corridor behind Mandeep. Once far enough away, he squatted on a doorstep and put his face in his hands.

The others gathered around to gaze down at him with concern.

'My wife is quite superstitious,' he began in a low voice. Raising his head, he swept them with a guilt-ridden gaze. 'I should not have brought her here.'

Clasping and unclasping his hands he fixed Byron with anxious eyes. 'I do not believe in such things, but Randeep is certain there is evil here. The incense is not enough, she says, and will not keep us safe for long. She wants us to return home, even though our holiday has only just begun.'

At his words a fraught stillness settled on the group.

'Did something happen to frighten Randeep?' Madeleine prompted, her voice gentle.

'She became terrified of being hunted by spirits, after hearing what happened to you,' and he jutted his chin at Jill.

At her audible gasp, Peter took her hand. 'It's alright, old girl,' he soothed. 'Not your fault.'

Byron and Madeleine shared a meaningful glance as Mandeep went on, the words spilling from his mouth at increasing speed.

'At first she merely stayed in the room, too afraid to pass through the door for fear of what awaited her outside. Then she wanted me to not leave either. Begged me to stay inside with her.' Pausing, he swept a wretched glance over each of them in turn.

No one spoke.

'And now,' he said flatly, 'she seeks further refuge. Only comes out from under the covers for rare moments of necessity. Still she finds no peace from her terrors.' With a resigned sigh he got to his feet and announced, 'I fear we must leave this place, and soon.'

Later, with the computer on her lap in screensaver mode, Madeleine sat staring into space from her favourite garden seat. 'A case of night terrors,' she mouthed, counting off on her fingers, 'a booze and drug-induced "vision" on a misty night-time lake, and now a woman scared out of her wits by … well … nothing.'

What would the fright buffet serve up next?

She gave a shiver and wrapped her arms around herself.

'Maddie!' Byron strode up the path, shrugging off his coat. 'You look cold. Here, take this.'

As he draped the coat, still warm with his body heat, around her shoulders, she smiled up at him. 'Thanks. I should've brought my cardie with me. Guess I wasn't thinking....'

When his fingers brushed her chilled skin, he frowned. 'Hey, you're freezing.' Dropping onto the seat, he wrapped his arms around her and drew her in against his side.

After a brief hesitation, she leaned into his reassuring warmth.

He rested his chin on top of her head and his words, 'Have you had lunch?' rumbled under her ear.

'I'm not hungry.'

'You're not still worried about the other guests? They're all fine, you know.' He gave her a squeeze. 'Just scared themselves with all that silly ghost talk.'

'Yeah, I know, though I can't help feeling sorry for Randeep. Locking herself away in their room too frightened to come out. And only 'cos she's scared of what *might* happen.'

'She needs to stop burning all that incense. I don't know how those two can stand it. They're probably suffering from smoke inhalation.' He clicked his tongue. 'After they leave it's gonna take the cleaners a while to get that unit smelling normal again.'

At Madeleine's soft chuckle against his shoulder, he smiled. 'It's not uncommon for people to get a bit freaked out when they stay here, especially when they talk about ghosts as much as this group has.'

'Yeah, but for so *many* to be freaked out....'

'People assume all castles are haunted, which is rubbish of course. They're just big old houses when you come down to it. Although,' and he winced, 'proprietors of commercially run castles like ours—and yes, we're just as guilty of this—have used that notion for monetary advantage. So I guess we all share the blame for any rash of "ghostly encounters".'

'I take it you're a sceptic?'

'Yep, though I keep my opinion to myself ... normally.' He gave a playful wink. 'What about you? Do you "believe"?'

'You're talking to a fellow sceptic.'

'Thought so. Anyway, enough about freaked-out folk. How are you going with that cold case you were working on?'

With a sigh she drew back to gaze into his face. 'Not making much progress I'm afraid.'

'Wanna fill me in on the details? I've got some time.' He

settled himself more comfortably on the bench, draping his arms along the backrest.

'Sure you want to hear this? Most people would think I'm crazy, talking about solving a mystery this old.'

'You're kidding, right?' He flashed her a meaningful glance and spread his hands wide. 'Remember me, part-owner of a supposedly haunted castle?'

She gave a lopsided grin. 'Okay, you asked for it. That mystery I've been trying to solve....'

'Yeah?'

'Well, the starring role goes to one Elizabeth Lorienne.'

He grew still and stared at her. 'So ... Edward Lorienne's wife was...?'

'My great, great grandfather's sister.'

'Your ancestor?'

'Yep.'

'So your mystery *does* involve the castle.'

She gave a tentative nod.

After a thoughtful pause his expression lightened. 'Well then, if you need a mystery-busting sidekick....' and he jiggled his eyebrows suggestively.

She laughed. 'Thanks for the offer, BM McAlister, mystery solver extraordinaire.'

'Glad you remembered my full name.' It was his turn to chuckle. 'And in case you're afraid some spectre will come gunning for you, after what happened to the others—'

'I thought we established that neither of us believes in ghosts?'

'You don't have to believe in ghosts to dislike being alone at night.'

'Are you offering to keep me company at night?' She flashed him a sideways glance. 'Is that what you're getting at?'

He raised his hands in surrender. 'Just saying it'd be perfectly understandable if you got a bit jumpy. I've spent nights in the castle and heard things going bump without obvious causes ... none I could find, anyway.'

'Thanks, but I'm fine on my own.'

'Well, if ever you're not, just remember I'm close by. You can knock on my door any time, day or night.' At her raised eyebrows, he hurried on. 'Hey, you haven't seen my cottage. How about you come for dinner tonight? I'll cook.'

'Won't you be doing your butler thing?'

'We haven't had any dinner bookings so far today, I think our guests are all a bit rattled by recent events. And if we only get light bookings we don't offer the full sit-down meal, just room service. Carl handles that on his own.'

'Do I assume you can cook?' She regarded him levelly. 'And by cook I mean more than boil water.'

'Enough to get by. So what d'you say? Shall I walk across and collect you at seven?' At her smiling nod, Byron glanced at his watch and rose to his feet. 'I'd better get on or Mum'll be dispatching a search party.' Bending to tuck a loose strand of hair behind Madeleine's ear, he gazed into her face. 'Warmer now?'

With a smiling, 'Yes thanks,' she passed him his coat.

. . .

Back in her unit, Madeleine stood staring in the bathroom mirror.

Another date with Byron, and this time at his place. Of course 'dinner' can mean so much more than simply a meal.

She chewed her lip.

Did she want it to be simply a meal shared with a friend, or something more?

Byron was charming, easy on the eye, and clearly interested in her. Probably only scoping for a holiday fling though, with little likelihood they'd cross paths again after she left.

Was that a bad thing though? Didn't she prefer short-term relationships after....

Resting her hands on the vanity, she leaned in to stare at her reflection.

Was it wrong to enjoy a charming man's company on a no-strings basis?

But ... look at how she'd treated the other charming man in her life.

She frowned into her reflected eyes as an image floated across her mind, of a blond head on a starched white pillow, pale arms tucked against the sheet-covered body.

Dropping her chin to her chest, she leaned her weight on the vanity.

And for once, let the memories come....

. . .

Tubes snaked from beneath the sheets to connect with nearby machines, their blinking screens emitting soft, regular beeps. From where she stood in the Emergency ward corridor, gazing through the window at the gut-wrenching sight, Madeleine took a shuddering breath and went to step into the room, only to find a stony-faced, designer-suited Mrs de Voss barring the way.

'What the *hell* are *you* doing here?' Her distress and animosity were almost palpable. 'How *dare* you come near my boy—' When the words caught in her throat, she yanked down her suit jacket and indicated the motionless form on the bed. *'You're* the reason he's in here.' She stabbed a finger at Madeleine. 'This is *your* fault.'

The livid words punched the breath from Madeleine's body. Her mouth dropped open and she stared in shock at Kris's mother.

'Your cruelty that sent him speeding into oncoming traffic.' Mrs de Voss took a ragged gasp of air. *'You* who almost killed my boy.'

'But—'

Thrusting up a hand, the older woman went on bitterly, 'You know, I tried to like you for his sake, but I *never* considered you worthy of my son. And in the most painful way imaginable, you've proven I was right to have a low opinion of you.' She shook her head. 'I don't like being wrong, but in this case I wish....' Swallowing, she glanced over a padded shoulder. 'Look what you've done to him. My son, my only ch-child....'

'Oh Mrs de Voss, I'm so—'

'Don't!' Flinching and jerking out of reach when Madeleine made to touch her arm, Mrs de Voss spat, 'You have no right to be here, you ... you ... *jezebel.*' She thrust a manicured finger toward the exit sign at the end of the corridor. 'Leave. *Now.* And don't *ever* come near my son again, or either of us if you know what's good for you.'

The vicious tirade had Madeleine staggering back as emotions writhed inside her.

Anguish, at the sight of the unmoving form on the hospital bed.

Hurt, from the accusations being so cruelly flung at her.

Resentment, at being held entirely accountable for another's rash actions.

Guilt, for her starring role in the tragedy.

She wanted to make amends somehow, but what could she do except shut her mouth, bow her head meekly, and leave? She had no come-back, was so overcome with remorse she could barely look Kris's mother in the eye.

At the brush of furry warmth against her calf, Madeleine glanced down to see Topaz winding himself around her legs. Swiping away unshed tears with an arm, she shook off the agonising memories and murmured, 'Hey, buddy. It's been quite a day, I could use a lie down. Wanna join me for an afternoon nap?'

As if understanding, Topaz graced her with a feline smile and followed her into the bedroom and onto the bed. With him tucked snug against her side, purring as he licked his fur smooth, she stretched out, sighed deeply, and closed her stinging eyes.

15

Fog billowed around her feet, bringing a deathly chill as she drifted toward the mossy stone balustrade. Pausing there to glance upward, she glimpsed a castle's battlements, barely visible above the mist.

Glancing down again, she realised vaporous, spider-like forms had crawled around her torso and over her shoulders. Her attempts to bat them away proved useless, and when a fey breath stirred the fog, creating hazy, claw-like eddies, she yelped and pushed herself back from the balustrade.

The clinging mist trailed after her, coiling itself into another form. One with sinister facial features, black holes for eyes and ears, and bony, grasping hands reaching for her....

With a gasp Madeleine lurched upright, heart

pounding in her ears, and took a rapid, wide-eyed scan of her surroundings.

Only the familiar walls and furnishings of her Lodge room.

She was alone.

No sign of mist anywhere.

Blinking, she sagged against the pillows, the movement rousing Topaz at the foot of the bed. He stretched and yawned, and she scooped him into her arms and hugged him close. Resting her cheek on his furry head, she felt his rumbling purr against her ear and blew a long breath.

'Oh, buddy, what a dream. Make that nightmare. I *have* to stop listening to all the spooky stories.'

From: Madeleine.Brande
To: Connie.Brande
Re: Not so 'Breaking' News

I wish I had more to report, Mum. It's a relief to hear Gran's doing okay now, but I know how intense she can be with her questioning. And while I understand her 'No green bananas for me' impatience, I'm sorry you're copping the brunt of it.

Sadly, my searches have so far come up empty, apart from the odd painting and photo. So where does that leave us? I haven't been able to access all the castle's areas, some are closed off and others are used as private quarters. I doubt I'll get a chance to nose around there. So apart from the various outbuildings, I don't know where else I can look.

I did make one discovery you might find interesting. You know your quest for a project to replace hands-on management of CRB Consulting? Well, a little bird told me the McAlisters might consider selling the castle.

It would mean a substantial capital outlay initially, which would probably scare off most interested parties, and the renovations required to make it a more successful going concern would likely scare off the rest. But it has loads of potential, and I can't help thinking that buying Lorienne Castle would be like returning it to the family....

Oh, and speaking of returning things, I think we should consider reverting to our original surname, whether my quest here is successful or not.

Luv,

Maddie de Brande Barlow xxx

She gave a start at a loud chime from the landline phone in her room.

'Hello?'

'Maddie? It's me.'

'Mum?'

'I just read your email,' Connie Brande gushed.

'Wow, that was quick—'

'Such an exciting opportunity....' She paused to take an audible breath. 'But first, how are you, love?'

'Fine. And you?'

'Great. My recuperation's going brilliantly. So much so, I'm thinking of joining you at the castle, and inspecting the place while I'm there.'

Madeleine's eyebrows shot up. 'Oh, really? So ... you're seriously considering—'

'I'll book a flight as soon as I've checked with the doctor that I'm okay to fly. In the meantime, I'll be talking to my estate agent and the accountancy firm.' She sniffed. 'I know the bean counters' first reaction will be to suggest there aren't enough beans in the barrel, but they'll come around.'

Madeleine gave an indulgent smile. It was so like her go-get-'em mother to think positive, and to sometimes get ahead of herself. 'The castle won't come cheap, Mum.'

'Of course, but I'll decide for myself if I can afford it.'

'Then I guess I should book a room for you.'

'Please do, once I have an ETA. You can always cancel if our plans don't work out, though I have every expectation they will.'

'Before you go to all this trouble, Mum, I think you should know one of the reasons the current owners are considering selling.'

'Go on.'

'They've done some restoration work on the castle but it'll take a whole lot more to get the place up to scratch, requiring another large injection of capital.'

'Ooh, just the kind of project I'm hankering for, love, with challenges aplenty. And I simply *adore* the idea of us, you and me, owning, renovating, and maybe even living in a castle. As for the money side of things,' she added, sounding less like an excited girl and more like an astute business woman, 'I'll look into the possibility of drawing from CRB's resources. Not sure the accountant will like that idea, but he's clever at writing off costs.'

'I only heard about this possibility on the grapevine, don't forget,' Madeleine warned. 'The property's not officially on the market—'

'The best options rarely are. Staying one step ahead is a key to success.' Connie gave a delighted titter. 'This is the most excited I've been in ages, love, thank you.'

'Well, I hope something comes of it.'

'Bound to. And speaking of the grapevine, I have some news for you.'

Good news judging by her tone.

'What about?'

'Kris.'

Madeleine's eyes clouded and she lowered her head.

'You knew his mother took him overseas for specialist treatment?' Connie prompted.

Madeleine's quiet, 'I did,' was a while coming.

'He responded so well to the treatment,' Connie bustled on, 'she's been able to bring him home. Isn't that wonderful?'

Madeleine's head snapped up. 'Oh yes, wonderful. Wait

... how did you hear? Every member of our family is *persona non grata* to Mrs de Voss, so it couldn't have come from her.'

'As I said before, I like to stay one step ahead of the game .. and the competition. Anyway, I'll keep you posted on Kris?'

'Please.'

Apart from the odd cobweb in some of the leadlight windows, Byron's house was neat, clean, and cosy. It smelled old but in a nice, wholesome way, Madeleine decided. And as for the aromas wafting from the kitchen ... mm mm mmm!

She sat on the worn though comfy sofa, legs tucked beneath her and a glass of wine in her hand, watching flames dance in the fireplace and listening to the John Butler Trio album playing in the background.

Her gaze roved to a group of framed photographs on the age-shabbied timber dresser in the corner, and she unfolded her legs and wandered across the well-trodden rug to take a closer look. They were mostly family shots, featuring Emma and Byron as children. But there was one of an older Byron posing beside a shiny new Ducati, with a man Madeleine assumed was his father. Picking up the frame, she examined the two subjects more closely. While they shared the same grin, Byron's father was taller, rangy, and more sinewed than his son.

Peering into the older man's face, she saw more differences. Where Byron's frank gaze held self-assuredness, intelligence and amusement, his father's was closed, unreadable. His body language held an innate restlessness, in keeping with what Byron had told her about him.

She replaced the photo as another toward the back caught her eye, and she reached over to pick it up. This picture featured all four McAlisters, huddled together on a windy point overlooking a beach. Was that Witchcliffe Bay in the background?

In what appeared to be a candid shot, perhaps taken by a visitor to the family, or a passing tourist, Kathryn was laughing up at her husband while he gazed fondly back at her, one sinewy arm around her waist, the other hugging his two youngsters close.

All four appeared relaxed and happy, so much so that Emma was barely recognisable.

No wonder the bay was special to Byron.

'All taken in the good old days, before any talk of castles,' Byron muttered drily from the kitchen doorway.

Replacing the photo, she turned to face him. 'Sorry, I wasn't snooping, just....'

He shrugged. 'It's fine. Photos are meant to be looked at.'

'You take after your dad, you know.'

'Y'think so?' He gave a hollow smile.

'And your mum looks so happy in that shot. I ... well ... almost didn't recognise her.'

'Yeah. She was always happiest when he was around.'

'By the way she's gazing at him I'm guessing she loved your dad a lot.'

'Make that *loves*. Even though he walked out on us, she's never stopped loving him.' Byron paused before adding, 'Probably never will. It's a shame he doesn't feel the same way about her. About us. For which the damn castle's partly to blame....'

The 'damn' castle.

Madeleine eyed him keenly.

Was it possible he was as willing as Emma to offload it?

'From that photo, I'd swear your dad cares about you all as much as you care about him.'

Byron didn't answer, merely gave a thoughtful frown. Then a timer went off in the kitchen and he announced, 'Ready to serve up. Make yourself comfortable at the table.'

'Can I wash my hands first?'

'Sure. Bathroom's down the hall. There's a clean towel in there you can use.'

'Ever the attentive butler.'

This met with an amused snort as he headed for the kitchen.

Madeleine made for the cottage's bathroom, which proved to be spacious and well appointed. Above the pedestal vanity, the prisms of glass in the medieval-style leadlight window caught and reflected sunlight in an array of colours. In the centre of the room a claw-foot bathtub sat encircled by a dark green shower curtain, an old-fashioned shower rose suspended above it.

Beside it, a pair of towels, one brown and the other pink, hung from a brass rail.

Gazing at the towels, Madeleine found herself likening them to that popular wedding gift, the 'His-n-Hers' towels set. She ran the front edge of the pink towel through her fingers, picturing its textured fabric embroidered with the initial M in satiny thread, a B on its brown partner....

Whoa!

She dropped the towel like a burning coal.

Where had that soppy thought come from?

Scowling into the mirror, she washed her hands and splashed water on her face, then once again reached for the pink towel.

Back in the lounge room, she settled herself on the sofa and took a gulp of wine. It was a rather splendid drop— Byron really did have good taste—and had the desired effect of helping her forget she'd even had those soppy thoughts.

Her stomach growled when he emerged from the kitchen carrying two bowls of fragrant chicken curry over basmati rice, and she licked her lips as he indicated a seat at the table.

'Dinner is served, Madame,' he announced in butler voice. *'Bon appétit.'* Setting down the bowls, he grinned into her eyes while pulling out the chair opposite. 'After dinner, I want you to fill me in on this mystery you're trying to solve. The way you've been dodging my questions it'll be worth hearing about. So I expect full disclosure.'

To avoid his gaze she bent her head to breathe in the aromatic steam. 'Mmm. This curry smells absolutely delicious.'

Setting down her coffee mug some time later, she sat straighter and smiled at Byron seated beside her on the sofa. 'Dinner was wonderful, thank you.'

'You're welcome. Can I tempt you with another after-dinner mint?'

She patted her tummy. 'Couldn't fit another morsel.'

'So it's time then.' He eyed her over his mug. 'For that full disclosure we talked about.'

'Yes, that. Um ... I have ... there's something ... I should tell you.'

He froze, coffee mug half way to his mouth. 'Oh no. You're not *married?*'

'Of course not!' As if I'd be doing ... I mean ... as if I'd be here ... if I was at all spoken for.'

'That's a relief. So there's nothing stopping us....' Leaving the sentence hanging, he set his cup down on the coffee table and moved closer. Taking her face in his hands, he rubbed his thumb along her cheek while staring into her eyes.

His breath was warm on her quivering mouth as he ever-so-slowly bent his head.

The kiss lasted a long time, and left them breathless.

Familiar, long-suppressed yearnings arose, but the prodding of her conscience rose above them. It was time to be honest with him, to lay everything—well, almost everything—out in the open.

She moistened her lips. 'I do have a confession ... of sorts ... to make.'

'Oh?' His grin took on a teasing slant. 'Have you burgled some of the castle silver, my love?' It's only silver-plated, I'm sorry to say, so you won't get much for it.'

My love.

Kris had called her that too.

She swallowed and thrust the painful memory aside. 'No, nothing like that.'

Moving closer still, Byron brushed fingers up and down her arm and whispered, 'Can't this wait?'

So tempting! But she couldn't go any further without clearing the air. He was bound to find out, and better he heard it from her first. 'I need to tell you....'

Her tone and expression had him sitting back to search her face. 'Go on.'

'See, it's ... well ... it's about the castle.'

'What about it?'

'You described it as the "damn" castle.'

'Did I?'

'Yes.'

'Okay. So?'

'So ... am I right in thinking you might feel the same as Emma about it?'

He pulled back further to stare at her. 'About the castle?' At her nod, he frowned and cracks opened in the sensuous atmosphere between them.

'Yeah, I ... um ... heard she was interested in selling, and wondered if you also—'

'Want to sell?' Realisation dawned on his face. '*Our* castle? My family home?'

Oh-oh.

He gave a sharp shake of his head. 'Maybe Emma has her own ideas, but Mum and I have no intention of putting Lorienne Castle up for sale.'

When Madeleine fixed him with a guilty wince, the atmosphere turned prickly and he muttered, 'Out with it.'

'Nothing's definite yet, but....'

'Yet?'

'Yeah, look it's possible ... actually more than possible ... likely ... that ... my mother's an interested buyer. Connie Brande,' Madeleine blustered, 'that's her name.'

The last vestige of warmth left his eyes and he shuffled along the sofa, putting more distance between them.

'She's considering embarking on a new project,' Madeleine hurried on, 'and is well placed financially. So I ... we ... thought ... maybe....'

'That she could buy our castle, our livelihood and our home out from under us.' He crossed his arms, his expression stony. 'You heard gossip about my family's monetary situation and thought you'd take advantage of it.'

'No, I—'

'You don't need to say anything more, Madeleine.' The butler was back. 'I know now where we stand. And I think it's time we said goodnight.'

16

Hour after dismal hour Madeleine lay, mind and stomach churning, longing for first light when she could finally rise. As a tiny glow of the sun's rays breached the horizon, she got up and stood staring outside while the kettle boiled.

Later, sitting hunched at the table, she squinted bleary eyes against the steam rising from her cup while the evening's events ran on constant replay in her mind. And with each replay, the same result – there was no mending the damage her words had caused to her relationship with Byron.

Oh, to retract those words!

If wishes were horses, beggars would ride....

Of course she'd tried to mend things, but the flurry of explanations about the Brande family's connection to the

Loriennes, Gran's yearning for the mystery surrounding Elizabeth's downfall to be solved in her lifetime, and the— clearly wrong—impression Madeleine had gleaned from Byron's reference to the 'damn' castle, had made no difference. He'd sat in hurt, disapproving silence throughout, only moving when she ran out of breath.

With a tight-lipped, 'I'll walk you to your unit,' he'd gone to the front door and swung it open.

The message was clear – the date was over. Despite what had happened between them mere minutes before, Byron was back in butler mode, all arms-length formality.

That walk should've been taken with arms around each other, heads together murmuring sweet nothings, but instead was spent in hostile silence from him and miserable, contrite silence from her.

And after leaving her at her door with a formal, 'Good night, Madeleine,' he'd marched off without once looking back.

Rising with a sigh she went to the sink, tipping out the dregs of her tea and rinsing the cup on autopilot.

If not for her 'do-the-right-thing' compulsion, would she still be with Byron right now instead of alone in her Lodge room?

Inhaling deeply, she stuck out her chin and pushed herself back from the sink. She couldn't change what had gone down last night, and fretting over what-ifs wouldn't get her anywhere. She needed fresh air and exercise. Maybe another tour, or some window shopping in town ... a barista-made cappuccino in a pretty café—

She clicked her fingers.

Aha.

'He's not-a our son by blood.' Ada's voice took on a wistful note. 'But we worry about-a Byron like-a he *is* our boy, and want him to be happy.' Setting Madeleine's coffee on the checked tablecloth, she flopped into the chair opposite.

'Gino, he like-a to see café full of customers all-a time, but me....' and she swept an arm to indicate the empty tables around them, 'I like-a the lulls, a chance to take-a weight off my feet.'

With a smile Madeleine took her first sip of the foam-topped, chocolate-dusted coffee. 'Mmm. Sorry for coming so early.'

'Is-a no problem.'

'Still, thanks for letting me in.'

'What I'm a-gonna do, leave you waiting outside looking hungry?' Ada waved away her thanks. 'No, no, no. Anyway, was-a time to open door. Lotsa people wanna early coffee, like our Maddie-Rosa,' and she reached across to squeeze Madeleine's arm.

As guilty heat blossomed in her neck and face, Madeleine held the cup in front of her lips and prompted, 'You were saying ... about Byron?'

'*Si, si.*' Ada's smile faded. 'Our boy, he was-a meat in the sandwich. His-a real father was against buying the castle, and he want-a Byron to side with him. He say, "We gotta stick-a together, son".'

Madeleine nodded and took another sip.

'The mama, she appeal-a to Byron too. She say "I need-a you, son. How can I do this without-a you?" They each pulling at him, like tug of war, you know?'

She didn't wait for a response. 'It's-a no win. Byron, he love-a both, but he gonna hurt-a one or the other. He knows papa will be okay, whatever happens, but mama....' She threw Madeleine a significant glance and patted her hand. 'He's a good-a boy. He do right-a thing by his mama ... and-a his Rosa.'

'So he went into the venture because of loyalty to his mother, not because he really wanted to own the castle?' At Ada's nod, hope glimmered in Madeleine's eyes and she rushed on. 'What about now? If he had the chance to move on ... to leave the castle?'

'Siding with mama cost-a him his papa.' Ada paused, thoughtful. 'So giving up castle ... be like he lost-a papa for nothing, and this I think he could not-a stand.'

The tender buds of relief wilted in Madeleine's chest.

Standing in the café doorway, Ada watched as Madeleine walked away. When Gino came to stand beside her she looked up at him with anxious eyes. 'I'm a-worried about them.'

'Our boy and his-a Rosa?'

'*Si.*' She returned her gaze to Madeleine's disappearing back. 'I think maybe they having problems.'

'Problems?'

'*Si.*'

'How you know?'

'A woman can tell-a when someone has...,' and she put a hand to her chest, 'heartache.'

Gino wrapped a floury arm around his wife's shoulders. 'Just-a be patient, Mama. These young people, they sort-a themselves out. Not every love-a story has a smooth path.'

Ada smiled and patted his cheek. 'And not all men pop-a the question on second date, like-a my Gino.' She sobered. 'But Rosa is the right-a one for our Byron, this I feel in-a my bones. He mustn't let her get away.'

'Don't-a worry my romantic *cara,*' and Gino gave her a squeeze. 'The boy will do the right-a thing.'

'How you know this?'

'A man can tell-a these things.' When she gasped and slapped his arm, Gino gave a tummy-jiggling chuckle and led her back inside.

Madeleine stood outside Byron's cottage chewing her lip. Silence had once again greeted her tentative knock. She hadn't really expected to find him home—at that time of day he was no doubt in the castle or the Lodge's kitchen—but it was worth a try.

After what Ada had told her, she needed to talk to him ASAP, tell him she understood now what the castle meant to him, and ... apologise?

For being up-front about what was going on?

No, not that. Maybe for the way she'd given him the news? Yes, she could've handled that a *lot* better. Needed to do better next—

She gasped and leapt to the side as something dashed past her.

Followed by something else.

The first was a tabby streak—Topaz?—and the second, a large black dog. A Doberman or similar, it was breathing hard, jaws slobbering, ears pricked, rapacious eyes intent on its prey.

Topaz?

With a cry of, 'Oh no you DON'T!' Madeleine leapt into a sprint after the animals. On rounding a corner she glimpsed Topaz scoot into Byron's shed, the dog not far behind. She dashed in after them, and once her eyes adjusted to the darkened interior, spotted Topaz cowering behind a pile of boxes.

No sign of the dog though.

Muttering, 'That's right, run away you big coward,' she moved to where Topaz crouched, fat-tailed, fur raised in a vertical line along his back, in a dusty, webby corner near the front tyre of Byron's Ducati.

'C'mon buddy,' she crooned, reaching for him, 'that rotten dog's gone. You can come out now.'

She was rewarded with a warning hiss as the cat continued scanning for his canine attacker.

'Hey buddy, it's me.' At the bang of a nearby door she gave a start, and urged in a harsh whisper, 'Come on, Topaz, let's get out of here. Before Byron finds us snooping around in his shed. I have enough explaining to do without adding that to the list.'

Reaching into the corner she grabbed the traumatised cat, who gave another hiss and dug his claws into what looked like an old rug, partly-buried in the dirt floor.

'Let go, buddy.'

At her tug he dragged a corner of the fibrous, darkly-patterned rug part-way out of the dirt.

'What's that you've dug up?' Hugging the cat close to calm him, Madeleine gently released the rug from his grip. It dropped to the ground again and she remained on her knees, staring at it.

Setting the cat down by her side, she grasped the rug's edge, gave it a firm tug and felt it give. With one more yank a square of the decaying, fetid carpet came away in her hand. Screwing up her nose, she tossed it to the side and shot Topaz a dark look.

He remained sitting beside her, licking his fur.

'Glad you've finally stopped hissing at me,' she

muttered, 'while I'm here, in the dirt, cleaning up your mess ... sort of.' Turning back, she caught a metallic glint in the newly exposed soil. When she brushed away the dirt, a box-like shape emerged.

Buried treasure?

The scent of mystery had her nose twitching as, heart thumping, she wiped away the remaining soil and lifted the box free.

It was a battered tobacco tin, probably long emptied of its original contents. She shook it. Definitely something inside.

She tried the lid.

Jammed fast.

It would need to be levered open. And there, on the work bench less than a metre away, lay a flat-blade screwdriver perfect for the job.

It seemed her luck might be on the improve....

Rising, she set the tin on the bench and quietly got to work. The lid popped open after the third attempt, releasing a puff of stale air mixed with musty old tobacco. Wrinkling her nose, she waved away the smell and held her breath as she peered into the tin.

A piece of paper, yellowed with age, its folds stained and fraying, lay in the rusted base.

With eager fingers Madeleine lifted out the fragile paper and carefully unfolded it.

A hand-drawn map.

Though smudged in spots it was still legible, and the

scribbled place names recognisable.

Spyglass Hill – Jeff had pointed that out on the tour.

Wild River – also mentioned by Jeff.

Le Froid township – within cooee of where she stood right now!

Dray Road – that was new. She traced the track with a finger. On Crown land, it ran from the water's edge up the hill to the eastern border of the Lorienne estate. The twice etched circle over a section of the road had to mean something important, surely.

Additional scrawled notes lay across a fold, but the paper's deterioration made them unreadable.

She turned the paper over to check for the back.

Nothing.

Still, what a fabulous find, an old map!

A map showing the way to ... what?

'I've made an exciting discovery, Mum.'

'About Elizabeth?'

'Sadly no, nothing new there. This discovery does have castle connections though.'

'Well don't keep me in suspense.'

'It's the Bedazzler, the necklace Fred Chalmers, AKA "The Oyster", stole from the throat of a dignitary's wife!'

Phone clenched between her ear and right shoulder, Madeleine held the stunning pearl and diamond necklace in front of her face and jiggled it so the gems sparkled in the sunlight, sending coloured glints around the room like a disco ball.

'How can you be sure it's this "Bedazzler"?'

'It has to be. Chalmers holed up in the castle after the robbery, and when captured he refused to tell the authorities what he'd done with the necklace. It stayed where he'd stashed it.'

'How did you find it?'

'I ... make that Topaz and I ... stumbled across a clue to its whereabouts, buried in an old tobacco tin.'

At the other end of the call Connie sucked in an audible breath. 'What clue?'

'A hand-drawn map, of the local area.' Madeleine's excited wiggle unbalanced the phone and she had to make a grab for it.

'Go on.'

'I guess Chalmers didn't trust his memory, or had so many stolen items in secret caches he was afraid he'd forget where they were all buried. Of course he never got the chance to find this one again.'

'So where, and what, did the map lead to?'

'I'm getting to that, Mum.'

'Please hurry.'

Madeleine gave an amused huff. 'I managed to follow the map to what Chalmers called Dray Road. It's little more than a steep, overgrown track but he'd circled a section of it, so I figured that was the place to start looking.'

'And?'

'I followed the track for a bit and came across a burial cairn near a tight corner on a rocky incline.'

'A memorial cairn? Whose?'

'I found "Dray Man, RIP" scratched on one of the stones. I suspect it's the spot where a driver was crushed to death when his dray overturned, spilling its cargo of marble intended for Lorienne's ballroom extension.'

'Oh dear.'

'Yeah, sad, especially considering his personal circumstances. Anyway, I figured it was a likely spot for a thief to hide his stash, and after lots of peering into crevices, moving stones and hoping the whole burial mound didn't come down on my head, I spotted—'

'Something glinting?'

'No, fabric. An old pouch. Cleverly hidden inside the cairn. I found it when I pulled a bush out of the way and dislodged some stones.'

'A velvet jewellery pouch?'

'Well, it might've been velvet ... once.'

'Containing the necklace?'

'You got it.'

'Ooh, I can't wait to see it.'

'It is an impressive piece of jewellery,' and Madeleine jiggled it again. 'All sparkling diamonds and gleaming pearls.'

'Well, well,' Connie mused aloud. 'I wonder what it's worth. Could be a significant amount considering its age and colourful history. We can get a proper valuation from Sotheby's.'

Madeleine grinned, imagining the wheels turning in her mother's head.

'Then again,' Connie went on, her tone pensive, 'the right thing would be to return it to the original owners, if any of their descendants are still alive. And if so, there's probably a handsome reward for the necklace's recovery.'

It was so like her mother to be both shrewd and kind.

'To think it's been buried in that cairn all this time. And it took my daughter to find it.'

'Me and Topaz,' Madeleine corrected her. 'It'd still be buried if he hadn't led me to that exact spot in the shed. This is like his legacy.'

'A legacy that might help fund the purchase and maybe even the renovation of our ancestral home. Good work, both of you. Now leave it with me, I'll find out what the deal is.'

So, it was a certainty. Her mother was seriously considering making an offer to buy the castle.

Frowning, Madeleine lowered the hand holding the necklace and slowly hung up the phone.

From: Madeleine.Brande
To: Connie.Brande
Re: About the castle....

Hi Mum.

I've been thinking, and am starting to wonder if the castle is as good a prospect as I first thought. I'd hate to give you a bum steer. The grounds are in tip-top shape, but as I said before, the building still needs loads of renovations. The McAlisters have only scratched the surface on that score. And the kind of renos it needs would be HUGELY expensive. Just FYI.

Talk soon.

Luv,

Maddie xxx

She wasn't smiling as she pressed SEND. She longed to offload to her mother about everything, but all things considered, that wasn't a good idea.

At least not yet.

To avoid an awkward encounter with Byron she decided to skip breakfast. She took a pot of tea onto the balcony and sat sipping distractedly, staring moodily at the sun-kissed harbour until it was time to phone her mother.

'You sure you're alright, love? You sound ... flat. Anticlimax after finding the necklace?'

Madeleine cleared her throat. 'I'm fine, Mum.'

'Good. Now, tell me why you've gone cold on the idea of buying the castle, after earlier suggesting we should bring it back into the family fold.'

'I just don't want you to be disappointed.' Madeleine

chose her words with care. 'You know, if things don't work out.'

'Don't worry, love. I'm excited, yes, but also aware of the need for due diligence.'

There's that shrewdness again.

'Well ... okay.'

'I should know my arrival date in the next few days. And in the meantime....'

Madeleine grimaced.

Here it comes.

'I'm hoping you might sow a seed about this venture?' When her daughter didn't answer straightaway, Connie prompted, 'It's easier for you to put out feelers, being on the ground and all.'

'Well....' Madeleine sighed. 'If I must.'

'Thanks, love. And trust me. I know what I'm doing.'

Which was no doubt true about most aspects of the venture ... but not all.

17

'We have plenty of availability for around that time. Shall I proceed with a reservation?'

'Thanks, but I'll need to get the exact dates from Mum first.'

With a dip of her head Emma closed the guest register and turned away.

'Right now I think I can help you with something.'

At Madeleine's words Emma paused and glanced over a shoulder. 'Oh yes?'

'My mother owns a large and successful Australian company.'

'How nice for her.'

Ignoring the droll response, Madeleine charged on. 'She's currently on the lookout for a new business venture.'

'I see.' Emma turned to fix her with a calculating gaze.

'It's possible she might be interested in buying Lorienne Castle,' Madeleine went on, 'hence her forthcoming visit, to view the estate.'

Emma's eyes glinted and she moved to stand hard-up against the counter.

'I have reason to believe you may not be averse to selling?'

Emma continued eyeing her. 'You're saying your mother might be prepared to buy us out?' and she swept an arm to indicate the castle.

'Yes, assuming all the pieces come together of course.'

'I see,' Emma said again, this time with a hint of breathiness. Then a shadow crossed her face. 'Have you mentioned this to anyone else?'

It was obvious who she meant.

'I thought perhaps you'd want to give your mother the news.'

'She might prefer hearing it from a stranger. Better still, from a real estate agent.'

'Mum's agent has already been advised there may be an offer pending.' Seeing Emma's eyes light up, Madeleine cautioned, 'You do realise this is just a possibility, that it might come to nothing.'

With a hasty, 'Yes, yes. Of course,' Emma glanced around and tapped her lips with a finger. 'For that reason, could we keep this between ourselves for now?'

'Bit late for that I'm afraid.'

'Oh?'

'Byron knows.'

'My brother knows? But ... he hasn't said anything.' Emma's face fell and she stiffened. 'How did he hear?'

'I told him.'

'When?'

'A couple of nights ago.'

'Two nights ago ... that'd be—oh, wait.' Emma peered sceptically at her. 'You weren't the date he cooked dinner for?'

'Guilty as charged.'

Guilty.

That was exactly how she felt about her involvement in the 'scheme' to buy the castle. But she'd been asked to plant the seed, a bitter-tasting seed as it turned out, and she'd done it. Whatever came next was between her mother and the McAlisters.

'I don't mean to be rude,' Emma was saying, a bevy of emotions crossing her face. 'It's just ... you're not my brother's usual arm-candy type—'

As if realising the person she was speaking to wasn't just another castle guest but a link to a thrilling possibility, she flashed an apologetic smile.

'I'll take that as a compliment,' Madeleine said over-brightly while turning on her heel. 'Soon as I've heard from Mum I'll get back to you with those dates.'

'Before you go?' When Madeleine glanced back Emma said, 'You mentioned on checking in that you wanted to have a proper look around the area.'

'That's right.'

'Well, there's a bus calling in soon to collect some other passengers for a tour, one I think you might enjoy. The tour company phoned to say there's room on the bus if anyone else is interested.'

Madeleine eyed her for a long moment, thinking that putting her tourist hat on again could be a welcome distraction from all the wheeling and dealing she'd been coerced into doing on behalf of her mother. 'How soon is soon?'

Emma checked her watch. 'Should be here in just under an hour.'

With a thoughtful, 'Enough time to get ready,' Madeleine smiled her thanks. 'I might take you up on that.'

This holiday had gone from being a pleasant break and fact-finding hunt—a less than successful hunt, sadly—to the precursor of a major acquisition.

Distracted by her thoughts, it took Madeleine a moment after climbing the stairs of the red double-decker tour bus to recognise the face grinning at her from behind the wheel.

Jeff's grin broadened as she handed him her fare, and he announced over the microphone, 'Okay folks, this lovely lady is our last pick-up. From here we head to our first stop, the lookout, and then to historic Gilston House, followed by a stroll in the botanical gardens. Then it's off to the brewery to end the tour with a splash, figuratively speaking of course.'

As the door rattled shut behind her Madeleine found a seat, and the bus set off with a rumbling groan of mechanical liberation.

Once at the lookout, with the boisterous wind whipping loose strands of hair around her face, she leaned over the railing to eye the castle. From that vantage point, in its peninsular setting with sunlight glinting off its aged silver-grey stonework and candle-shaped leadlight windows, the home Richard Lorienne had created for his family looked elegant ... and deceptively innocuous.

Of course the building itself was harmless. It was what transpired—past and present—beneath its steeply-pitched slate-tiled roof that tainted its existence.

A clap of hands and a jolly, 'All aboard to Gilston House,' jolted her back to the here and now.

As the bus trundled up the hill and parked in front of Gilston House, Madeleine pressed her nose to the window to take in the heritage estate's well-preserved grandeur. It was easy to imagine the property in days past, with the city's elite—including the Loriennes, perhaps?—strolling the extensive grounds in their suits, top hats, Victorian gowns and pretty parasols.

Finding herself alone on the bus, she rose to join the group gathered outside around an animated 'Gilston Guide', a smartly dressed young woman whose name tag identified her as Adele.

'Gilston House is the result of one progressive man's dream,' she announced with an appropriately proud, well-practised smile. 'Jonathon Gilston's home provides a glimpse of the suburban lifestyle of a privileged Taswegian in the early 1900s. Now, if you'll follow me?'

Stepping out with purpose and indicating points of interest along the way, she led the group up the stone pathway to the main entrance.

'The house and outbuildings were designed by a prestigious London architect. The home is centrally heated, has an internal phone system, and a service lift linking all four storeys. A workforce of servants maintained its thirty-plus rooms and large grounds, which made the perfect setting for entertaining VIPs, colleagues, and friends.'

Spinning on her high heels to face the group, she continued with the commentary. 'Few homes, even today, have a balcony that can accommodate a minstrel's gallery. Gilston also boasts a roof-opening device to vent cigar smoke from above the billiards table. And if you look up when we enter the great hall, you'll see a small "Juliet" window in the wall of the upstairs sitting room. Adults used this vantage point to check on their young charges in the hall below, the aim being to preserve decorum.'

She grinned. 'Kinda like a version of "Big Brother", only in this case they *didn't* want any hanky-panky.'

There were quiet chuckles among the group as, walking forward again, Adele carried on. 'The property remains in its original condition because the Gilstons had no surviving children. Jonathon died a widower and donated the house to the town's fathers, complete with a grand piano, which visitors are invited to play....'

As the group made their way through the impressive front door Madeleine trailed behind, soaking up the historic sense of family in the gracious old home. Last to enter the drawing room, her gaze fell on the grand piano enjoying pride of place.

'As you can see,' Adele said, stopping at a long wall hung with numerous artworks, 'the family accumulated a collection of original paintings. This one by Darcy Doyle, featuring the signature purple-flowing Jacaranda, is a fine example....'

After glancing at the artworks, Madeleine strolled to the piano and brushed her fingers across its gleaming black surface.

A hand-written sheet on the decorative music wrack bore the title, *We Call to Thee*. She ran her eyes over the simple score and lyrics in the first verse.

We call to thee who bears the gift,
Please, save us from sad eternities.
Listen now and listen swift,
To sorry tales and mysteries....

'Do you play?'

She spun around to find Adele behind her.

'A bit.'

'Well then, give it a go.'

'Oh, I don't know. I'm awfully rusty. It's been a long time ... and I don't know the song.'

By this time the rest of the group had crowded around the piano, some chorusing, 'Go on!'

'It'd be better than having young Alex here pound out Chopsticks,' a stout man announced, eyeing the over-excited youngster tugging impatiently at his shirttails.

'Surely we have a real pianist in our midst?' On being greeted only with silent, eager expressions, Madeleine winced and reluctantly perched on the stool.

After running her eyes over the score, she put her fingers to the keys and began to play, slowly at first and then with growing confidence. The piano's excellent tuning released the beautiful, haunting melody of *We Call to Thee* with a rare sweetness. Everyone, even the hyperactive youngster Alex, fell silent as though entranced by the simple but evocative melody.

There was a moment of awed silence when Madeleine finished playing and lifted her hands from the keyboard, followed by enthusiastic applause.

'Thank you, that was lovely. Now everyone,' Adele prompted, 'we have lots more to see.'

While the group moved on to the next point of interest, Madeleine remained seated, staring at the sheet music in front of her.

We call to thee.

Like Elizabeth's call to her descendants from across the decades....

. . .

'Now here, ladies and gents, we have an auditory oddity, if you'll pardon the parlance.' Jeff grinned at the tour group, gathered around him in the aromatic 'perfumed piazza' of the botanical gardens. True to its name, the fragrances of rose, jasmine, and orange blossom caressed every olfactory sense within reach.

Pointing at two large disks, like satellite dishes, positioned at opposing ends of the piazza, Jeff announced, 'Those dishes aren't just architectural features, they have a purpose. They're like tin can phones without the string, otherwise known as "whisper dishes". If you whisper in one, the person standing near the other one, right down there,' and he pointed, 'will hear you.'

Strolling on, down the path, Madeleine admired the well-tended garden beds filled with sweet-smelling boronia, lavender, and rose blooms, all gleaming with sunlit droplets of water. Mentally comparing the flower beds with those on the Lorienne estate, she gave a start when a tinny male voice said close by her ear, 'I'm whispering at a dish, from a dish, to another dish.'

She whipped around, and realising she was right next to a whisper dish, peered at the other one. At Jeff's broad grin and theatrical bow, she gave him a wave before bending to inhale the perfume from a particularly beautiful Double Delight rose blossom.

At a whispered, 'Stay the course,' from the dish, she clicked her tongue and glanced over at Jeff.

Only he wasn't there now. Was back with the group.

No one was anywhere near the dish. And no guilty side-eyed glances from among the group either.

Come to think of it, had the whisper sounded more like a woman's? So who was the whisperer? And what did 'Stay the course' mean?

Was it a message from Elizabeth, wanting her to keep searching?

A chill ran up Madeleine's spine.

'I can take you all the way to the castle if you like? You're my last passenger.'

'Thanks Jeff. Hey, would you mind making a brief stop on the way? After all those beer tastings I feel like pizza for dinner.'

'Yeah, the brewery's generous with their servings.' He flicked on the indicator and it ticked as he waited to make a left turn into the town centre. Flashing her a grin in the rear-view mirror, he said, 'I know a great little pizzeria and it's right on the way.'

'Sounds good.'

'So ... you're not eating in the castle tonight?'

'No.' Madeleine gazed out the window. 'Not tonight.'

'Hey, I heard another snippet on the grapevine about the castle, from a real estate assessor friend of mine.'

She stiffened. 'Oh?'

'He confirmed what I thought, that Emma McAlister's been wantin' to sell up for a while now. And she's just had a serious nibble on the line, from some Aussie company exec, apparently.'

Madeleine continued staring out the window, avoiding his questioning gaze in the mirror.

'Don't know if she'll be able to convince her mum and brother to sell up, though,' he went on, returning his focus to the road. 'But if the word 'round town is right, maybe they won't have much choice.'

What would the 'word around town' say about her, Madeleine wondered, after the details of the castle's acquisition came to light? Maybe something like, 'The manipulative Aussie girl who almost killed a previous beau, and then used the castle's "blue-eyed boy" to pursue a mercenary agenda'.

She closed her eyes and slumped in her seat, letting her chin drop to her chest.

What if people she cared about, people like the Capaldis, came to doubt her integrity, to suspect she was without scruples? That would be a dreadful outcome ... though not the worst.

The worst had already happened. Byron now saw her as little more than a callous, manipulative user.

She sucked in a breath and raised her head, her expression hardening.

Why should she care if the thing between them was

over? It was only ever supposed to be a holiday flirtation, nothing remotely serious.

So why was a fat tear tracing a path down her cheek?

'Okay, here we are. The best pizza joint in Le Froid.' As he spoke, Jeff changed down gears and the bus rumbled to a stop.

Swiping an impatient hand across her cheek, Madeleine rose and hurried down the aisle and out of the bus. 'Won't be long.'

'No rush,' he called after her. 'It's home for me after I drop you off.'

As Jeff lumbered the bus away from the castle, Madeleine trudged to the Lodge's common area, pizza box in hand. Eating there would keep her room from smelling like pizza for the rest of her stay, and possibly the next millennia.

Pulling out a chair, she dropped the box on the table and opened the lid, then sat staring into space. Even the mouth-watering aromas of salami, mozzarella cheese, mushrooms, olives, and capsicum couldn't break through her dismal thoughts.

But why so dismal at the loss of her budding relationship with Byron, unless....

Engrossed in her musings, she didn't notice the dark eyes watching her from the gloom of the kitchen doorway.

. . .

Having just turned out the kitchen lights, Byron heard a bus drive off, followed by footsteps on the common room's flagstones and sounds of a chair being pulled out. Now he stood in the shadows, leaning on the door jamb, arms crossed over his chest, contemplating the source of both the sounds and his inner turmoil.

She sat alone at a table with what appeared to be a pizza box in front of her.

Why did the sight of her bring on such a swell of resentment, longing, disappointment, and yes, passion in him, damn it? How could he regard her with anything other than loathing after she'd blatantly used him to pursue her objective, of buying the castle out from under his family? A castle they'd sacrificed so much for, even losing a husband and father over it.

And now Emma's push for them to sell the estate had gained momentum. That was no doubt thanks to a well-placed word in her ear, and his eyes narrowed as he gazed at Madeleine, sitting motionless and silent at the table.

Then he sighed.

Emma was right, though. The family was being swamped by a looming tide of debt, a situation their mother had refused to acknowledge ... until now. As always he'd supported her stance, but it seemed Kathryn's attitude had changed. She'd even begun weighing in to the argument to sell, leaving him feeling under attack from all quarters.

He scowled and bent his head.

Why was he opposing this chance for them all to move on? Surely it made sense to cut their losses and sell what their dwindling resources could no longer sustain, at least not in the open-cheque way the historic estate so richly deserved.

He dragged an agitated hand through his hair and glanced again at Madeleine.

Her dejected body language and the untouched pizza ... was she miserable too?

As concern for her joined his other swirling emotions, Byron retreated into the dark kitchen. When it came to Madeleine Brande, he clearly couldn't trust himself to do the right thing, by either of them.

Whatever the right thing was.

And what about his family, was he doing right by them? Or had he become a liability, an obstruction stopping them from moving on to better things?

The leadlight entrance doors opened with the usual puff of air, flash of daylight, and awed intake of breath. Then a voice announced, 'Well, well,' and Emma looked up from the counter, to see a striking older woman standing inside the doors, smiling as though charmed by what she saw.

Tall and well built, the woman carried herself with an air of gracious authority. Her tailored pant suit, chic hairstyle, and tasteful—obviously not paste—jewellery, all projected sophistication ... of the snobbery-free kind, Emma intuited with a tinge of envy.

Still smiling, the woman strode to the counter and set down her case, a waft of French *parfum* following in her wake. When she rested a hand on the counter top, Emma's eyes were drawn to the long, elegant fingers, their manicured nails buffed to a clear shine.

'I'm here sooner than expected,' the woman announced, 'but am hoping to surprise my daughter. I believe she mentioned I'd be arriving this week?'

As she met the woman's perceptive gaze, Emma noted the unusual colour of her almond-shaped eyes.

A colour that had lately become familiar.

'Oh yes, and we'll be happy to accommodate you.' Emma's own eyes lit up and genuine pleasure coloured her polite receptionist's smile. 'It's my pleasure to welcome you to Lorienne Castle, Mrs Brande.'

18

'Hello? Is that Hacks for Hire? It's Madeleine Brande here.' From inside her mother's unit in the Lodge, she pressed the mobile phone against her ear. 'Look, I'm gonna have to reschedule today's booking. Sorry to mess you around, but can I change it to tomorrow please?' She paused to listen. 'Super, thanks. See you in the morning.'

Shutting the phone with a snap, she said to the open bedroom door, 'It's lucky you caught me now, otherwise I'd have been out all day.'

'Sorry to spoil your plans, my darling.' Connie's voice drifted from the bedroom, accompanied by the swish of a suitcase zipper. 'But it sounds like you were able to reschedule.'

'Yes, luckily.'

'Anyway, I don't know why you'd pay to ride some hired

nag when you have the beautiful Razoo at home. He's fine, by the way. I called in at the livery stable to check on him right before I left.'

'Thanks for doing that, Mum. And about today, I just felt like going for a ride. There's nothing like seeing the countryside from a saddle.' Madeleine didn't add that she found trail-riding a salve for troubled heart and head. 'And this place doesn't hire out "nags".' Her tone was sharper than intended. 'Only well schooled horses.'

Connie emerged to stand in the bedroom doorway. 'You *are* glad to see me, aren't you?'

'Of course I am.' Madeleine darted over to give her mother another hug. 'It's just ... I wasn't expecting you to arrive quite so soon.'

'Well, after the promising reports from my real estate agent and financier—and a less promising 'if you must' response from my doctor—I decided why wait? Luckily Celia was able to book me a seat on the next available flight.' Connie sniffed. 'Just a shame it had to depart at such an awful time.'

Madeleine glanced at her watch. 'Still, it got you here by eight am.' Thinking of her mother's efficient and ever-tolerant executive assistant, she grinned. 'Celia works wonders for you, I hope you know.'

'Mmm.' Turning, Connie ran her eyes over the unit's kitchenette. 'Any chance you could make me a tea, love? That awful stuff they serve on the planes....' She shuddered.

'I'm simply dying for a decent cuppa, and maybe something to eat?'

'Breakfast's available in the common room—' As she spoke, Madeleine's heart leapt with hope ... but just as quickly fell.

Lately Byron had been avoiding her as diligently as she'd been dodging him.

The replay of his deep voice in her head, 'Having someone else make the tea will be a pleasant change,' rekindled the hollow inner ache she'd been trying to douse.

'I'll ... um ... put the kettle on.'

'Thanks love.' Moving to the French doors, Connie threw the curtains aside with a flourish. 'Oh, just look at that view.' Opening the doors, she stepped out, taking a lungful of ocean air before resting her hands on the balcony railing.

Madeleine swallowed, picturing Byron admiring the view the day he'd called in, and recalling her struggle to stop ogling his wide-shouldered, slim-hipped physique.

At a whistle from the kettle she shrugged off the memories, and busied herself filling the teapot. 'Shall we have it out there, Mum?'

'Please,' Connie called over a shoulder. 'I don't want to turn my back on all this.'

After setting the tray on the small outdoor table, Madeleine handed her mother a steaming cup.

Connie continued gazing at the sun-kissed view while

murmuring her thanks. 'I can see why you've fallen in love with this place.'

And not just the place, perhaps....

Wait. What?

Madeleine's brow creased.

She'd fallen in love with the Lorienne estate, sure, but that was as far as her being 'in love' went. Anything else was just a ridiculous notion.

Cup in hand, she joined her mother at the railing. 'You were saying you've had favourable reports about the castle?'

'Yes.' Connie turned with shining eyes. 'And I'm positively rapt, especially now I've had my first glimpse of the property. Can't wait to see the rest.' She pulled her daughter in for another, one-armed hug. 'Thank you my darling, for finding this treasure.'

'My ... pleasure. Though it might not prove to be the treasure you're hoping for, Mum.'

'Oh I know. But it's exciting to even be considering it.' Connie held her daughter at arm's length and gazed into her eyes. 'Now, where are you at with Elizabeth's case?'

Madeleine's shoulders slumped. 'Nothing new to report, sadly. And I'm all out of places to search. The only other option would be to knock holes in the castle's walls to check for secret hiding spots, and we both know that's not gonna happen. Seems I've reached a stalemate.'

'Oh well, at least you can tell Gran you tried.'

Tried wasn't good enough. Was a long way from good enough.

'Now, what were you saying about the breakfast arrangements?' Connie's focus had clearly moved into the gastronomic sphere.

'It's served in the common room 'til nine am, so we can head over whenever you're ready.'

'Which is right now,' and Connie set her emptied tea cup on the table. 'Let's go.'

'Wait. Before I forget....' Madeleine darted back inside, to emerge moments later holding the tobacco tin, now cleaned almost to a shine and containing more than just a grubby map.

With a breathy, 'Ah, yes.' Connie took the tin from her. 'The famous Bedazzler.' Lifting the lid she extracted the ragged silk pouch, handed back the tin, and carefully tipped the necklace into her palm.

'I haven't mentioned the find to the McAlisters yet.' Madeleine watched her mother hold the necklace to the light, which the diamonds caught and reflected in a sparkling kaleidoscope, while the pearls delivered a discreetly lustrous, come-hither shine.

'It really is ... exquisite,' Connie breathed.

'Yes. So ... the McAlisters?'

Informing them of the find was the right thing to do, but—and Madeleine suppressed a wince—she hated the idea of owning up to what Byron would assume to be more 'snooping around'.

'What about the McAlisters?'

'Well ... I only found the necklace after discovering that,' and she pointed to the tin, 'in Byron's shed on the castle estate, which is still McAlister land.'

After carefully cupping the necklace in her hand, Connie tapped her lips with a finger before saying, 'We should have it valued first, and find out if there's a reward for its return. Then we'll have the full story to share with the McAlisters, if that's what you want to do.'

And it *was* what she wanted to do, despite being unlikely to heal the rift with Byron. Madeleine pretended to gaze out at the vista so her mother couldn't read her expression. 'And if there is a reward?'

'To still be on offer so long after the loss ... hmm ... I have my doubts. Let's wait and see.' Connie dangled the necklace in front of her eyes again. 'This beauty could fetch an even more significant price if put to auction.'

'And the proceeds?'

Connie tilted her head to eye her daughter. 'You found it, love, so that'll be your call.'

'We're helping ourselves to a buffet brekkie this morning,' Jill Fox announced after introductions had been made. 'The hot food's in the bain-marie, and the continental stuff is beside it, along with crockery and cutlery. Help yourselves whenever you're ready.'

No sign of Byron anywhere....

When she spotted chef Carl emerge from the kitchen with fresh trays of hash browns and sautéed mushrooms, Madeleine steered her mother over to the stack of clean crockery.

At her cheery, 'Morning Carl,' he glanced up, nodded, and continued swapping out the spent trays.

'On your own this morning?' she pressed.

'Yep.' A distinct sour edge to his voice.

Her smile wavered. 'Where's your partner in crime?'

'Byron?' Turning to peer at the pretty young woman in front of him, Carl gave a 'that'd be right' humph before growling, 'Your guess is as good as mine. He was *kind* enough to lay out all the breakfast settings last night, but no sign of 'im this mornin'.' With an irritated clanking of trays, he loaded up and bustled back to the kitchen.

Madeleine stared after him until aware she was standing alone, empty plate in hand. Hastily fronting up to the bain-marie she began piling on toast, grilled tomato, hash browns, mushrooms, bacon and scrambled eggs.

'Wow! There I was thinking *I* was the hungry one.' Coming to stand beside her, Connie eyed her daughter's full plate. 'Is one lifetime enough for you to eat all that, or are you taking the ancient Egyptian approach and also preparing for the afterlife?'

Freezing mid-scoop, Madeleine blinked at the pile of food she'd served herself. 'Oops. Didn't realise....' She flicked her mother a sheepish glance. 'Guess I was a bit heavy-handed.'

Connie took a clean plate from the stack. 'Here,' she said, gazing quizzically at her daughter, 'put some on mine.'

'So, Connie,' Jill piped up when the two women returned to the table, 'what's on the agenda for your first day here?'

'A tour of the castle and grounds this morning,' Connie replied with a smile, 'followed by a "nana nap" this afternoon to recover from a shatteringly early start. And dinner in the castle's dining room tonight, of course.'

Madeleine's fork clattered to her plate, making everyone jump. Flashing an apologetic wince, she mumbled, 'Sorry,' and turned to her mother. 'I thought we'd have dinner in town tonight? There's a great little Italian café—'

'Oh, but I'm *dying* to experience a castle dinner after everything you've told me. Maybe we can go to the Italian place tomorrow night?'

Madeleine opened her mouth ... then closed it and forced a smile.

When Byron leaned over to serve their bowls of soup, Madeleine caught her mother eyeing him. And he *was* worth a second look, no denying, with his slicked-back hair, handsome features, and those wide shoulders under the stylish butler's garb.

Connie's eyes held a mischievous gleam when she 'whispered' way too loudly, 'You didn't tell me he was movie-star gorgeous, love. This Byron of yours is quite delightful. But Kris—'

'He's not "my" Byron, Mum,' Madeleine hissed, with a hasty sideways glance in his direction. 'Not by a *very* long shot.'

He had his back to them, was moving down the table, but ... had he heard?

She cringed inwardly.

Having no choice but to serve them—her—with a smile must be tough going. While an awkward situation for them both, was it worse for Byron?

Catching her mother's knowing smile, Madeleine hastened to distract her. 'What was it you were going to say, about Kris?'

'Only that he's back from overseas.' Connie bent her head over her bowl. 'Mmm, this smells divine. Is the food and entertainment,' and she indicated Kathryn presiding in black-and-gold Victorian finery at the head of the table, 'always this good here?'

Noticing Kathryn cast a probing glance her mother's way, Madeleine's lips tightened. Were the two women exchanging subliminal messages after meeting that morning? Following her tour—make that inspection—of the castle, her mother's only comment was an annoyingly vague, 'It was wonderful.'

Wonderful? Oh sure, the Lorienne estate was that and more, but was it also worth shelling out millions to own? On that subject, her mother's equally vague, 'We'll see,' had spoken volumes. She would not have held back from saying if the castle hadn't lived up to expectations; that was just who Connie Brande was.

Snatching up her soup spoon, Madeleine was about to plunge it into the delicate swirl of sour cream in the centre of her pumpkin vichyssoise when her mother leaned in to ask, 'You seem subdued, my darling. Is something wrong?'

Drawing back to twirl the spoon in her fingers, Madeleine replied, 'I'm fine, Mum,' and stilled the spoon to stare at her reflection in its polished silver surface. 'Just … a bit tired.'

'*Tired?* You're young, and on holiday! If anything you should be totally refreshed, even jumping out of your skin.' Without taking her eyes off her daughter, Connie snatched a bite of her bread roll spread with whipped Tasmanian butter.

'I think all the sightseeing has worn me out.' Madeleine gave a half-hearted chuckle.

'Ahem.' As he came to stand at Connie's elbow Byron presented a bottle of red, one gloved hand at the base and the other supporting the neck. 'More wine, madam?'

'Please.' As she reached for her glass Connie threw a

wide-eyed, isn't-he-delightful glance at Madeleine, who groaned inwardly.

'And the white for you, miss?'

She had no choice but to look at him. Despite his hooded, unreadable gaze and the stiffness of his smile, having him so close took her breath away. Raising her glass, she stuttered, 'Y-yes ... thanks ... B-Byron,' and tried not to pull a face at her gaucheness.

Awkward? Only *excruciatingly* so.

After he'd moved on to the next table, Connie fixed her daughter with a probing gaze. 'I sense sparks and a prickly atmosphere between you two.'

Madeleine took a hasty mouthful of soup, noting after swallowing that the delicious vichyssoise deserved a more respectful appreciation. Sitting back when her mother turned to speak to another diner, she blew a resigned sigh.

Surviving this awkwardness, and all that was bound to come, was going to require some serious emotional armour....

On his return to clear their bowls Byron enquired with butler-esque formality, 'I hope you enjoyed your soup, ladies?'

Madeleine's pulse quickened at the sound of his deep voice, and when her nose caught a whiff of his familiar aftershave, she was transported to his cosy lounge room and the equally cosy—albeit sadly brief—time they'd spent there.

'Please pass on our compliments to the chef,' Connie was saying. 'That was the best soup I've had in a long time.'

'Happy to. And are you enjoying your stay with us?'

'Very much so, thank you.'

After a loaded pause, he enquired with what sounded to Madeleine like studied coolness, 'And what do you think of our castle?'

She risked a peek but his carefully non-committal expression gave nothing away.

'Marvellous, simply marvellous,' Connie enthused. 'I spent most of the day exploring it.'

'Naturally.'

Was there more than politeness in that one word? Madeleine tried not to frown. Condemnation perhaps? Was he thinking, *how nice for you to be enjoying a pleasant inspection of the castle you're planning to buy out from under us?*

Let's face it, if their roles were reversed....

'So, what do you have planned for tomorrow, Connie?' Sally's question floated from across the table.

'It appears I'm a free agent,' Connie replied with a sigh. 'My daughter's abandoning me in favour of doing an Annie Oakley impersonation.'

At Sally's 'Oh?' Connie grinned. 'She's going galloping around the hills on a hired hack.' Madeleine's eye roll only made Connie's grin widen. 'Although she did recommend the harbour cruise, so if the weather's nice I might take her advice.'

'*Vas* is *dis* "hack" you speak of?' Thomas interjected.

His question received soft chuckles from around the table, and Connie turned to him with a smile. 'Hack is another name for horse.'

'So, *vun* hires a horse ... er ... hack, like *vun* hires a car?'

'That's right, Thomas.'

'*Undt vere* is *zis* place?'

When her mother indicated for her to answer, Madeleine said, 'Next door to the castle. The ride takes in the peninsula and its fabulous scenery. Perhaps you and Selena would like to come along?'

'*Danke,* but *ve* are doing *ze* harbour cruise.'

'Well that settles it,' Connie announced, 'I'm going cruising tomorrow.'

As Sally and Alan launched into glowing descriptions of the harbour's highlights, Byron finished piling the soup bowls on his trolley.

Madeleine tried not to stare at his stiff, closed-off back as he quietly wheeled the load into the kitchen, letting the door swing shut behind him.

19

'Morning Mum.' After dropping a quick peck on her mother's cheek, Madeleine dashed back into the bedroom. 'Sorry about this, gotta finish dressing. I'm running late for my ride.'

Connie glanced at her watch. 'You've eaten already?'

'Yep, had to make an early start this morning.'

'I was looking forward to our having breakfast together again. Why didn't you come get me?'

'Thought I'd let you sleep.' Pulling a long-sleeved polo shirt over her head, Madeleine stepped into the doorway of her bedroom. 'You're on holiday, remember?' She nipped back into the room calling over a shoulder, 'And still recuperating.'

'Recuperating? Pish posh!' Connie gave an affected sigh

and raised her voice. 'I'll go for breakfast and leave you to it, shall I?'

'Okay. Have fun on your excursions today.'

'You too.'

Inside the bedroom Madeleine sat silent and unmoving, one foot raised, sock in hand, the toothbrush in her mouth dripping white froth on her jodhpurs.

Would the results of her mother's 'excursions' make this a red letter day? Would she find still more to consider 'wonderful' about the castle? A shrewd businesswoman, she was still capable of overlooking the downsides of an exciting prospect, like the amount of work the castle still needed. And when it came to the acquisition of Lorienne Castle, 'excited' was an understatement.

Another glob of froth fell on her joddies.

Tossing the sock to the floor beside her riding boots, she hurried to the bathroom.

'Did you hear me, love?' Connie called from outside the bedroom doorway.

Oh. Hadn't she gone already? Not that Madeleine wished her mother somewhere else ... of course she didn't. It was just....

She whipped the toothbrush from her mouth. 'Thorry, Mum.' Her semi-coherent response splattered froth on the bathroom mirror.

Damn.

'Gotta rush.' The splatter oozed down the glass and she swiped it away with a hand, leaving a milky smear behind.

Damn.

'I'm late-late-late! Can we talk when I get back?'

'Of course. Bye, love, you be safe now.'

The chocolate-brown gelding nuzzled her as Madeleine slipped the bridle over his handsome head and fastened the throat strap.

She rubbed the white star between his eyes. 'You're a beautiful boy, Abraham.'

He stood quietly while she finished saddling him, only tossing his head with an expectant snort when she slipped her foot into the stirrup. Once in the saddle, she bent to adjust the stirrup leathers. 'Wow, you're taller than Raz, big fella.'

The guide, a middle-aged man, ambled up beside them on a liver chestnut quarter horse, followed by two other riders, one on a showy Anglo Arab with a wide blaze and four white socks, the other on a high-stepping brown thoroughbred.

Watching Madeleine make her adjustments the man said, 'Watch Abe, 'specially when he's fresh. Likes to stretch his legs.'

Madeleine nodded and leaned forward to pat her mount's velvety neck.

'There'll be another rider joining us but we won't wait around for 'im. He knows the route and can catch up. Right then, let's go.' The guide urged his horse into a lope and the other three followed him out of the yards.

They passed a yarded grey thoroughbred, which charged around, pig-rooting and rearing at the fence, clearly unhappy at being left behind.

Headstrong at first, Abraham settled into a smooth, easy-on-the-buttocks gait as the group set off at a canter down a shady, leaf-strewn path. The morning sun shafted through the thickets of trees, and a gentle breeze lifted Madeleine's fringe as she tipped her face to the sky.

'Everyone up for a jump?' the guide called from the front of the group. 'Just a low gate.' At an eager chorus of Yeahs he grinned and veered left at a fork in the path, toward the timber gateway of a partially wooded field.

All four horses pricked their ears as their riders gathered them to take the fence. Madeleine felt Abraham's muscles bunch beneath her as they waited their turn, and he only needed the slightest pressure to leap into a canter and head for the obstacle. His powerful hindquarters had them sailing over the gate with ease, and on the other side she reined him in, smiling broadly while he snorted and tossed his head.

'Nicely done,' the guide called from where he'd stopped by the side of the track. 'He's not for everyone but you handle Abe well.'

As Madeleine bent to pat her mount's warm shoulder, the drum of galloping hooves reached her ears. Abraham stirred beneath her, his black-tipped ears flicking back and forth.

'Just our late arrival,' the guide called. Spinning his horse around, he yelled, 'Let's give him a run for his money!'

Infected by the excitement in the air and the sound of a fast-approaching horse, all four mounts leapt into a gallop. With the guide in the lead they flew along the path, and soon Madeleine had to check Abraham from taking the lead.

'Go on ahead if y'want,' the guide yelled, 'this track goes for miles.'

She nodded and let Abraham have his head. The horse responded immediately, stretching his long legs and powering forward. Tucking herself into his neck, Madeleine watched as the ground below his flying hooves became a blur. The air rushed past them, whooshing in her ears and whipping Abraham's mane into her face.

Laughing at the sheer exhilaration of the moment, she sensed another horse coming alongside them. The grey thoroughbred raced up with all the fire and pace of a Melbourne Cup favourite, ears and head forward, sweat foaming on its neck. It wasn't until they drew level that Madeleine glimpsed the rider.

And gave a start that had Abraham's ears flicking back at her.

Leaning low over the grey's neck, Byron looked for all the world like he'd been born in the saddle.

They raced along, until it became clear neither competitive animal would let the other 'win', and their riders reined them in. As their blowing mounts slowed, Madeleine's stirrups clanged agains Byron's and the brief touch brought on a familiar arc of energy. Glancing over, she found him studying her through narrowed eyes.

'Hey,' was all she could think to say, and got an unsmiling, 'Hey,' in response.

'I didn't think—'

Damn, her mouth was so dry. From the wind in her face, or....?

Or nothing.

She licked her lips and tried again. 'I didn't think you could ride ... horses?'

'I never said I couldn't, only that I prefer bikes.' Byron gave a ghost of a smile before returning his gaze ahead.

'You look at home in a saddle.'

'Knowing how to ride has come in handy at times.' He nodded toward the group now a way behind them. 'And this place has decent horses at least.'

'Yes, they do.'

She'd never had trouble talking to him before, but now ... her mind just wouldn't come up with anything remotely intelligent to say.

After an awkward silence he cleared his throat. 'You'll be pleased to hear that Emma has finally convinced Mum to sell the castle.'

Madeleine's insides clenched.

'You've certainly done a number on my sister.' His tone soured. 'And she's done one on Mum. Now they're both insisting I agree to sell if we get an offer to purchase.' His jaw set in a tight line. 'And I won't stand in their way, or yours. I'll add my signature to the contract of sale ... under sufferance.'

She opened her mouth, but what could she say at this point that didn't sound trite or insincere?

Nothing.

Approaching hoof beats reached their ears. The other riders were catching up.

'Anyway,' Byron said with an air of finality, 'I thought you'd want to know how the land lies.'

Still the right words—or any that might not make things worse—wouldn't come to her.

At her continued silence he cast a final accusing glance and dug his heels into the grey's side. It gave a startled grunt and leapt into a fast trot.

Madeleine didn't need to urge Abraham to match the pace. As she rose to the trot she puffed, 'Byron! Wait, please,' and drew level with him again. 'Let's talk about this.'

'So now you wanna talk.' He kept his eyes fixed ahead. 'Don't bother. As far as I'm concerned the deal's done, so you don't have to waste your time with me anymore.'

'What do you mean, waste my time with you? That's not ... I don't....' She frowned and tried to gather her thoughts. 'Look, I didn't ... come here to instigate a buy-out, or a hostile takeover, or whatever you want to call it. I came here for a holiday.'

'And to case the castle,' he threw back.

'Well ... I....' Wincing, she gritted her teeth. 'It was only when I heard you might be forced to sell that things changed. To be honest, I didn't think Mum would be all that interested in buying the castle. Then again, with our family connection to the place—'

'*Your* family connection? What about mine?'

'Of course, your family owns Lorienne Castle, but it also has a place in my history.'

'History?' With a harsh snort he flicked her a sideway glance. 'That's what it's about to become for us too, history.' Fixing her with a bleak smile he added, 'And the castle's not the only thing I'm losing.' As he spoke he glanced over a shoulder.

The other riders were almost upon them.

Feeling him shorten the reins, the grey gathered itself expectantly. 'I think we've said all we need to, Ms de Brande Barlow.' Eyeing her with a mixture of resentment, regret, resignation and grim resolve, Byron ground out, 'Goodbye, Madeleine, and best of luck with ... everything,' and put his heels to the thoroughbred's sides.

The keyed-up horse leapt into a standing gallop and thundered away, its racing hooves throwing clods of dirt into the air.

'Byron!' Her cry was lost in their swirling wake as she struggled to steady an excited, spinning-on-the-spot

Abraham. When he finally settled, she took a shuddering breath and watched, wretchedly, as Byron hurtled past the other riders.

His parting words sounded dreadfully final.

Her breath caught in her throat.

Hadn't Kris said something similar, and in the same relationship-ending way, right before storming out of her apartment?

Toward an accident that almost claimed his life.

No, please, not again.

'Hey, Gino, look-a who's here!' Ada rushed over to throw chubby, garlicky arms around a grinning Madeleine.

'Lovely to see you again, Ada.' When she could extricate herself, Madeleine introduced her mother, who smiled and extended an elegant hand. Ada ignored it, choosing instead to draw Connie into a robust hug, managing to smear tomato paste on the other's cream linen dress in the process.

Connie noticed the smear.

Ada didn't. 'Maddie-Rosa's mother,' she gushed, 'so glad to meet-a you!'

Smiling over the effusive woman's shoulder, Connie raised eyebrows at her daughter.

Madeleine looked past her to Ada. 'We haven't booked, so if you don't have a table—'

'Don't-a be silly! We always have a table for Byron's Rosa.'

Oh no.

Madeleine squirmed inwardly as Connie's eyebrows rose higher.

'He's not with-a you tonight?'

'No.' Unable to think of anything more to say, and fearful of being at the mercy of two skilled interrogators, Madeleine was relieved when Ada simply said, 'That's a shame,' and led them to a table for two.

'I get-a you some menus.'

When Ada made to bustle off to the kitchen, Madeleine caught her hand. 'We already know what we'd like to order.'

Anything to delay her mother's inevitable grilling....

Connie's whispered, 'We do?' coincided with Ada's, 'You do?'

'Yes, two of Gino's famous carbonaras and your yummy salads, please?'

When the man himself emerged through the kitchen's swing doors and spotted them, he made straight for their table where they once again launched into introductions.

'Ah, the mama! So we get to meet-a-Rosa's family.' Gino took Connie's extended hand in his and bent to smile into her eyes. 'And-a so beautiful too, *si*, like-a her daughter.'

The two women shared a self-conscious grin.

'I always-a say to Byron,' Gino enthused, 'you wanna know what your girl be like when she's-a older? You look-a at the Mama.' He opened his arms in a flourish and inclined his head toward Connie. 'And now Byron, he's-a know he's-a found a prize.' Beaming, he swept a glance out to the footpath. 'Where is-a our boy?'

Madeleine took a breath and murmured, 'He's … not with us tonight.'

'Oh, that-a boy,' Gino grumbled. 'Should-a be spending time with his future family, not a-working.'

His *future family?*

Madeleine managed to swallow a gasp but couldn't help screwing up her face.

Connie stared open-mouthed first at her, then at Gino, Ada, and back at her daughter again.

As if sensing tension, Ada said loudly, 'We need-a two carbonaras and-a salads, Gino, *grazi*. I get-a the wine.'

'Excuse-a me, lovely ladies. *La cucina,* she calls.' With a regretful bow of his head, Gino returned to the kitchen.

Before following him, Ada took Madeleine's hand and leaned in to say softly, 'We very glad-a to see you, and-a to meet your Mama.'

At Gino's, 'Ada!' from the kitchen, she called, 'Coming!' and flashed another smile at Madeleine before hurrying away.

With a breathy, 'Well,' Connie watched Ada's broad back disappear through the kitchen doors. 'In the words of you young people, WTF?'

'Simply a misunderstanding. Can we leave it for now?'

Dragging an agitated hand through her hair, Madeleine met her mother's perplexed gaze. 'Please?'

Why had she thought bringing her mother to the café was preferable to another awkward dinner in the castle? Talk about a *bad* idea.

And what if her mother's plans worked out? Would Madeleine be able to eat here again once the Capaldis knew the part she'd played in the ... scheme, for want of a better word? No ... at least not until she'd made her peace with Byron, and through him, the Capaldis.

And was that even possible? He'd made it clear he didn't want a bar of her.

Her heart rose into her throat.

Could she sit him down and make him understand that despite how it appeared, she'd never meant to hurt him or his family?

Would it help to admit that by hurting him, she'd also hurt herself?

Or was that giving too much away?

20

'I've set the ball rolling,' Connie waved the signed contract at her daughter. 'There are a number of conditions to be met prior to settlement, but all going well Lorienne Castle will soon be ours.'

Madeleine stared at the contract.

How to respond? With a hypocritical 'That's wonderful'? Could she make it sound sufficiently sincere? Her mother was so damn perceptive. Though ... it *was* wonderful news, wasn't it? Not only for her family but also for the castle, which now stood a chance of being returned to its former glory. Shouldn't she be glad on that basis?

Her daughter's lack of enthusiasm obviously hadn't registered, for Connie went on gleefully, 'I have more good news too. Emma put me in touch with the building contractor who carried out the original renovation work.

Turns out he's always wanted to finish the castle job "properly" is how he put it, and will make himself and his team available when the time comes.'

She gave a delighted shiver. 'I just *adore* when a plan fall into place like this. Feels like ... affirmation.'

Madeleine remained silent, struggling to keep the tangle of emotions from showing on her face.

So, it was happening.

They were indeed, as Byron had alleged, 'buying the castle, their livelihood and home,' out from under the McAlisters.

And there was no stopping Connie Brande once she had the bit between her teeth.

'In other news, I've had an update on the Bedazzler,' she went on. 'Apparently the family of the original owners has died out, so that puts paid to any monetary reward for its return. I've already contacted Sotherby's to arrange a valuation, so there may be more funds coming our way to help pay for the renovations. Assuming,' and she arched an eyebrow at her daughter, 'you decide to put it up for auction.'

With barely a pause she charged on. 'Oh, and one final thing. I've instructed Celia to draw up the paperwork to formalise transfer of management of CRB Consulting. So celebrations are definitely in order don't you agree, love?'

Madeleine sighed. 'Of course.' True to form, there was no stopping or even slowing the Connie express train once it left the station.

. . .

'Ms Brande ... er ... Madeleine, good afternoon. What can I do for you?'

Emma's cool demeanour had definitely thawed. It was amazing what offloading a problem can do to a person's spirits.

Madeleine took care to keep her tone light, free of cynicism. 'I was hoping to speak to Byron but haven't seen him around. Any idea where I might find him?'

'You're asking me?' From where she stood behind the reception counter, Emma's eyes narrowed. 'I thought you two were seeing each other?'

'We'd ... um ... gone out once or twice. Whether you'd class that as seeing each other—'

'Either way,' and Emma shrugged, 'I would've thought he'd tell you if he was going away.'

Madeleine swallowed her annoyance. 'So he has? Gone away, I mean?'

'Took a few days off, to clear his head or some such thing.' As she spoke, Emma flicked a significant glance over Madeleine's shoulder and raised a 'just wait' finger at her. 'Hello, and welcome to Lorienne Castle,' she said brightly, slipping into the usual spiel. 'Checking-in, are we?'

Madeleine stepped back to make room for the newly arrived guest, only to bump into a firm body. Then a pair of hands grasped her arms and a man's voice above her head said, 'Hello, Madeleine.'

She froze.

It wasn't Byron's voice, but familiar all the same.

A voice from the past....

With a gasp she whipped around, shock, dismay, guilt, all rising suffocatingly as she stared at the fair-haired man gazing fondly down at her.

The man whose scarred face she'd thought she'd never see again.

The man whose life had almost ended, thanks to her.

Dr Kris de Voss.

They stared at each other for a long moment.

She, open-mouthed in disbelief, emotions in turmoil, questions colliding in her mind.

He, with an unsteady smile, and a touching uncertainty in his eyes.

'You missed it.'

'Missed what?'

Emma eyed her grim-faced brother, perched on the corner of her desk. Just back from two days away, he appeared as restless and unhappy as before he left. Girl trouble again, no doubt. He could be such a sucker for a pretty face....

'A bloke with a fancy double-barrelled name checked in a short while ago,' she went on. 'He would've been drop-dead gorgeous if not for the scars, and partly shaved head.'

Byron frowned. 'So why should that interest me?'

'Madeleine was here when he arrived, and you should've seen her expression. It was ... *awkward!* Like ... well ... like she was seeing a ghost. And I know that look,' Emma added with the twitch of an eyebrow, 'only too well.'

'And you believe this bloke is...?'

'A past ... or maybe,' and she pursed her lips in thought, 'not so past, flame.'

'You think he chased her here?'

'Can't know for sure, but it looked that way to me.'

'What did Madeleine say to him?'

'I didn't catch much of it. She saw I was listening and lowered her voice, and then she rushed off. But I could tell she was shocked to see him.'

'And pleased?'

'More stunned I think, though I could be wrong about that. It's possible she didn't want to let on that she was pleased to see him, in case it got back to you through me.'

Byron lifted his chin. 'Not that it's any concern of mine.'

'Weren't you two—?'

'No.' He fixed his sister with a stony gaze. 'We weren't anything.' His expression darkened. 'And even less of anything now.'

Emma frowned. 'What's that supposed—' At his loud expletive, she barked, 'Hey! Don't use that language here,' and swept an angry glance around the reception area. 'Someone might hear you. And if that someone was Mum, she'd say you're not too old for a tongue peppering.'

'Yeah, yeah. Sorry.' He hung his head. 'It's just that there's even less holding me here now.'

'You mean now we're selling the castle?'

'Selling ... yes.' When he raised his head, Emma noted the brooding, faraway look in her brother's eyes. 'And buying our freedom,' he added.

'What—'

With a growled, 'Leave it, Em,' he pushed away from the desk and marched off.

The sky held a mere promise of daylight as Madeleine strode along the pathway, the clinging tendrils of early morning fog swirling in eddies around her feet, dampening her footfalls.

Feeling like the only person awake on Earth was an empowering sensation, one that helped her put other issues, especially one with fair hair and a scarred face, aside.

If only briefly.

The castle loomed in the dimness, eerily silent, as she took the fork in the pathway toward Byron's cottage.

Walking on, she dragged a hand across her forehead. No amount of makeup could cover the dark circles under her eyes after another poor night's sleep. Presenting herself to Byron in this sleep-deprived state would be humiliating but necessary. She had to bare her soul to him, or she might never enjoy unbroken slumber again.

He needed to understand her innocent—mostly innocent—involvement in the castle's purchase. Also where Kris, whose arrival Emma was sure to have described to her brother, fitted in her life. Though ... did she fully understand that herself? She shook the question away as the cottage loomed out of the fog, bringing with it pangs of uncertainty.

Emma had said Byron was back, but would he be home now?

Would he be awake?

Would he be pleased or angry to see her?

Would he be alone?

From the gate she paused to eye the cottage. It looked its age in the fog; shabby, and heart-sinkingly dreary with no smoke curling from the chimney, no cheery glow of light spilling from the windows. With all the curtains drawn the place appeared shuttered, cloaked with a chill sense of desertion as if its warm heart had grown still and cold.

Murmuring, 'Oh no,' through leaden lips, Madeleine hurried up the path and knocked on the front door.

The sound reverberated hollowly, before a heavy silence settled again.

She tried once more.

Same result.

Maybe he was over at the Lodge, preparing to serve breakfast to the guests?

Although ... that wouldn't explain why the cottage was all locked up, dark, and lifeless.

She stood staring at the door and chewing her lower lip.

The shed, of course!

Striding across, she stood just inside the entrance and after her eyes adjusted to the gloom, swept a searching gaze around.

The Ducati's parking spot was empty. The bike was gone.

And Byron with it.

The following day....

'He'd only been home for like twenty-four hours when he stalked into Mum's office in a huff, said something like "the castle's sold so you don't need me anymore" and took off.' Emma screwed up her face. 'Which is real handy, as it means we're short a butler and I'll have to stand in—'

Madeleine threw up a hand. 'Byron really said that?'

'That we don't need him anymore? Yes, he really did. And that he'd call us when he got there.'

'Where's "there"?'

'You don't know?' Emma eyed her warily. 'So once again you have no clue where he's gone, or how long for?'

Madeleine held her gaze and said nothing.

'If he wanted you to know wouldn't he have told you himself?'

'We did have something of a ... falling out.'

'Let me guess. Over your mother buying the castle?' Emma's eyes glinted. 'Or was it about that Kris bloke?'

'I didn't ... he wasn't ... he's not....' Madeleine blinked hard and swallowed. 'Look, can you at least tell me where Byron's gone? It's not like I'll go chasing after him like some crazed stalker.'

When Emma merely arched an eyebrow at her, Madeleine clicked her tongue. 'The reason I need to contact him is that we have a job offer we'd like him to consider.'

'What sort of job?'

'Once the transfer of ownership is completed, we hope he'll take up the position of overseeing manager.'

'Oh, I see. Lucky old By. Well, that changes things.' Emma chewed her lip. 'He's gone to the mainland, to find Dad.'

'Byron's gone to look for your father?'

Emma nodded.

'Why now?'

'Dad always said he'd come back if Mum gave up the castle. And now she has.'

Madeleine stared at her without speaking.

It made sense for Byron to go looking for his father. Like Humpty Dumpty, he wanted to put his family back together again. And a desire to mend his family was totally understandable.

Not wanting to mend his relationship with her, also totally understandable. And totally upsetting, for reasons she refused to examine.

Some weeks later....

The brown-gold, green-flecked hazel 'Brande Topaz' eyes gazed back at Madeleine from the restored painting. It sat on the floor of Elizabeth's music room, leaning against the wall, waiting to be hung.

The restorer had done a wonderful job of bringing Elizabeth Lorienne back to life in dramatic swirls of oil paints on canvas. Her classic features, the rich maroon of her velvet gown, the elegant fingers gripping the diary with its ink-tipped quill and ribbon bookmark, the cat at her feet, all so ... lifelike.

The room too had been brought back to life. The oval mirror was still in place, milky glass and all, but had been cleaned and re-hung in its original spot as a testament to the passing of time. The peeling wallpaper was gone but the suit of armour remained, straightened and polished to a pewter-like shine.

The parlour chair, now sporting chintz upholstery, sat beside the grandfather clock still standing at attention where it had for an age but with a recently polished timber body, brass face cleaned of tarnish, and hands and pendulum happily ticking over the minutes and hours.

And as for Elizabeth's portrait … now it was fully restored Madeleine would ask if one of the builder's tradies could be spared to hang the painting above the fireplace in that room.

Why wouldn't the damn painting sit square? With an irritated grunt the tradie lifted it down again and ran a work-gloved hand over the stone wall.

That's why.

One of the bricks was out of alignment.

And … loose.

After working it free he lifted it out, to reveal a dark cavity in the wall. Yet another hidey-hole. This damn castle was full of them. Sadly none had contained anything worth pocketing so far. And even if they had, the boss was clear about anything they found being handed over to the new owners.

Tugging off his gloves, he reached into the hole and felt around with his fingers, jerking his hand back when they bumped against something furry.

A petrified rat carcass probably. Or worse, a live rat.

In the absence of frantic scurrying or other sounds of live rodent, he extended a finger again to prod the object. Didn't feel like there was a skeleton of any kind under the fur, so he grabbed hold of the object and tugged it out of the opening.

His eyes lit up as he studied the delicate velvet pouch cradled in his large workman's paw. Clearly old, it was covered in dust and swathed in cobwebs. He'd have to be careful handling it.

When he brushed away some of the dust the initials EDBB became visible, embroidered in gold thread on the crumbling velvet. Intrigued, he released the ancient silk drawstring, which promptly disintegrated in his hand.

Cursing under his breath, he carried on.

At least the pouch survived being opened. Taking extra care not to tear the fabric, he widened the neck and peered in at the contents.

Instead of the hoped-for sparkle of diamonds—a bloke can dream, and after all, finders is keepers—he found himself staring at a small, gold-leafed book.

A book? Was that all?

Flipping over the pouch, he shook out the contents.

When only the book tumbled into his palm, he put the pouch to his face and peered into it.

Nothing else.

This was not his lucky day.

His frustrated breath sent the dust in his hand into a swirling dance.

Noting the same initials on the book's leather cover, he opened it to pages of handwriting—a woman's judging by the neatness—with dates against each entry.

Just another diary.

He swore again.

How many did this one make? Three at least, all written by people who'd lived in the castle long enough to make or discover secret hiding places. Still, not the find of the century.

With a grunt he snapped the book closed and slipped it back into the pouch, which he jammed into his top pocket. It could stay there 'til he next caught up with the boss.

And whoever the boss passed it onto next was welcome to it.

21

From: Madeleine.Brande

To: Connie.Brande

Re: Castle Status Report and some news

Hey Mum.

How's the AGM going? Are you taking my advice and letting others get the odd word in? ;-) No need to rush back, I'm sure Gran's thrilled to have you on the 'mainland' for a while. As you can tell from that, my metamorphosis from Mainlander to Taswegian is progressing nicely (!) as are our renos, I'm pleased to report.

The builders keep discovering hidey-holes in the castle, so I'm accumulating quite a collection of fascinating old documents, letters, newspaper clippings, and other correspondence. The Loriennes (whose 'treasures' I believe these must've been) were skilled at finding little nooks and crannies in the walls and under the floorboards to hide their secrets!

The latest unearthed treasures are two leather-bound diaries, belonging to Edward and his father Richard. They're in excellent condition for their age. It appears father and son prided themselves on keeping detailed records in oh-so elegant handwriting, so the journals were quite the find. From what I've read so far, the entries deal mostly with the running of the estate and other business affairs.

Richard's contains pages and pages on the castle's construction—it was certainly a project close to his heart— but also mentions his daughter and Edward's younger sister, Genevieve. Did I tell you I found a portrait of her, hanging among the other paintings in the gallery? Apparently Richard had the portrait commissioned for her birthday, and later penned this poem for her:

A daughter we loved and tried so to save,
A sister so constant, so true and so brave,
A kind friend whose loss will e'er be bereaved,
We shall never forget you, sweet Genevieve.

Sad but pretty words, and a sad end for a pretty girl. Typhoid, what a nasty disease. Richard mentions Genevieve being 'in the grip of delirium, eyes glazed over, "rose" spots forming above her décolletage', before 'masked men' carted her away to an isolation ward.

She died soon after making what Richard calls a 'rash' promise to one Philip Mason, who he describes as 'unacceptably lower class'.

These diaries make fascinating, if often melancholy, reading. I've only skimmed over some of the entries, and wish I could stay awake longer to read more, but these busy days leave me struggling to keep my eyes open at night. Of course the end results of all this work will be totally worth it. And on that subject, the building inspector made an impromptu call at the site yesterday arvo (yikes!). Thankfully he left satisfied with everything. * wipes brow *

My room in the castle is still a mess of drop cloths, tools, and paint tins so I'll be staying in the Lodge a while longer. Your room's transformation is complete though. Gone is the dreary, dungeon-like black hole with horrid torn drapes, cracked lino, and peeling Victorian wallpaper, replaced by walls painted two shades of violet, and white furnishing and curtains to make a delightful contrast.

I don't know how Kathryn tolerated sleeping in there the way it was, and Emma's room wasn't much better. Guess they had to prioritise expenditures, especially before the castle started paying its way.

Back to my list of jobs.

I've started clearing the courtyard outside the kitchen ready for a flurry of plantings, which 'Kathryn-of-the-green-thumb' McAlister has kindly offered to oversee. I can't wait for that spot to be growing more than every type of moss known to man!

Speaking of Kathryn, she called in for morning tea yesterday and told us about the 'perfect home' she's found to buy. It's a cottage on a large block at the edge of town, with heaps of scope for her green thumbs. She's glad to be moving out of the rented flat – no doubt found it cramped digs after living in the castle.

As for Emma, she approached me about taking over Byron's cottage and I see no reason why she shouldn't live there, at least until he returns. She can look after it in his absence, and to be honest, it's handy having her readily available on site for late night call-outs from guests. We've drawn up a roster to share that responsibility between us.

I'm glad we decided to risk asking Emma to share management duties with me during the changeover. The new responsibility, along with coming out from under her mother's and brother's shadows, has been the making of her. I'm not suggesting she isn't still ... heavy-going ... at times, but I suspect that's brought on by her need to be needed. And she's definitely needed now. I couldn't cope without having her sharing oversight of castle operations.

Yeah, I know what you're thinking, that we should begin the recruitment process to appoint a permanent manager, but I keep hoping we'll get the chance to offer the job to Byron. He should at least have the right of first refusal before we go looking for someone else, don't you think? If for no other reason than that he'd be brilliant in the role.

Oh, one more thing about Kathryn's visit. She made a

point of thanking me, and you through me, for buying the castle and sharing the Bedazzler's proceeds with them. Maybe she sensed my concerns that she might hold a grudge, and wanted to put me at ease. Anyway, she said letting go of the castle and forging a new life has freed the three of them, and she does look like a new woman lately.

Apparently her garden design business is taking off, and she's loving working outdoors. Says it beats hands-down all the brooding over unpaid bills in a gloomy hole-in-the-wall office. That space is now the brilliant wine cellar we envisioned it could be, by the way, thanks to our talented building contractor Bob the Builder (I love that his name really is Bob!).

Isn't it fab that our buying the castle has freed Kathryn to realise her dreams? And before you ask, no, I haven't heard from Byron, but he has been in touch with Kathryn. She confirmed that he's in Australia with his dad. It took him a while to find his father; apparently Rob McAlister knows how to stay 'off the grid'.

Like father like son, I guess. Byron's certainly not making it easy for us to reach him.

Anyway, that's all for now. Looking forward to having you back 'home' at the castle soon.

Maddie xxx

As she signed off the email, an image of Byron galloping away flashed into her mind.

Not making it easy to find him? You bet.

'Madeleine!'

She flinched.

Damn. Wasn't he here only a day or two ago?

Ignoring the now familiar sinking feeling, she composed her face and turned to see him jogging up the corridor toward her. 'Hello Kris. To what do we owe the pleasure?' She refrained from adding, 'Again.'

She should count her blessings though. Having him here at the castle had been ... unnerving, to say the least. So it had come as a huge relief when he checked out after only a brief stay, no doubt thanks to her less than enthusiastic welcome.

For which she still felt guilty. And cowardly. She should've faced the situation head-on, but it was all so ... unexpected. Both his arrival and his obvious, if as yet unspoken, desire to rekindle their relationship.

A relationship already drenched in guilt.

Mostly hers.

And her relief when he checked out hadn't lasted long, was killed stone-dead when he announced his intention to settle in Le Froid.

Not to holiday but to *settle* in the closest town to what was now her home.

When that announcement left her staring open-mouthed at him, he'd given one of those crooked—even more so, thanks to the scars—smiles of his and explained that he'd been offered a position with the local hospital. A position he intended to accept.

Taken on its own, the job offer was no surprise. Like most regional hospitals, Le Froid's was always in need of more experienced medical staff. And Dr Kris de Voss had proven himself, before the accident, to be an excellent physician. So the hospital board had welcomed him with open arms, even offering him long-term accommodation for the duration of his tenure.

The board's eager reception had contrasted starkly with her own luke-warm greeting when he turned up at the castle, uninvited and unexpected.

And unwelcome?

There's that stab of guilt again.

And now he'd become a regular visitor to the castle, having decided—on a whim?—to leave his family, friends, and a thriving private practice on Queensland's Sunshine Coast to relocate to an out-of-the-way place in Tassie. While taking a job with a regional hospital could be viewed as a selfless act, the move was not consistent with the ambitious man Madeleine knew Kris to be.

No, he'd moved here to be near her. It was the only reasonable explanation; one that spawned the impulse to duck whenever she spotted him.

Which was tiring, time-wasting, and, let's face it, infantile.

Also tough to resist.

'Just thought I'd drop in for a quick chat.'

A less intimidating label for the 'serious talk' he'd been trying to have with her since arriving in Tasmania. She stopped herself from pulling a face.

'Glad I spotted you.' He slowed on reaching her side. 'You've been hard to find.'

On purpose, but the message hadn't got through to him.

Sensing he was about to take one of her hands she put it to her head, making a show of feeling for the ever-present wood shavings and sticky paint drips in her hair.

'Sorry, now's not a great time. I've been waiting to catch the plumber for weeks and he's just arrived, so....' She flashed an apologetic smile but slid her eyes away from the still-healing scars on his face.

'I won't keep you.' When she made to push her way through the glass doors, he followed her out. 'Just wanted to ask if you're free for dinner tonight?'

The icy sea breeze buffeted them as they stood on the front landing, making them tug their jackets closer. Madeleine glanced wistfully at the stairs, quashing the impulse to dash down them, and saw the plumber standing at the base staring expectantly up at her. She released an audible breath.

Talk about feeling trapped. And whose cowardly fault was that?

Pasting on a smile she turned to Kris. 'Thanks, but tonight doesn't work for me. I have a Chamber of Commerce meeting in town. And tomorrow night,' she added before he could suggest it, 'we have guests to entertain in the dining room.'

His expression lifted. 'In that case, I'll be one of them. And you'll be free one evening for a quiet dinner together, surely?' His mouth stretched into a hopeful grin, whitening the scars against his faded tan.

The sinking feeling returned as she took in his once-handsome face, the ample forehead under fashionably tousled short blonde hair, straight nose above a wide mouth, and strong, stubbled chin. The contrasting vulnerability in his deep-set blue eyes, and the fuzzy regrowth on a recently shaved section of his head made the guilt she'd been carrying around since his accident slice into her stomach like a blade.

It was obvious he wanted to talk about 'them', and considering all the trouble he was going to, she owed him a hearing at least.

With an apologetic glance at the none-too-patient plumber, she said hastily, 'Wednesday night?'

'Super.' Kris beamed at her. 'How about I take you to that Italian place in town, the one I heard you and Connie raving about?'

Gino's? No way! She cared too much for the Capaldis' good opinion to dine at their café with 'another' man. And what if it led to an all-out interrogation? That would be awkward for everyone.

'We'll sort that out later,' she threw over a shoulder

while descending the stairs two at a time. 'Right now I've gotta dash. The plumber's here at last.'

Kris waited while she shook hands with the plumber and led him away, before throwing an exultant air punch once they were out of sight. He was finally going to have the tête-à-tête he'd been planning since waking up in the ICU.

Although his mother was against his plan to win Madeleine back, talk of a wedding and grandchildren would bring her around. Especially after Madeleine demonstrated her willingness to settle into the dedicated role of doctor's wife, something she must be ready for by now.

It was high time she came out from under Connie's skirts, gave up her childish interests in horses and sleuthing, and became the responsible wife and mother she was meant to be....

From: Madeleine.Brande
To: Connie.Brande
Re: Some big BIG news

HUGE news! One of the men working in Elizabeth's music room found something hidden in the wall. It's another diary, a very *special* diary – Elizabeth's!

I'm staring at it right now, not quite believing what I'm seeing.

I would've rung with the news only I wanted to share an extract with you (and Gran, who I figure you'll read it to). Turns out our Lizzie *was* falsely accused. The 'scandal' was based on a pack of malicious, fabricated lies, according to her account. Here it is, from an entry dated shortly before Edward died in the shipwreck....

Is today the blackest day of my life, or is that yet to descend upon my fraught soul? I have received news of such devastating import, I can barely write of it. Word has reached us of a vile tale propagated to discredit me and my beloved Edward and his family, and all while Edward is not here to defend my honour.

It is said, and I almost fail in the writing of it, that, for the purposes of financial gain, I have had 'dalliances' with another man, and that a child has ensued. Such villainous lies! I cannot think that someone could wish to bring us all into such terrible disrepute.

Oh diary, how am I to declare my innocence when my situation appears to give credence to this wicked story? Of course it is my beloved husband's child whose presence becomes more obvious each day. I eagerly await Edward's return to impart these glad tidings first to his ears, but now my joyful expectation has been tarnished by this slanderous tale. Those jealous of Edward's success and high standing will view my condition, and the fact I have not publicly announced it, as proof of the lie, of that I am certain.

My heart swells with a pain unbearable at the thought of

this vile falsehood finding its way to my beloved Edward's ears. He is so far away from me in Paris, so out of reach of the truth. I must find the fortitude to write to him the facts, for I cannot endure the thought of his thinking ill of me for even the briefest of moments....

I have to admit to a tear or two while reading the account, Mum. When you get to read the diary for yourself, you'll see how her handwriting becomes less neat, more wretched, as she embellishes on the spiteful accusations against her.

I'm sure Edward would've sorted things out lickety-split if he'd made it home. How sad for them both that he died unaware his wife was not only innocent of the awful allegations, but also carrying his first child.

There was a newspaper clipping tucked into the diary's back cover, yellowed with age and badly smudged in places, but still legible. It's a brief account of 'Tasmanian Timber Merchant Edward Lorienne' cutting short his stay in Paris to hurry home to Tas, having no doubt heard the slanderous allegations made against his wife.

I checked the article's date against Lizzie's diary entry, and reckon he departed France around the time she was writing to him. So while she was putting pen to paper in Tassie, Edward was boarding the next vessel leaving for Australia, the *Polly Brown*, carrying a load of his timber. And so Edward Lorienne Esq. died not knowing the truth about the woman he loved.

In her diary Lizzie noted the date of his death in a

spiderweb-thin hand. The ink is smudged in places and there are water marks on the page, from her tears no doubt. In the next barely legible entries she writes of her 'unendurable heartbreak', and of the family's efforts to have her seen by a doctor. In the final entry she simply professes her undying love for her husband, who she 'shall miss for eternity.'

A tragic tale, hey? And not the only one being unearthed, though the most relevant to our family. Anyway, at least now we have Elizabeth's side of the story.

Ooh ... I just peeked outside and think the carpenter might've arrived. I'd better scoot and grab him before he gets away.

Topaz sends a purr, and lotsa luv from across the briny from me.

Maddie xxx

She hadn't mentioned Kris, wasn't ready to tell her mother about his arrival in Le Froid. The situation was all so ... upsetting, and embarrassing. She'd have to own up before Connie returned though. And what would her mother make of this development?

Would she see it as a positive, a catalyst for her daughter to settle down? She'd been dropping hints along that line since Madeleine's mid-twenties, and was in favour of her relationship with Kris until it turned pear-shaped.

Madeleine frowned and blew a long breath.

She'd have to pull on her big girl pants or, better still, sort things out with Kris before her mother's return, so she could speak of it as a *fait accompli.*

But whose *fait accompli?*

Hers or his?

Or were they one and the same?

22

From: Connie.Brande
To: Madeleine.Brande
Re: 'Mainland' news

First to Gran. You've made her the happiest I've seen for ... I can't remember how long, love. Reading her the extract you sent of Elizabeth's diary was like giving her a tall glass of life-juice. Even the cardiologist remarked on her improvement at today's check-up.

Oh, and she asked me to tell you she can't wait to see the diary for herself, the other two as well. She keeps asking me to read your email again, while she sits in her wheelchair smiling and smiling. I almost know it word-for-word! She's even talking about travelling to Le Froid after she's regained her strength, so she can finally see the castle for herself. Considering her delicate condition and aversion to air travel that's a big deal for her, as you know.

I could go on and on about how thrilled we both are with your discovery, but I have another meeting starting soon so will have to keep this brief.

Yes, I'm glad things have worked out so well. Sotherby's nose-bleed valuation of the Bedazzler, and the consequent sale to some fat cat with bottomless pockets, has set us all up wonderfully. Our share of the proceeds should fund the castle's renovations, while theirs, in addition to the sale of the castle, appears to be doing wonders for the McAlisters.

I call that a win/win, for all involved. And that's it for now, my love. It's off to the next round of meetings for me.

Mum xoxo

In the dream, Madeleine stood in front of the portrait, reading the inscription on the plaque beneath. *Genevieve Lorienne, daughter of Timber Merchant Sir Richard Lorienne, circa 1895.*

On the canvas, Genevieve's hair, sprinkled with tiny flowers and coiled high in a chignon with precise side braids, allowed her gown's ruffled 'Bertha' neckline to reveal her bare shoulders.

She stood with face aglow, eyes lit with coquettish anticipation and her head inclined ever-so-slightly toward a tall young man standing side-on at what might pass for a discreet distance behind her.

Then, in front of Madeleine's slumbering eyes, the images on canvas began to move. An unhealthy flush blossomed on Genevieve's cheeks and beads of perspiration formed on her brow. Her dainty cough into an embroidered handkerchief left a crimson smear on the fine white fabric, and a glistening red stain oozed darkly from one of her delicate nostrils.

On the floor below her white satin-slippered feet, a sinister fog slithered upward to engulf the entire picture, dispersing a moment later to reveal a much changed depiction of the young woman.

Slumped on a chaise longue, eyes glazed over and cheeks an unhealthy shade of cerise, Genevieve muttered and twitched feverishly, one trembling hand plucking frantically at the sheet covering the chaise. Her chest rose and fell with increasing speed, as alarming 'rose' spots appeared, sullying the hitherto creamy skin of her décolletage.

In the dream the foul vapour reappeared, this time taking an almost human, entirely monstrous, form. Bending over Genevieve's wasted body, the apparition blew toxic fumes into her nostrils and clawed at her with wraithlike fingers.

As her body twisted and arched, defenceless against the malady robbing her of life, a doctor flitted in and out of the picture. Then two faceless men in white appeared and took up what had been the chaise longue but was now a stretcher. Their guttural voices uttered harsh words,

'Typhoid. Contagious ... keep away. Isolation ward ... best for all.'

As they bore the insentient Genevieve away, Madeleine glimpsed a slender arm fall limply from beneath the sheet to dangle, pale and lifeless, over the edge of the stretcher.

The slender hand open, palm up, as if in surrender.

'And you recognised the girl in the dream?' The woman's eyes were bright with curiosity as she leaned across the dining table to fix Madeleine with an eager gaze.

Swallowing the impulse to change the subject, Kris instead spooned another mouthful of the *soup du jour* into his mouth. While savouring the creamy texture and delicious flavour, he recalled Madeleine saying how relieved she was the castle chef—Carl was it?—had stayed on. Apparently he was a lot happier now they only offered dinners in the castle three nights a week instead of five, or even seven.

Not for the first time Kris found himself wishing Madeleine would speak on subjects like that more often. Surely she was as sick of talking about hidden treasures, or some dream or other she'd had, as he was of hearing about them?

He blew a sigh.

Things weren't going quite as he'd envisaged but at

least they were dining together, even if flanked by the castle's current set of house guests.

When she glanced at him he assumed an expression of interest, only to drop the pretence when she turned to answer the woman. Introduced to him as Penelope, the woman referred to herself as Loppy, or Loopy ... or something equally ridiculous.

'It was Genevieve Lorienne,' Madeleine said with a smile. 'There's a painting of her in the gallery, and she's described in detail in her father's diary, which we found secreted away in the castle. Actually, I think his descriptions of her battle with typhoid might've triggered my dream.'

'Ooh, this is fascinating,' Loppy crooned. 'And there's some mystery about her, this Genevieve?'

'No mystery. She died from typhoid, end of story.' Kris winced, realising his careless words had killed the smile on Madeleine's lips and earned him a glare from across the table.

Not that he cared about the latter.

'I take it you're not much interested in history and suchlike ... Kris is it?' The woman didn't wait for an answer. 'The oh-so-interesting, not to mention dishy castle butler would be, but he's a hard act to follow.' Flashing Madeleine a wink, she added with exaggerated sadness, 'It's a shame Byron's away for my visit this time.'

Kris gaped at her.

Surely the ridiculous woman wasn't comparing him, a

medical doctor, to some butler dude? And her wink ... what did that mean?

Bending his head over the soup bowl again, Kris reminded himself to be patient and guard his tongue. The last thing he wanted was to get Madeleine offside by coming on too heavy.

Look where that got him last time.

Unaware he was doing it, he put a hand to his face and fingered the deepest of his scars.

Loppy was right, Kris was no Byron. All the same, Madeleine flashed her a quelling look when Kris leaned in to ask 'So, this butler guy?'

How should she answer?

If she wanted to give their relationship another try she'd have to be open and honest with Kris, about everything including the 'thing'—how to describe it?— with Byron. But ... trying again after she'd called quits on their relationship first time round?

She searched inside herself for the frisson of excited anticipation, the flicker of desire one would expect on being pursued by a man like Dr Kris de Voss.

She didn't find it.

Why not? His looks might not be what they were—and whose fault was that?—but he was still what most people, even Sir Richard Lorienne, would consider a worthy life partner.

She thought back to their time together, recalling how Mrs de Voss's constant interference in their lives fuelled most of their arguments, with Kris always ending up siding with his mother. Those arguments, instead of clearing the air, only confirmed Madeleine's suspicion the interference would continue and probably escalate if she married Kris.

Which made her all the more frustrated and angry with him.

Still ... had she rushed into splitting up with him? Or had she dodged a bullet, one that now appeared to have been reloaded?

And how did the formidable Mrs de Voss feel about her son rekindling a liaison that had physically and emotionally 'broken' him once before? It was surprising she'd even let her son come to Tasmania, considering his intentions while here.

Madeleine gave a silent snort.

He'd stood up to his mother in the past, though, when he really wanted something. And was she, Madeleine, what he really wanted now? Or did he only think so?

Feeling his questioning gaze, Madeleine flushed and reached for a crusty bread roll. 'Byron?' She kept her tone carefully casual. 'He's the head butler here, away at present. Also one of the castle's past owners. And something of a mystery hound,' she added with a hint of a smile.

All true, but a far from comprehensive description of the man who'd had her in stitches by reciting 'The Boy Stood on the Burning Deck' with just the right amount of pompous ceremony. The same man who'd arrived on his sexy black Ducati to take her to meet the delightful Capaldis, and whose behaviour toward her had been nothing but honourable and respectful.

And romantic.

That was back before her betrayal, of course. What he took to be a betrayal, anyway.

Perhaps their relationship was never meant to be anything more than a fling? That didn't explain the hollow sense of loss since his departure, though.

'Well I hope this butler dude knows I'm going to stick around.' Kris leaned in to fix his eyes on hers. 'For as long as it takes to become part of your life again.'

She had to stop herself squirming at the unwanted declaration, and was pleased when the waiter arrived to clear away their soup dishes, overseen by a hovering Emma. Scowling when the young trainee fumbled and clattered the crockery, Emma flashed Madeleine an eye roll that said Byron's debonair style and first-class butlering skills were sorely missed.

Unaware of the wordless exchange, Kris smiled at Emma and asked, 'If you had to choose between dating a butler or a doctor, who would win? Not that it's a competition,' he added in a tone that implied it totally *was.*

His words irked Madeleine but appeared to impress Emma, who replied with a flutter of eyelashes, 'No competition at all. The doctor wins hands-down.'

Madeleine stared at her, bemused, as she moved away.

Then again, Emma had always struck her as someone who valued status. And was there anything wrong with that, or did it simply differ from Madeleine's own attitude? In that way at least she was more like the tragic Genevieve. If she loved a man, his status wouldn't enter the equation.

She would love him no matter what.

As if sensing her displeasure, Kris ran fingers down Madeleine's arm until she moved it away. 'So, getting back to this dream you were talking about,' he prompted. 'What do you think it all means?'

'Just my overactive imagination filling in the details.' A slow grin formed on her lips. 'Which happens when a subject really grabs my attention.'

'I don't get why you're so interested. Those events happened a long time ago.'

She picked up on his thinly-veiled scepticism and responded tightly, 'Which only makes them more interesting.'

Ignoring the warning signs, he asked, 'Aren't you past all this?' and leaned forward to take her hand.

'All this what?'

'You know, solving mysteries, dreaming about dead people from long ago.'

When she snatched her hand away he frowned and sat back again. 'Sorry, I don't mean to be flippant. It's just ... I feel like I'm on an episode of that TV show, *Ghost Whisperer*.'

Madeleine stiffened. 'So in your opinion, this is all just

trite nonsense,' and she swept an arm to indicate the castle and all it entailed.

'I didn't mean—'

'Sounded to me like you did.'

And right then Loppy piped up again. 'Excuse me for interrupting, but I wanna hear more about Genevieve Lorienne.'

The following evening....

Madeleine stifled a yawn. 'I'm done in, can we call it a night?' Her courage had once again failed her. She still wasn't ready for *that* conversation, even though constantly having to steer Kris onto safer subjects was tiring.

As was keeping an eye out for the Capaldis.

Despite having convinced Kris to eat at The Prima Donna instead of Gino's Café, she remained on edge, fearful the Capaldis might catch sight of her on what was obviously a date.

With a man who was not their 'adopted' son, Byron.

Why should she feel guilty, though? Byron had chosen to leave. And as for the Capaldis, their café was enjoying increased patronage thanks to Madeleine's arrangement with Jeff. He was now ferrying castle guests to Gino's up to four times a week, armed with discount vouchers courtesy of the castle.

She glanced across the table at Kris. He wasn't

bothering to hide his displeasure at her request they call it a night. A typically selfish reaction that, instead of inspiring a sense of guilty obligation in her, brought on a flash of resentment.

It was alright for *him* to have a late night. He wasn't wearing himself out trying to co-manage and grow a business, put on a happy face for troublesome guests and staff, and project-manage major renovations.

Seeing his lips compress with disappointment, her resentment subsided and she reached out to touch his hand. 'I know you wanted to talk about ... us. I'm just not ready for that discussion yet.'

'Right then,' he snapped.

'I'm not saying we *won't* have that conversation. Just ... not now.' Sagging in her chair, she murmured, 'I'm just so busy with everything....'

He exhaled and his mouth softened. With a nod, he gestured for the bill. When the signal went unnoticed he gave an irritated huff, pushed his chair back, and marched to the counter.

Glad of the chance for some fresh night air, Madeleine made her way out of the restaurant and onto the chilly footpath.

'Maddie-Rosa?'

Her breath caught in her throat.

Oh no.

Not here, not now.

Hastily composing herself, she turned as a woman

bustled toward her, beaming widely. 'Ada,' she rasped, and then gulped. 'How ... lovely to see you.'

'*Cara,* I thought it was you!' Throwing open her arms, Ada drew Madeleine into a familiar garlicky hug, then pressed both hands to her flushed cheeks. 'I have-a news,' she announced, with barely suppressed excitement. 'About our Byron.'

Reaching into a pocket in her floury apron, she extracted an envelope which she shook at Madeleine. 'A letter, from Australia.'

Neither woman noticed Kris step out of the Prima Donna and stop to watch from the shadows.

'A letter?' Madeleine sucked in an eager breath. 'From Byron? Where is he? Is he alright? When's he coming home?'

Ada chuckled. 'I tell you if you give-a me a chance, *cara.*'

'Sorry. Please, go on.'

'You might-a know this already, but our Byron has found-a his papa. His-a *blood* papa,' Ada added, her tone wistful.

'That's great news.' Madeleine clapped her hands. 'So, where is he now?' Her stomach clenched when a crease formed in Ada's flour-dusted brow.

Was Byron's 'Ma' wondering why her *figlio* hadn't kept his girlfriend apprised of his movements? Only natural if she were...

'In-a Queensland,' Ada said slowly. 'He track-a down his papa, and got a big-a surprise. He found—' She stopped abruptly when Kris moved out of the shadows to slip an arm around Madeleine's waist.

'Aren't you going to introduce us?' he enquired pleasantly.

Ada stared at Madeleine, dismay written across her round face.

With pleading look that said *please trust me*, Madeleine swallowed and said, 'Kris de Voss, this is Ada Capaldi. Kris is an old ... friend of mine, on holiday from the mainland.'

The older woman, seeming to get the silent message, extended a hand and said slowly, 'Nice-a to meet you, Kris.' Her questioning gaze never left Madeleine's face.

23

'So much still to do.' Madeleine sipped her coffee and ran her eyes around the mess of the partly cleared courtyard.

From his perch on one of two overturned crates in what Madeleine optimistically referred to as the 'courtyard garden' Kris frowned. She didn't appear to care he was seeing her in such an unsightly state. Not only was her face smudged with dirt, her boots mud-caked, the sleeves of her loose shirt rolled haphazardly to grimy elbows, but, and his frown deepened, her paint-stained cargo pants were secured with *twine,* no less!

And as for the potpourri of paint stripper, turpentine, and other unnamed odours ... it was all truly appalling, and totally out of character for the Madeleine he knew. That Madeleine smelled of gardenia and patchouli, and dressed with panache. Nothing like this ... disaster ... in front of him.

His criticism must have shown on his face for she rose, saying rigidly, 'This was only meant to be a quick coffee break. I can't afford extended time-outs with jobs piling up around me. Better get back to it.'

Maybe she was busy, but who wasn't? And hadn't he gone to some trouble to track her down, once more traipsing through this gloomy old castle to find her?

He leapt up. 'Before you go—' The sudden movement tipped his mug, and dark dregs of coffee spilled down his silver-grey Ralph Lauren polo shirt.

He swore under his breath and hurriedly brushed off the drops that hadn't already soaked into the fabric. On lifting his gaze again, he caught sight of Madeleine's back as she strode away. Without even offering a cloth to help clean his shirt! Didn't she care that it might be ruined?

And how did she always manage to slink off just as he was about to broach a serious subject? This time it was the conversation he'd overheard between her and Ada Capaldi, and the bloke they'd spoken about with such obvious affection; the butler dude that woman Loppy had gushed over at dinner.

So did this ... Byron?... mean more to Madeleine than she was letting on?

He stepped onto the tarmac with a rush of pleasure, feeling the touch of crisp afternoon air on his face.

So good to be back home in Tassie.

Inhaling deeply of the much cooler, way less humid air, Byron made for the terminal, his long-legged stride overtaking the passengers ahead. It felt good to stretch after the longish flight from Brisbane.

Brisbane ... where a little group had waved farewell from the airport's departure gate, looking for all the world like his loving family. Only one of them could claim blood ties with him though, and 'loving' wasn't a term he'd use to describe Rob McAlister.

But his relationship with his father wasn't uppermost on Byron's mind right now. The news he had to break to his mother, just as she was getting on with her life, was what had him on edge.

His mouth tightened. This trip to the mainland was bound to have rekindled her hopes the family could be reunited, damn it. Was she even now waiting expectantly for their return, her son and his father, the men she loved?

A spasm crossed his face, replaced an instant later by the stern expression that had become the norm since....

No, he wouldn't think about that, or about her.

Madeleine Brande was just a brief mention on a closed page in the book of his life.

Forcing his thoughts back to the long and dusty car ride into Brisbane, he mused on the stilted snatches of conversation along the way. The only occupant immune to the charged atmosphere and unspoken words was the little boy. Sitting beside Byron in the four-wheel-drive, the likeable little tyke had chatted happily, if often unintelligibly, for the first part of the trip before falling asleep on Byron's lap.

It had been a surprising wrench to hand over the sleeping child when the time came to board the plane. And when Rob took the little boy from him, a glance had passed between the two men. In it the son read his father's heartfelt regrets for the hurts caused by his actions in abandoning them, and the father saw his son acknowledge the wider personal cost, to more than those abandoned.

On entering Hobart Airport's arrivals hall, Byron dragged a hand through his hair. It'd been a bumpy flight, not conducive to catching up on some shut-eye. He needed a shower too, judging by a tentative sniff of his underarm. But first, a visit to the airport bar. A drink would help him unwind, and think.

As if he hadn't spent the whole flight thinking....

His expression morphed into a scowl.

Sure he was back home, but what should his next move be? Where to from here? His whole life had been turned upside down, and not by his own hand. Letting resentment determine his actions was pointless, though. He was better off focusing on more pressing issues.

Like the fact he no longer had a place of his own.

Dumping the heavy duffle at his feet, he caught the barmaid's eye. 'Johnny Walker, on ice. A double, thanks.'

'Don't go drowning your sorrows, boy.' His father's recent words echoed in his ears. 'Take it from me, it won't help. Only make things worse.'

Byron blinked his dry, stinging eyes and reached for his wallet. Amid the half-hearted chatter of other travel-weary patrons around him, music pumped from wall speakers, and the words of a current hit song filtered through to his mind.

... our time apart, like a knife to the heart ...

Why had this time apart not done what he'd hoped? Why was he still seeing her face in crowds, finding himself wondering where she was at that moment, wishing they'd....

He stiffened and bent his head.

Madeleine belonged in the past, so why wasn't he able to leave her there and move on?

A drink appeared at his elbow, and the barmaid collected the twenty dollar note he'd thrown on the bar. Taking up the frosted glass he swirled it in front of his eyes, and the ice blocks clinked against the sides.

'Here's your change,' a throaty voice purred.

The pretty barmaid was eyeing him with interest, her highly-glossed lips parted in a wide, sensuous smile, a coquettish tilt to her chin and an invitation in her deep blue eyes.

Another time, perhaps.

He paused with the glass part way to his mouth.

Another time? Was that his new mantra?

He'd come across some lovely girls on the mainland, but the only mainland girl who meant something to him didn't live there anymore.

Draining the glass and thumping it on the bar, he mumbled, 'Thanks,' and collected his bag from the floor. With a jaded half-smile for the barmaid he strode away, joining the exodus of somnolent travellers from the airport.

Behind him, the barmaid collected his glass, now empty of all but melting ice cubes. As she watched him stride toward the taxi rank, she ran admiring eyes over his outdoorsy tan, open-necked cotton shirt, snug-fitting moleskin pants, and dusty riding boots. Add to that his craggy, brooding air, and her current movie crush sprang to mind.

Mm mmm....

She sucked in her bottom lip and pictured the manly hand her departing commuter had rested oh-so briefly on the bar. There'd been no evidence of a wedding ring on his finger, not even a pale reminder.

Damn.

Another good one—and those were *definitely* in the minority—had got away.

With a long, regretful sigh, she went back to work.

From: Madeleine.Brande

To: Connie.Brande
Re: 'Stuff'

Everything's okay here at castle central, and it appears our marketing activities are paying off. No cause for worry there. I know you have things to do while you're in Oz, and Gran needs time with you too, so don't rush back.

I do have a bit of news, though ... about Kris.

He's here.

Yes, you read right.

Kris is here, in Le Froid, and not for the short term apparently. The local hospital has snapped him up to be their Career Medical Officer.

I know, what a shock, right? And what's even more shocking, it seems he's scoping for us to get back together, despite how things ended before.

Now, while his arrival came as an unwelcome surprise, it also made me confront my feelings about him and ... well ... everything that happened between us. As a result, I've come to terms with the fact the accident wasn't entirely my fault, that we share responsibility for the outcome of our actions.

I couldn't have predicted that Kris would go charging off in a rage following our argument. He made that decision for himself. And to his credit, he doesn't appear to blame me for what happened.

He might be a snob and a hothead on occasion, but he isn't a bad person and deserves to be loved, Mum.

By the right woman.

I just don't think that's me.

If I'm reading him right, Kris wants a quintessential doctor's wife, someone like his mother (shudder). A 'little woman' he can crow about to his colleagues, be proud to show off at highbrow soirées, and who'll provide him with good-looking, high-achieving children. And I'm not saying that's a wrong or unhealthy goal, in fact it's a life choice lots of women are more than pleased to make.

I'm just not one of them.

It'd be nice to have kids of my own one day, but what I want first is what you and Dad had; love, respect, shared interests, and a true friendship free of pretence. What interests do Kris and I share? And does he love the real me or just the woman he wants me to be?

He's been dropping in at the castle, often without calling first, and you should've seen his face when he caught me in my working clobber! He stared at me in total disbelief, like the grubby person in front of him couldn't possibly be the same woman whose glamorous picture he carries in his head. Another indicator he doesn't know the real me.

Now for confession time.

I can't help comparing Kris with Byron, Mum. We didn't spend a lot of time together but I got a strong sense of the kind of man Byron is, and felt a connection with him I never had with Kris. We were *good* together, and not just in the superficial 'flowers-n-chocolates' way. He even has a nose for mystery almost as big as mine (actually he has a handsome nose, as I'm sure you recall). Was there more to our relationship than a shared interest in mysteries, though? If he doesn't come back to the castle I may never know....

Anyway, I feel better for unloading on you, Mum, even if by email! Please give Gran a huge hug for me.

Luv,

Maddie xxx

In the late-night quiet, the fat raindrops slid audibly down the window pane to plop into puddles on the ground below. Occasional gusts of a sodden wind howled around the battlements, carrying with them a bleak sense of damp. From where she sat alone in the office, it was easy to imagine whispers, moans, and sighs as the castle wound down from another day of tourists traipsing along its corridors, filling its rooms, and stomping up and down its stairs.

Madeleine slumped against the chair's backrest and glanced at her watch's illuminated face.

Almost ten pm.

An unlikely time for anyone else to be in the castle, particularly on an off-dinner night. Then she recalled her own clandestine late night explorations when the castle still belonged to the McAlisters, and her lips twitched into a wry grin.

When something warm and furry brushed against her leg, she gave a start and then bent to scoop Topaz into her arms, murmuring, 'How do you always know when I can use some company, buddy?'

His throat rumbled in a pleased purr as he settled on her lap, tucking his paws under his body and gazing up at her with contented topaz eyes. The half-closed, drowsy-eyed gaze had her own eyelids drooping.

She yawned....

'You're here, great.'

She jerked upright with a gasp.

'Were you asleep?' Kris stared down at her.

Madeleine frowned, rubbed her eyes, and swallowed. 'Guess I nodded off.'

'Dreaming about me maybe?' His grin radiated hope, along with an irritating assuredness.

Instead of the sharp comeback on the tip of her tongue, she gave a perfunctory smile. Any other response would result in the indulgent, condescending look she'd always found annoying.

And even more annoying now.

She blinked and exhaled. 'What are you doing here so late?'

'Thought I'd drop in on the off chance you were still working. I've been out at the club.'

That explained the alcohol on his breath, but not why he was here. Although that was pretty much a given....

'Your Emma was there too, at the club. And looking pretty swish I must say.' Something about his dreamy tone, the way Emma's name rolled off his tongue, piqued Madeleine's interest.

'She's not "my" Emma, but go on.'

'She was there with an older couple.'

'Her mother probably. I wonder who the man was with her.'

Could it be Kathryn's husband, returned to the fold?

Had Byron succeeded in reuniting the family?

'Whoever he was, she was on his arm,' Kris said. 'So I'd say they were on a date.'

Promising....

'And Emma? Was she on a date too?'

'Don't think so.' One corner of his mouth tipped upward.

'Hmmm.' Madeleine looked at him sideways. 'Say, how did you know I'd be here, in the office?'

'When you weren't in your bedroom—' Seeing her head jerk back he blustered, 'I knocked first,' as if that made up for the invasion of her privacy. 'Anyway, I figured I'd find you here.'

She continuing eyeballing him. 'Well, you found me. What was so important that you had to come by so late?'

'I have a message from my mother.'

Madeleine's stomach clenched.

Mrs de Voss wasn't here too, surely? It wouldn't be out of the question for that woman to follow her son wherever he went.

'She rang earlier,' he said carefully, bending to rest both hands on the back of a spare chair.

Madeline blinked. 'Oh yes? And ... how is she?'

'Fine.' He gave a nervous chuckle. 'Everything's okay, she just wanted me to pass on her regards.'

'To me?'

'Of course to you.' He pretended to gaze around the office. 'There's nobody else hiding in the dark here, is there?'

Without thinking Madeleine glanced into the dim corners, and then frowned. What was she expecting to find? A ghostly visage hovering in the dimness, or the infinitely more scary sight of Mrs de Voss lurking there?

She gave a silent groan.

It was clear she was spending *way* too much time alone in the castle....

24

T he following morning....

'So, what's the deal with you and the dishy doctor?' Sinking into the chair opposite, Emma admired her recently manicured fingernails under the light of the restored Victorian desk lamp.

Her co-manager's smart corporate attire, carefully styled hair and flawless makeup somehow conjured up an image of Mrs de Voss, and Madeleine blew a long breath through pursed lips. Swivelling her office chair she said resignedly, 'And here I was, hoping to get some work done this morning.'

At Emma's unrepentant grin, Madeleine fixed her with a mock-reproachful gaze. 'And did you just describe Kris as dishy?'

'Dish-*eee*. That's what he is.' Emma's eyes twinkled.

Smiling despite herself, Madeleine once again marvelled at Emma's transformation from disgruntled employee to professional manager material. And since taking on the co-manager role she'd become more than a colleague, was fast becoming a friend. One inclined to an affected poshness perhaps, but a friend no less.

'Dishy, hey?' Madeleine quirked an eyebrow and crossed her arms. 'So ... the facial scars?'

'What about them?'

'They don't ... put you off?'

Emma's tilted thinking face, a mannerism she shared with her brother, sent Madeleine's stomach twinging and twisting into the now familiar 'missing Byron' tango.

'Not at all. They make him look ... like he could use some tender lovin' care.' Receiving a measured glance from Madeleine, Emma prompted, 'So ... you and Kris?'

'There's no deal. He's just an old friend from Queensland.'

'Friend? With benefits?'

'Once, a while ago. Now we're just ... friends.'

Emma eyed her shrewdly. 'That's all?'

'That's all.'

'I doubt he'd say the same.'

A small crease formed in Madeleine's brow. 'What makes you think that?'

'It's just that for an old "friend" he comes here a LOT.' Making a point of gazing at her nails again, Emma went on with studied innocence. 'I wonder what Byron would make of that.'

Madeleine's frown deepened. 'Why would your brother care about who comes to visit us here?'

'Visits *you* here, don't you mean?' Emma arched an eyebrow at her. 'Look, I know you and By have a "thing" going, no matter what you say.'

Madeleine stared at her, stomach in a twist and her mind a jumble of thoughts. *Did* they have a thing, she and Byron? Or was *had* a thing more accurate?

'Why are you so interested in Kris?'

'No reason, just curious is all.' Emma's attempt at nonchalance didn't quite come off. As if realising that, she blustered, 'Oh, there goes my phone again!' and leapt up, whipping the chiming mobile from a pocket in her tailored pants and putting it to her ear. 'Hello? Yes, thanks for calling me back. Look, I want to talk to you about the new trainee you sent us....'

With a roll of eyes at Madeleine she strode to the doorway, high heels clicking on the recently refurbished, chocolate-red floorboards. 'We're not running some greasy spoon *café* here, you know.'

The air of proprietorship and authority in her plum-in-mouth tone had Madeleine hiding an indulgent grin.

'We're trying to leave our clientele with a good impression, so I'm sure you understand the importance of having competent staff....' Still speaking into the phone, Emma gave Madeleine an affable flick of a hand as she left.

With a smiling shake of her head Madeleine returned to the paperwork littering the desk, only to have her own mobile chime. Glancing at the screen, she groaned and switched off the alarm.

Having already missed one appointment with local accounting firm Beenleigh, Keep and Badger, which she'd nicknamed Bean-counting, Bookkeeping and Badgering, she didn't want to be on the receiving end of another—totally warranted—stern-faced greeting. And with parking in town often a time-sucking nightmare, being driven there was altogether faster, easier, and more efficient.

She dialled the number for Jeff's shuttle service.

A beaming Jeff leaned across to open the passenger door, releasing a woodsy scent of pine air freshener. 'Where to m'lady?'

'Main Street, please.' As she settled into the seat beside him Madeleine added, 'And could you put the pedal to the metal? Don't want be late for my appointment.'

He nodded and accelerated down the drive. 'Off to see the wizard are we?'

'Guess you could say that. The financial wizard.'

'Say, speakin' of money ... how're things goin' at the castle?'

'Coming along.'

'Ah,' he breathed, 'y'gotta love the noncommittal response.'

Madeleine gave a wry chuckle. 'I just don't like to tempt fate.'

'So when you say it's coming along...?'

'It really is. Guest numbers are up, and we're even having to turn away some dinner bookings. Having your shuttle service transport the overflow to Gino's Café is so handy, and means another business can benefit from the custom.'

'Always happy to oblige. And I'm sure the Capaldis would say the same.' He glanced warmly at her. 'You 'n Emma still managing the place together?'

'We are.'

'And the prodigal son?'

'On the mainland, apparently.'

'Right.'

When Madeleine's nose picked up a hint of expensive aftershave, she ran her eyes over him. 'Say, what's different about you?'

'About me?'

'Yeah, something's changed....'

The amiable expression, boyish grin and smattering of freckles across his nose were the same, but his trademark mop of sandy hair had been styled into a modern step cut with a straight-up fringe. And in place of the usual tee shirt and jeans, the smart polo shirt and chinos showed off a pleasingly manly physique. Something she hadn't noticed before.

'Your hair's different,' she murmured, 'and are those new clothes?'

'Yep.' He flashed a proud grin. 'So, what do you think? Is Jeff Mason lookin' better or worse?'

'Looking good.' Smiling, she tilted her head to study his profile. 'Say, I forgot that your surname's Mason.'

Like Genevieve Lorienne's unfortunate beau. Was it a coincidence or a thread to pull on?

His grin widened. 'Only for my whole life,' and he puffed out his chest. 'So, what's the verdict? Better or worse?'

'Better. Not that you looked bad before.'

'I'll take that as a complimen—' The tyres squealed as he stomped on the brakes and at the same time, thrust a protective arm across Madeleine's chest. Winding down the window he bellowed, 'Look out, ya crazy bugger!' at the chagrined driver of the car in front.

Gazing at the arm still pressed against her chest, Madeleine enquired mildly, 'Isn't that what seatbelts are for?'

With a jerk Jeff withdrew his arm and flashed a sheepish grin. 'Yeah ... um ... sorry about that. Old habits, from drivin' kids around.'

Despite his apology there was a look in his eyes that brought warmth to her cheeks.

And a vision of Byron to her mind's eye.

The meeting with the accountants ran longer than expected and ended, to Madeleine's irritation, with the scheduling of a follow-up meeting the next day. It also made her late for dinner. So by the time she slipped into the castle's dining room, Kris was already seated at the table with Emma by his side.

As she approached, Madeleine heard him ask a question, and when Emma leaned in to answer him, her silky, low-cut blouse revealed an eye-catching—and for Madeleine, an eyebrow-raising—amount of cleavage.

On seeing Madeleine, Emma jumped as though zapped by a cattle prod. With a pink flush climbing up her neck, she shuffled her chair to put more distance between herself and Kris, who seemed unaware of any awkwardness.

Catching sight of Madeleine, his expression brightened. 'I was starting to think you weren't dining in-house tonight.'

'I was held up in town.' Madeleine settled herself in a chair, her thoughts on Emma's reaction.

Was she feeling guilty?

Had she been flirting with Kris?

She *had* been asking about him, and their connection.

Interesting....

Alone in the office the following morning, Madeleine released a long breath and stretched her arms above her head. There was so much happening, she couldn't make progress on any one thing. That was how it felt, anyway.

Tossing her pen on the desk, she watched it roll until coming to rest beside her mobile phone, which promptly chimed another reminder.

The follow-up meeting with the bean counters.

Oh, great.

After shutting off the reminder she scrolled to a number in her contacts list. 'Hello, Jeff? Any chance you're free in half an hour to ferry me into town again?' A pause and then, 'Thanks heaps. I'll be waiting by the front stairs. And yes, I probably will be up for a coffee after all the number crunching.'

A coffee, with a touch of snooping on the side. Time to tug on that Mason thread....

'When I told Mum you were asking about our family history she seemed chuffed that someone was interested.' Jeff grinned at her from across the outdoor table at his 'all time favourite' street-side coffee shop.

Madeleine sipped her flat white. 'She didn't think I was poking my nose into your family's business?'

'Not at all. She only knows what was passed down by her grandma, but is happy to share it. And she said you'd probably find the story really interesting.'

'She did? Why's that?'

''Cos there's a connection with the Loriennes.'

'Ooh.' Madeleine's skin prickled. 'Do tell.'

'Well, the story goes that great grandad George had a pretty tough life until a substantial inheritance from some far-flung relative landed in his lap. By all accounts the Masons had dropped off the high society radar, so more than anything else George wanted their newfound wealth to reinstate the family's social standing. Being a frail old man by then he knew there was only so much he could do in his lifetime, but that was okay; his only son, Philip, would pursue the goal once he inherited the Mason money.'

Philip Mason?

Madeleine sucked in a breath.

Was it possible he was Genevieve Lorienne's unfortunate beau?

Jeff took a mouthful of coffee before going on. 'Of course George's plan went belly-up when Philip died young, from typhoid.'

Typhoid!

Her mind racing, Madeleine murmured, 'Oh. Sad.'

'Yeah.' Draining his mug, Jeff kept hold of it, twirling it in his hands. 'Philip's death sent poor old George off the rails, apparently. He drank to excess, squandered his money, created trouble wherever he went ... you get the picture. And speaking of pictures, this is where the Loriennes enter the frame. Somewhere along the way,

George developed a real beef with that family, though Mum doesn't know why.'

Hope fluttered in Madeleine's chest. Perhaps George had blamed Genevieve for exposing his only son to typhoid. But did Philip catch it from her, or was he the source of the disease that ended both their young lives?

'Must've been a doozy of a feud, 'cos the old boy went so far as to spread vicious rumours about the Loriennes, hoping to discredit the family.'

There it was, the vengeful action Elizabeth had written about in her diary.

'Anyway, that's pretty much what Mum thought you'd find interesting about our family's chequered history.'

'Please thank her for me.'

'Sure. You know, she reckons what George did is the source of the "Mason curse".'

Madeleine's eyes widened. 'Your mother thinks your family's cursed?'

'Nah, not really.' He gave a wry chuckle and set down his mug. 'Though for folks who should've inherited a fortune we still have to work for every crust, not that we let it bother us.'

Leaning his elbows on the table, he rested his head on both fists, gazed into her eyes and with a teasing wiggle of eyebrows said, 'Don't mind if our sad story scores me some brownie points with the girls though.'

. . .

'Thanks, mate.' After paying the driver, Byron collected his duffle and watched the taxi speed away, before gazing across the street at the lace-curtained windows above Gino's Café. This was the only place, apart from his mother's, where he'd be welcome to stay as long as he liked.

And although she—and she alone, he reminded himself tersely—was the reason he was back, he wasn't ready to face his mother yet.

Firming his grip on the duffle, he was about to cross the street when a familiar voice floated out at him from among the hum of street-side cafés. Stopping in his tracks, cursing the way the hairs on his arm rose in response to the sound, he scanned for the owner of the voice.

A voice he'd know in a chorus of hundreds.

And there she was, outside a nearby coffee shop. Seated at a table with a man.

A man who was leaning in, smiling at her. Into her eyes, in fact.

'Oh, you silver-tongued so-'n-so.' Laughing, Madeleine leaned across to slap Jeff on the arm. 'It's lucky I know you're just scoping for more business to come your way.'

'Damn, you've seen through my clever plan.'

'Clever? Not so much.'

They laughed together, and then she glanced to the side.

And gasped.

Leaping to her feet, tipping her chair so Jeff had to make a grab for it to stop it crashing to the floor, she threw a rushed apology over a shoulder while dashing out.

'Byron!'

Turning to see her running toward him, face aglow and topaz eyes shining, he dropped his duffle, preparing to wrap her in his arms.

But....

No.

This was Madeleine Brande, the sneaky schemer who'd played his family for fools. The woman who'd set in motion events that would break his mother's heart all over again.

Hunching his shoulders, he thrust both hands into his pockets.

She must've read his body language, for her steps faltered and she slowed to a tentative walk. Stopping a short distance in front of him she said simply, 'Hey.'

'Hey.'

'You're back.'

'Yep.'

'It's good to see you.' Surprising them both, she stepped in, and putting her hands on his forearms, rose to her tiptoes to drop a kiss on his cheek.

He instinctively drew her in for a hug, only to hastily drop his arms and step back.

They stood staring at each other.

He watched her gaze rove over his face, no doubt taking in his five o'clock shadow, before skimming over his eyes to the new military-style cut of his hair. Her nostrils flared a little as she breathed in what was bound to be his 'Eau de Outback' scent – dust with, and he gave a mental wince, a top note of whisky.

At the slight parting of her lips the breath caught in his throat, and he dragged his eyes away from her mouth and up to those cute damn freckles across her nose. Freckles he recalled counting while lounging beside her on the picnic rug overlooking Conquest Beach. Of course the freckle stocktake was merely a distraction from what he'd really wanted to do at the time, which was to kiss her.

An urge he was fighting right now....

With a gruff, 'It's good to be home again,' he took another step back.

'You've been gone a while.' Her voice wasn't quite steady and her cheeriness sounded forced.

He nodded silently, eyes locked on hers.

'We've m-missed you.'

Seeing colour suffuse her cheeks, he bent to collect his bag to hide his own reaction to the heartfelt declaration. Murmuring, 'Good to know,' he straightened, adding with stiff politeness, 'Great seeing you.'

He was about to walk away when she grasped his arm.

'Byron, wait. I ... we ... I ... need to talk to you.'

Squinting down at the slender fingers, pale against his skin's outback tan, he felt a familiar ache and stiffened. 'I've had a long flight preceded by a long drive, and I'm stuffed. Anyway, I doubt we have anything to talk about,' and he jerked his head pointedly in Jeff's direction. 'And I wouldn't want to keep you.'

She followed his gaze and slowly withdrew her hand. 'We *do* have something to talk about, as it happens.'

'Oh? Like what?'

'Like ... a business proposal.'

'I thought our business dealings were done with.'

'This is ... new business.'

When he dithered, she rushed on. 'A proposal I ... that is *we*, Emma and I, want to discuss with you. Are you available to meet with us at the castle tomorrow morning?'

'You and Emma?' He lowered his bag to the ground again.

'Yes. She and I are co-managing the business.'

'I see. You and my sis, partners in crime.' His jibe garnered no obvious reaction.

'So you'll come?'

Exhaling, he dragged both hands down his face and tipped back his head. There was gear stored at his old cottage he'd need to collect at some stage, so why not tomorrow? And although it galled him to admit it, he was curious to see what they'd done to his ... the ... cottage, and the castle.

Staring unseeingly at the sky he muttered, 'I've returned from a ridiculous father-chasing mission with no job or home to go to, and a bank balance that could use some replenishing.' Dropping his gaze, he met her questioning eyes. 'So I guess I can make myself available.'

'Great. Ten o'clock suit you?'

Did her lips just twitch like she was suppressing a smile? His own lips tightened and he wavered, before giving a curt nod. 'By the way, I'm planning to surprise Mum so I don't want her to know I'm back yet.'

'If I happen to see her I won't say anything, though I can't speak for Emma.'

'I'll phone Em and let her know what's happening.' After retrieving his duffle he paused to add in a gentler tone, 'Thanks, Madeleine. See you tomorrow.'

She stood watching him stride away.

There was a new, wary grittiness about this Byron, an air of maturity that left her breathless. She watched him reach the alleyway leading to the rear of Gino's café where he stopped to glance back at her, his expression unsmiling and intense, before disappearing into the shadows. Forcing her leaden feet to move, she made her way back to the coffee shop.

Jeff rose to pull out her chair, his face alight with curiosity. 'Was that who I think it was?' At her distracted nod, he murmured, 'The prodigal son has returned.'

'So it seems.'

'What does that mean for you? At the castle, I mean?'

Madeleine sank into the chair with a sigh. 'I ... we ... have a job offer to put to him.'

'You want him back as head butler?'

'As overseeing manager.'

'Wow.' He gave a drawn-out whistle. 'And how does Emma feel about that? 'Cos the two of you have been handling things 'til now, right?'

'She was okay about it before. As for now....' Placing her elbows on the table, Madeleine rested her chin on her hands. 'I guess we'll find out tomorrow if that's still the case.'

25

Ada opened the door to his knock, releasing a warm gust of garlic-laden air into the alleyway. With a cry of, 'Gino! Our Byron, he's-a back!' she threw chubby arms around him, pulling him close against her ample bosom.

From in front of the open oven Gino jerked upright, almost spilling the tray of buttery, freshly baked garlic bread over the counter. The near miss didn't quell his broad smile, which only broadened as he hurried to join them at the door.

Wiping his large hands on a stained apron, he boomed, '*Mio figlio*, you-a back at last!' and thumped Byron on both arms before drawing him into a bear hug. 'Why you away so long? We-a missed you.'

'Gino, don't-a leave him standing on the step,' Ada

chided from beside them. Spying the duffle at Byron's feet, her eyes lit up. 'You come-a to stay with us?'

At his smiling nod she sobered and clasped his face in both hands, peering into it with motherly concern. 'You look-a tired.'

'I just flew in from Brisbane—'

'Ah! You need-a to rest.'

'Well—'

'Rest?' Gino threw his hands in the air. 'He just-a got here.'

Ada gave her husband's chest a dismissive pat. 'Let him catch-a his breath at least.' Flashing a fond smile at Byron, she said, 'Your room, she's-a all ready,' and indicated the staircase. 'Always I keep it made up, in case our boy,' and she patted his cheeks, 'need-a to use it.'

'Thanks, Ma.' He dropped a kiss on her forehead. 'You're the best. What would I do without you two?'

'Oh, get outta here,' she scolded with a fond slap on his arm. 'We bring-a you something to eat when you ready.'

With a quick squeeze of Gino's arm and a grateful peck on Ada's cheek, Byron climbed the stairs, his weary footsteps heavy on the well-trodden wood.

Watching from below, Ada waited until he was on the landing before turning to Gino with an anxious frown. She touched her nose and he nodded, miming glug-glugging from a bottle as they exchanged a worried glance.

From: Madeleine.Brande
To: Connie.Brande
Re: More news

First of all, Byron's back. I ran into him in town today, freshly arrived from the airport. He's coming to meet with me and Emma tomorrow morning, and I'll let you know what eventuates. Before you ask, it appears he and I are still a long way from being friends again. But we don't have to be friends to work together now do we?

And speaking of friends, Kris had dinner here again last night and I heard him telling Emma about a shocker of a nightmare he'd had, apparently waking from it hollering and throwing punches. While he didn't say what the dream was about, I have a sneaking suspicion—one he probably shares—that all my talk of mysteries and dead people might've brought on the nightmare. * sigh * When is he going to realise I spell trouble for him?

Anyway, wish us luck with our offer to Byron tomorrow. BTW, with the bang-up job Emma's doing she's proving to be a real asset to the company. Would you have any objections to keeping her on in a managerial support role? Of course that's assuming Byron accepts the top job, which might be assuming too much. Tomorrow will tell.

Luv,

Maddie xxx

'Lorienne Castle, please mate.' Shaking droplets of rain from his hair, Byron dropped into the seat behind the driver.

Having woken to a bleak, drizzly morning, he'd been tempted to phone and request the meeting be rescheduled, if not cancelled altogether. But here he was, in a shuttle, on his way to the castle.

He stared unseeingly through the raindrops skidding across the window. If this weather continued he'd need his Mazda, currently stored in the cottage's shed. The bomb of a car had been sitting idle for weeks, and would probably be hard to start. Harder still the longer he left it there.

At a bouncing thud when the shuttle hit a pothole, he glanced up at the driver and caught the man, of around his own age, studying him in the rear view mirror.

'Nearly there, mate,' he said with a grin. 'I'm Jeff, by the way.'

'Byron.'

'McAlister, right?'

'Right.' He met the driver's curious gaze with one of his own.

Flashing a cocky grin in the mirror, Jeff quipped, 'Been getting heaps of fares from the castle lately, thanks to the new owners. We have an ongoing arrangement, and the lady managers themselves use my service all the time, even if there's a cab closer.'

With an offhand, 'Good for you,' Byron turned to gaze out the window again.

'Yep, seems I'm "in" with the lovely ladies running the show.'

Something twigged and Byron focused his gaze on the mirror once more. A crease formed in his brow, not at the bloke's boasting about ferrying around his sister and his ... and Madeleine. That didn't upset him one iota. What bothered him was the realisation he'd seen the smug sod recently, cosily ensconced at a table for two in a street-side coffee shop.

Gazing into Madeleine's eyes.

An icy blast of damp, salty air from off the ocean lost none of its chill as it slithered across the castle's stone floors and along the passageway. It set candles flickering and curtains twitching as it made for the rear of the building, where a windowless arch in the metres-thick outer wall waited like an open mouth ready to exhale.

Seated in her office chair, Madeleine shivered, drew the cardigan closer around herself, and cursed the craftsmen for taking so long to install the replacement leadlight window panels in various spots around the castle.

Was the chilly draft a portent of trouble to come?

She gave a wry sniff. Clearly her imagination hadn't lost the ability to fly off on tangents, even with her mind so taken up by other—

'Hey, hon. Got a minute?' Kris appeared in the office doorway.

The 'hon' reference grated and she eyed him coolly.

'I ... um ... want to talk to you about something,' he went on. 'Something important.'

'I have a ten o'clock meeting, so don't have much time right n—'

'It's *always* some appointment or other with you.' His face darkened. 'All I'm after is a few minutes of your precious time. Is that too much to ask?'

Narked by his bossy 'don't argue, I'm a doctor' tone, she bit back an angry retort and settled for staring at him in silent condemnation.

'Sorry, hon, didn't mean to shout.' He dragged a hand across his forehead and blew a long, audible breath. 'It's just I ... really need to talk to you.'

She peeked at her watch.

Nine forty-five. Please don't be early, Byron.

Sitting back with a sigh, she clasped her hands in her lap. 'I have fifteen minutes at most.'

Kris pulled up a chair and leaned forward to place both elbows on his thighs and rest his chin on his clasped hands. 'I can't do this any more, Madeleine. All the pussy-footing around, waiting for the "right" moment to tell you what I came here to tell you.'

When she made to speak he raised a halting hand.

'Nor can I stay in Le Froid forever. Mum has been able to appoint a locum to fill in for me at the practice but I'll have to get back to it, and my normal life, at some point. And sooner rather than later.'

Her heart sank.

There was now no escaping the conversation she'd been avoiding ever since he arrived.

It was crunch time.

Time to put aside all the conflicting thoughts and decide if she wanted, or simply felt obliged, to try again with Kris. He appeared prepared to do whatever it took to re-establish their relationship, but it would require more than a sense of obligation for her to even attempt it.

And did she feel anything other than obligation?

The answer was there, she didn't have to dig deep inside herself for it. If only the right words came so easily. Words that made plain her feelings while being gentle with his. Unlike last time....

She blinked and swallowed.

'Madeleine ... hon.' Kris leaned across the desk to take both her hands in his. 'Before, when I thought I'd lost you, I went a bit crazy. I....' Frowning, he cleared his throat. 'After the accident, it was the thought of seeing you again that kept me going through the treatments and convalescence.'

He fixed her with an intense gaze. 'Let's put that silly fight and what happened after it behind us. I came here to be with you. And to tell you that I....' He took a deep breath. 'I'm serious about this, hon. I want us to be together. Forever.'

So ... no declaration of undying love? Then again, Kris had never been the sentimental type.

When she said nothing, he gave a self-conscious chuckle and let go of her hands to sit back. 'I'll understand if you want to stay close to the castle ... for a bit.' A grimace flittered across his face. 'Then, once the renovations are completed and you're happy with everything here, we'll return home to Queensland.'

In the awkward silence that followed—a silence bound to be confidence-eroding for him—Madeleine blew a long breath and shook her head. 'Kris ... you know I care about you, right?' At his frowning nod she went on without flinching. 'I think you also know, deep down, that I'm not the right woman for you.'

His frown turned into a scowl. 'I know my own mind, thank you very much.'

'I wasn't suggesting—'

'If anyone doesn't know their mind it's you.'

'Kris, I—'

'What do I need to do to convince you ... propose?' To Madeleine's chagrin, he dropped to one knee beside her chair. 'Mum always says diamonds speak louder than words.'

Stunned by the move she gaped at him, not noticing when he once again took one of her hands in his.

Just as a tall shadow darkened the doorway.

Madeleine's startled eyes flew to the new arrival.

Although his face was in shadow, his stillness spoke volumes.

Oh no....

Realising Kris was still holding her hand, she jerked it away.

About to protest, he followed her shocked gaze to the man standing, silently staring. 'Is this your ten o'clock?' At her curt nod Kris rose, brushing imaginary dust from his pants.

Leaning down to say in a low, intimate voice, 'I'll be back for your answer later,' he planted a kiss on her stiff cheek before striding to the door, giving the man who'd rudely interrupted them the briefest of glances while squeezing past.

The sounds of Kris's footsteps faded as the two stared across the office at each other.

Wishing herself anywhere else, Madeleine gave a start at Byron's scornful chuckle.

'If that bloke was worth his salt,' he drawled, 'nothing would've stopped him from finishing the job right here and now.'

She bristled. 'Thanks for the uninvited opinion. As if this isn't awkward enough. And that "bloke's" name is Kris.'

Byron sauntered into the room and she could finally see his face. His eyes were unreadable but a mocking grin hovered around his mouth.

'And does your *other* bloke know about this Kris, I wonder?'

'Other bloke?' She frowned. 'Y-you? I-I mean ...' Mortified, she gave a strangled cough and blustered, 'Who? Who do you mean?'

Dropping into the seat Kris had vacated, Byron stretched out his legs and laced his hands together behind his head. 'So many you can't remember them all, hey? Seems you're stealing hearts all over Tas.' His lips split into a cynical grin but his eyes remained hard. 'I'm talking about your personal chauffeur.' When she stared at him, mystified, he added, 'You know, Jeff, the infatuated shuttle driver.'

'Infatuated, with me?' She gave a snort. 'Hardly. Anyway, how do you know Jeff?'

'I don't *know* him, just seen him around. And he drove me here this morning.' At her puzzled frown he added, 'I'm planning to drive my old Mazda back to town.'

'Oh. Right.'

Though his expression didn't change, his eyes glittered darkly. 'Your buddy Jeff was at pains to tell me how he's your personal driver. Yours and Emma's, apparently. Seems you might have some competition for his affections from my little sis. Then again, lover-boy Jeff has competition too,' and he nodded in the direction Kris had gone.

Her lips compressed into a thin line.

'I guess marriage proposals and romantic rivalry are flavour of the day.' A mock-innocent tone crept into his voice and he returned her indignant gaze without flinching. 'So tell me, are congratulations in order?'

'What? No! He ... Kris ... wasn't proposing,' she blustered. 'Just ... um—'

'By!' Emma appeared in the doorway. 'You're back!' Skipping over to her brother she threw her arms around him and planted a kiss on his cheek.

'Hey, squirt.' He grinned and patted her hand.

The guarded look on his face melted away, replaced by genuine fondness for his sister. It was the same look Madeleine herself had glimpsed, fleetingly, when he'd turned to see her running up to him the day before.

Only the look was quickly gone, leaving her wondering if it had happened at all.

26

'We're all here so let's get started.' Pushing everything that wasn't work-related to the back of her mind, Madeleine grabbed a folder from the tray on her desk. 'Emma and I have been sharing the role of overseeing manager on a temporary basis, but the position needs a more dedicated and consistent approach.'

She glanced at Byron. 'That's where you come in. We'd like you to consider taking on the role, with Emma providing ongoing managerial support if that arrangement suits you both.' Holding out the folder, she went on in the same businesslike tone. 'This offer document contains the role description and employment package.'

He took the folder from her with a dip of his dark head.

'I can go over the duties and terms with you now if you'd like?'

'Thanks.'

'And afterward,' Emma interjected, 'we'll take you for a look at the improvements to the castle.' She nudged him in the side and grinned. 'We've been busy while you were away.'

She nudged him again later, as they strolled to the cottage with Madeleine following a short distance behind. 'You haven't said yet if you'll accept the position.'

'You're right, I haven't.'

'Oh, you can be so annoying, By.' Emma punched him on his nearest arm. 'Whoa. You been working out?'

'Just working.'

When they reached the cottage Emma took a key from her pocket and, grinning, dangled it from a finger. 'I'll go open up.'

He watched her skip off, and said without looking at Madeleine, 'I suppose you've also made lots of changes to my ... the ... old place?'

'See for yourself.'

Pausing at the gate, he ran his eyes over the cottage. Sunlight glinted off the open, cobweb-free windows, their lace curtains twitching in the breeze. Flourishing potplants and freshly painted eaves graced the front porch, and the garden sported a smooth lawn, neatly trimmed paths, and well-tended garden beds. A vine curled over the wrought iron gate, dripping a mass of buds and purple flowers.

'Mum took care of the garden for you,' Emma called from the open front door. He joined her on the porch and stood gazing around until she grasped him by an arm. 'Come on.'

'Will I recognise the inside?' He flicked Madeleine a glance. 'Or have you given it a modern facelift?' Not that he cared, it wasn't his home any longer.

'See for yourself,' she said again.

At Emma's insistent tug he stepped through the front door. Once inside he blinked in the lower light and swept a wary glance around.

Nothing had changed, in that room at least. All the old furniture was still there, everything was as he'd left it, only cleaner.

He moved into the kitchen, where his pans still hung from the ceiling pot rack, and his appliances sat in their assigned spots on the counter. At the window above the sink the newly laundered café curtains were caught back to allow fresh air and sunlight into the room.

It was as though the cottage was pouring on the charm.

He turned to his sister with a bemused frown. 'You didn't change anything.'

'Of course not.' Emma beamed at him. 'Why would we? This is your home.' Darting a glance at Madeleine she added, 'Assuming you take the job, that is.'

'Who's living here now?'

'I have been, temporarily, to look after it while you were away.'

'So, my old room in the castle?'

Emma spread her hands. 'A storage room now. What it should've been all along. I never did understand why Mum put you in there.'

'The other rooms weren't liveable. And it wasn't long before she let me move into the cottage.'

'So she did.'

'You were okay with keeping the cottage as is?' He directed the question at Madeleine but it was Emma who responded.

'What d'you mean? It was Maddie's idea to not change anything. She wanted the place kept just like it was, ready for your return.'

All he'd said was, 'Thanks ... Maddie,' but with a depth of meaning that, along with his use of her shortened name, had set Madeleine's heart a-flutter.

Recalling the earlier scene she heaved a sigh, but the tender moment was cut short by an indignant, raised voice.

'So that's all you think I deserve, a "thanks but no thanks", after I had to once more chase you down for an answer.'

It was true she'd been away from the office when Kris called back as promised. Not on purpose, though. He just picked a bad time. And she hadn't kept him waiting for her final answer.

At the time he'd simply walked out, face flushed with disappointment, without saying anything. Now it seemed he wanted to talk.

'I've been dancing attendance on you, putting up with being shrugged off time and again. And all for nothing?'

Déjà vu washed over her as her mind flew to the scene in her old apartment; of the argument that led to—

'I think I deserve a better reason.' His voice rose. 'More than just "I'm not the right woman for you, Kris".'

'But it's true.' Her lips formed a tiny, sorrowful smile. 'I never meant to hurt you—'

'*Twice*. This is your second knock-back.'

'I am sorry about that.'

'So, after everything I've done, all I get is an "I'm sorry"?'

Stung by his condemnatory tone, she retorted, 'I didn't ask you to come here, remember, and I did nothing to lead you on.' When he remained tight-lipped, she went on more gently. 'I assumed, after we ended things all those months ago, that you'd accepted "we" were a thing of the past.'

At his scornful snort she said firmly, 'I've never been anything but straight with you.'

His shoulders sagged and he ran a hand over his face. 'If it's Mum you're worried about, you should know she's prepared to forgive and forget what happened before.'

At the mention of Mrs de Voss, Madeleine's face clouded. 'How generous of her.'

'Yes,' he said with a note of pride, 'very generous, considering.'

Her sarcasm was clearly lost on him. She frowned and compressed her lips.

Misreading her silence as vacillation, he went on with an air of renewed hope. 'It was Mum who suggested I propose, something she said I should've done much earlier.'

Madeleine winced as Byron's mocking words, '... if he were worth his salt, nothing would stop him from finishing the job,' echoed in her ears. And when it appeared Kris might be about to repeat the toe-curling performance, she threw up a halting hand.

The hopeful light died in his eyes and he muttered, 'You don't need to say anything more. It's written on your face what you think of my offer ... and me.'

'I didn't mean—'

'Oh I think you do.' Rising to his feet and shooting her a wounded glance, he growled, 'Don't worry, I get the message.'

As he marched stiff-backed from the room, Madeleine gave a drawn-out groan and sagged over the desk, banging her head repeatedly on its teak surface. Amid the inner turmoil though, there was a sense of release.

It was done.

Kris de Voss no longer factored in her life decisions.

'Yes, I knew you were being offered a managerial position at the castle.' As she spoke, Kathryn leafed through the folder of documents Byron had passed her. 'I'm pleased to see it comes with a good salary and rent-free accommodation in the cottage.'

Raising her head to smile at her son, she took in his new air of maturity and the outward changes to his appearance. Perhaps the trip to the mainland had proven to be something of a rite of passage.

He flashed a rueful grin. 'So Emma still keeps you informed.'

'We may not live together now, but your sister and I talk on the phone most days. We talk more now than when we were all living in the castle.' Kathryn smiled wryly. 'After being at odds for what felt like an age, Emma and I grew close again while you were away, and now I look forward to our conversations instead of dreading them.' She watched his face for changes. 'Yet another benefit from selling the castle.'

'Another *benefit*?' His grin faded.

'You're not still harbouring resentment, are you?' At his scowl she reached for his hand across the table. 'I'm not, and you shouldn't either. In fact, I find myself thanking the Brandes every day for what they did for our family.'

'You *thank* them for what they did to us?'

'*For* us, not *to* us. And of course I'm thankful. You should be too.' At his sceptical snort she froze, eyes widening as she took in the stubborn set of his mouth. 'Tell me you're not thinking of declining this excellent job offer,' and she waved the folder in the air. 'Don't be a fool, son. You're too smart to go cutting off your nose to spite your face.'

Byron sat back to eye his mother, his expression softening as he took in her golden tan, shining eyes, and the short haircut that made her appear younger. 'Enough about me. You're looking great, Mum.'

At his words she relaxed ... slightly. 'I'm feeling great too, better than I have for a long time.' At a whistle from the kettle she rose and made for her compact kitchen. While the tea brewed she stood staring out the window.

'It took quite some time after we left the castle,' she said slowly, 'to not wake every morning dreading a phone call from the bank or one of our creditors. These days I leap out of bed knowing I'm free of all that, and can spend all day gardening if I choose.'

She flicked him a wry glance. 'And no more having to squeeze into one of those damn hostess gowns for the nightly performance. I was tempted to simply toss them out but they cost so much.... Anyway, the local amateur theatre group was pleased to take them off my hands, and I was pleased to see the last of them.'

Pushing herself back from the sink she wrapped the teapot in its hand-knitted cosy and set it on the tray. 'Now my son has returned to what I choose to regard as a hero's welcome.'

'Hardly that—'

'And I've resurrected my relationship with Emma. Oh, when I think of all the bickering we used to do, it's no wonder the dear girl became all starchy.' As she carried the tray to the table, Kathryn took in her son's unreadable expression.

Shaking her head when he made moves to pour the tea, she went on. 'It's true I was against selling the castle, despite Emma's ongoing pleas and the alarm bells jangling in my ears. I loved the old place, and our time there held moments of delight for me ... along with some of despair.'

She paused with the teapot suspended above the second cup. 'I held onto that dream long after I should've let it go. It was just ... I wanted to prove your father wrong, to make the castle a successful venture so he'd regret ... leaving ... us.'

Swallowing, she brushed a hand across her eyes and finished filling the cup. 'Emma was right, though, we were going under. It was wrong of me to ignore the seriousness of our financial situation, and to involve the two of you in my personal battle.'

'No, Mum, we—'

'It's alright, son.' She passed him a steaming cup. 'Luckily I came to see sense before we had to abandon the castle and leave it to fall back into decay.' She shuddered. 'If not for the Brandes' offer to buy us out, all the time and money we spent on the place, not to mention everything else we lost in the process ... well, it would've been a truly tragic outcome.'

'I get what you're saying, Mum.' When she set a plate of Monte Carlo biscuits in front of him, Byron couldn't resist taking two. 'But the Brandes making out they were our friends when to them this was simply a cold, calculated business transaction?' With a shake of his head he put a whole biscuit in his mouth, barely registering its coconut flavour and the filling of sweet jam and vanilla cream.

'Granted, they may not be our friends *per se,* but the Brands have been a Godsend to our family. Without them I wouldn't have been free to start my garden design business, or been able to buy this darling little house.' Kathryn indicated their cosy surrounds with a lift of her chin. 'Selling the castle didn't leave me with enough to buy this place though, after clearing all the castle debts. If the Brandes hadn't shared the proceeds from the sale of that necklace....'

At his quizzical look she frowned. 'You knew Madeleine discovered the Bedazzler, buried on the peninsular? On Crown land it was, so we really had no claim to it. Despite that, they insisted on sharing the windfall with us.'

She blew steam off her tea and watched as astonishment, scepticism, deliberation, and then begrudging gratitude—and something else she couldn't quite label but sensed was good—crossed her son's face.

'We were going to lose the castle one way or another, son. Then the Brandes came along, and you can see for yourself how well things have turned out, for all of us. I own an unencumbered home and a business that's already providing an income. My daughter is finding her feet and making her way in the world, becoming a confident, likeable young woman in the process. And now my son's been offered a great position at his beloved castle, with perks he may never have enjoyed otherwise.'

Frowning, Byron dunked the remaining biscuit in his tea.

Was his mother right about the sale of the castle being a saving grace for their family?

He took too long to eat the dunked biscuit, and a sodden fragment plopped back into his cup.

What his mother said had made sense, but it didn't change the fact Madeleine had come into their lives acting the innocent while planning to weasel them out of the castle. And he'd been foolish enough to fall for the act ... and her.

'Byron?'

Glancing up, he found Kathryn staring at him with questions in her eyes.

And he knew what those questions would be.

His heart sank, and the lyrics of a favourite song sprang to mind ... *wish I didn't know now what I didn't know then....*

It was time to give her the other piece of news.

Did she really *have* to know, though? Couldn't he keep it to himself and save her the pain?

As though sensing his inner turmoil, Kathryn took his hand. 'You managed to catch up with your father on the mainland?'

He stiffened and looked away, knowing she'd see the disappointment, compassion, and regret in his eyes.

'Byron?' she prompted again. When he turned to meet her gaze, she took a deep breath and said quietly, 'Tell me, son, I need to know.'

27

T *he following morning....*
   Leaning back to gaze at the stone wall of the manager's office, Madeleine traced the uneven mortar between the silver-grey stones with her eyes while her mind wandered. A knock on the doorframe snapped her back, and she swung her chair around.

'Come in, Byron.'

'Thanks for seeing me on short notice.' His tone was respectful but he didn't smile.

She watched him make for the chair opposite hers. 'Thanks for ringing first.'

Oh the stiffness of their exchanges! So different from how they'd been before. Now like two hawks circling above the remains of what had once been a thriving ... friendship?

As he pulled out the chair the overhead lights fell on

his face, highlighting new lines and dark smudges around his eyes. She couldn't help asking, 'Is ... everything alright?'

He sat with a grunt. 'Yes and no. I've been to see Mum, and—'

'Is Kathryn okay?'

'She's fine.'

'And thrilled to have you back, no doubt.'

'Yeah.' He lowered his gaze. 'At first.'

Madeleine frowned. 'At first?'

'I came back with some bad news....'

'About ... your dad?'

He gave a tense nod. 'I was hoping he'd come back here with me once he knew we'd sold the castle, to patch things up with Mum. He'd always said it was the castle that drove him away, so I thought ... and Mum thought....' Byron paused. 'Turns out she and I both thought wrong.'

'You found him?'

'Managed to track him down, eventually.' A bitter edge crept into his words. 'Living with his new—much younger —wife and their son, on a property in western Queensland.'

'Oh.' She gazed at him, unsure what else to say.

'Yeah. Anyway, after the initial shock of finding his first-born on the doorstep,' and Byron's lips twisted, 'I guess Dad felt obliged to invite me to stay. They needed help on the farm anyway, were in the middle of a big muster and short a few jackaroos. I figured it was an opportunity to convince

Dad to give up his "pretend" family and come home to us, his "real" family. So I agreed to stay on. More fool me.'

The edges of his mouth tilted downward. 'I tried to hate the new wife and their little bloke. Wanted to blame them for keeping Dad from making our family whole again, except ... they're innocent parties in all this.' He dragged a hand over his head. 'Dad's new wife must've known why I was there, but she was really good to me. And their little bloke took to me like he knew we were half-brothers.'

Byron's expression softened. 'I've never had much time for kids, but that little tyke was different. Made me think maybe some day....' He broke off with a wry grimace.

'So what happened with your dad?'

'Well, I discovered a few things about him. For one, he's happier now than when he was here, at the castle. It appears he's found his Shangri-la with this new family. I just hope he's learned from his mistakes and does the right thing by them.' The hardness returned to his face. 'I might understand him a bit better now, but I still don't think he deserves to be happy after running out on us when the going got tough, and forcing us into more debt to pay him out. And he certainly doesn't deserve to have Mum still carrying a torch for him.'

'So ... how did she take the news?'

He took his time answering. 'She was stoic at first, until I mentioned the little boy. Then her face crumpled, and she ... well, she did something I haven't seen her do for a long time. She cried. And not just a few tears, I mean *really* cried. Totally soaked the front of my shirt.'

'It might've been a release for her, so she can—'

'What? Come to terms with the fact she's been replaced by some other woman?' His voice rose. 'A woman who's not only sharing his life but has borne him a son? How the hell does someone *get over* something like that?'

Madeleine extended a hand. 'At least now—'

'We could've remained blissfully ignorant if I hadn't gone looking for Dad.' He thumped his thigh with a fist. 'And I wouldn't have gone, if you and your mother hadn't bought the castle. Now we have to deal with knowing we've been cast aside, swapped for another family as easily as a man swaps old shoes for new.' His voice cracked and he cleared his throat.

Her face paled. 'I'm so sorry, Byron—'

'Don't.' His shoulders sagged and he bent his head to blow a long breath. After a loaded pause he said, 'I should be the one apologising. None of this is your fault. It's just ... I feel rotten about dashing Mum's hopes.'

He raised distraught eyes to meet her sympathetic gaze. 'What was I thinking anyway? That Dad would be hanging around, holding his breath, waiting for a chance to come back to us? When he'd already had ample opportunity to make the move and chose not to?'

Madeleine couldn't resist reaching out to him, and as her fingertips made contact with his arm, she felt a spark that charged the atmosphere in the room.

It appeared to jolt Byron too, for he frowned and dropped his gaze to the hand resting on his arm. After a long, pensive moment he covered it with his own hand.

Sucking in a stunned breath, she blustered, 'Speaking of giving someone bad news ... actually, make that unwelcome news ... I've had to deliver some too, to someone I care about ... *cared* about.' She frowned. 'Still care about ... just in a different way.'

Byron withdrew his hand and sat back to eye her. 'You mean that bloke, Mr Pop-the-Question?'

'He didn't really ... it wasn't a....' Pausing, she gave a resigned sigh and nodded.

'Do I assume,' and he chose his words with care, 'that you answered his question?'

Another nod.

'And your answer was...?'

'No.' She gave a long blink. 'He didn't *actually* propose, but he did want us to get back together ... even though his mother openly dislikes me.'

'And you told him no.'

At her nod an aura of relief descended on them.

'Wait, did you say *back* together?'

'Like I tried to tell you, Kris and I were in a relationship a while ago. He started getting serious and I didn't feel the same, so I called it quits.'

'And ... he came here to try to win you back?'

She nodded again. 'After what happened before, I felt

obliged to hear him out, but nothing's changed. Kris still doesn't *get* me, not the real me anyway.'

'So what did happen back then?'

'I had no idea Kris would be so upset about the break-up.' She met Byron's solemn gaze with guilt-ridden eyes. 'It turned into a shouting match, and when he left my place, he ... had a bad accident. A *really* bad accident. Wrapped his car around a power pole down the street from the apartment.'

'Is that why his mother dislikes you?'

'And she's right to.' Madeleine's voice dropped to a murmur. 'Kris is her only child, and he very nearly died.' Taking a pen from the holder, she proceeded to click it on and off repeatedly with her thumb.

Dragging his chair closer, Byron leaned over the desk to take her hands in his. 'You know what happened wasn't your fault, right? You couldn't have predicted he'd react so badly.'

'It's taken me a while to accept it but yes.' She swallowed. 'I know I had no control over his actions.'

Byron gave her hands a shake. 'And he obviously recovered.'

'Only after a long treatment regime. You saw the healing scars on his face?' She closed her eyes as if to shut out the image.

'Didn't look that close, actually.' Byron sat back again. 'So, what is it about the "real you" he doesn't get?'

'Well, for starters, he thought my penchant for solving

"old case" mysteries,' and she freed her fingers to mime inverted commas, 'about "long-dead people" was a childish fad.'

'Sleuthing isn't for everyone, but the bloke doesn't know what he's missing.' Byron winked at her. 'As for me, I found working in a supposedly haunted castle fascinating.'

'Emma also appears unfazed by strange happenings, so it must be contagious. Or a family trait.'

'Have there been any further 'spectral' activities or freaked-out guests?'

'Not for a while now. And I'm sleeping better lately, no more nightmares.'

He quirked an eyebrow. 'Perhaps the spirits have been somehow appeased.'

'Well, I did solve my ancestor's mystery....' When he fixed her with a level gaze, Madeleine clasped her hands together on the desk and said crisply, 'Anyway, I'm guessing you're here to talk about the job?'

'Yes. And according to my mother, who's usually right about things like this, I'd be a fool to pass it by.'

'So ... that's a yes?'

'Yes,' and he gave an amused huff. 'It's a yes.'

Madeleine clenched a triumphant fist. 'Good on Kathryn.'

'Yes, good on Mum.'

A weighty silence fell. A silence fraught with ... questions? Revelations? Declarations?

It was Byron who broke it, his deep voice vibrating with

emotion. 'Maddie, I'm ... starting to see things a bit ... differently now.' His Adam's apple bobbed in his throat. 'And I'm—'

'Oh great, I caught you.' Bustling into the office with a swish of linen skirt and a waft of perfume, Emma slid to a halt on seeing their reactions. 'Oops, sorry! Didn't realise you had someone with you, Maddie.' Then her eyes lit up. 'By? You're here again?'

'Hey, squirt.' He flicked her a distracted grin.

'Hey.' Turning to Madeleine, Emma said with a wince, 'Sorry to burst in on you. It's just ... you can be hard to find sometimes.'

With a droll, 'So I'm told,' Madeleine sat straighter in her chair.

'I saw the office door open,' Emma went on, 'and I figured....'

'It's fine. Byron's just here to talk about the job.'

Glancing at her brother and finding him gazing at Madeleine with a tell-tale look in his eyes, Emma gave a drawn-out, 'Riiight,' and turned to her co-manager again. 'I'll be quick, then. It's about Friday's masquerade ball.'

Madeleine stared blankly at her.

'Don't tell me you forgot?'

'I knew it was coming up, but....' As she spoke, Madeleine leafed through the pages of her work diary. 'Oh wow, it *is* this Friday night. And Mum arrives on Thursday.'

'What's this ball?' Byron asked.

'Our first gala night,' Emma said with a lift of her chin.

'A masquerade ball, to show the world what we've achieved here. My idea,' she added, puffing out her chest. 'All the city big-wigs will be here.' She gave his nearest arm a sisterly punch. 'So it's totes terrific you'll be on board to handle the final preparations.'

When he said nothing, she frowned. 'You *have* accepted the job?'

'Well....'

'Oh, come on, By! What's the holdup?'

Grinning, he raised a hand. 'No holdup. I've accepted it.'

Emma gave a whoop. 'I was counting on having you oversee things at the ball, with your usual style and pizzazz!'

'Pizzazz?' He gave an amused snort. 'Don't know about that, but I'm happy to pitch in. Can even don my old butler's outfit for the occasion if you need another pair of hands.'

Emma beamed at him. 'You're a champ.'

'And you're a kid sis who knows how to wrap her brother around a little finger.' Turning to gaze into Madeleine's eyes he said, 'I'll call in again tomorrow to go over the arrangements. And grab my butler clobber. See you then.' Rising, he gave a dip of his head and strode out.

Madeleine watched him go, her mind reeling and her stomach doing handstands.

What was he about to say before Emma interrupted? Was it about the job ... or something else?

'Super, he'll be here on the night,' Emma said with a sigh. 'That's a relief.'

'Yes, super.' Madeleine took a deep breath and cleared her throat. 'So what was it you wanted to talk to me about?'

'Oh yeah, the ball. I ... um ... need to give the caterers final numbers by tomorrow.'

'Okay.'

'So are you bringing a partner?

'I'll be too busy schmoozing with all the big-wigs to keep a partner entertained.'

'Noted.' Screwing up her face, Emma moved closer to rest her hands on the desk. 'Hey, speaking of partners?'

'Mm?'

'I don't have one for the ball yet, and I was wondering ... about your ... um ... friend, Kris.' Emma's expression grew pained and she rushed on. 'I haven't mentioned it to him yet. Wanted to find out first if you'd have any objections?'

Objections to Kris partnering Emma at the ball? None.

Concerns it could be awkward, his being there? Heaps. Though it would seem churlish of her to refuse.

'No objections from me.'

Emma grinned. 'Great.'

'Do you need his contact det—'

'Nah. Got his number already.' Still grinning, Emma pushed herself back from the desk. 'Thanks. Now I'd better arrange for collection of our gowns from the dressmaker. I'll send Jeff, he knows to hang them in the van so they don't crease.'

About to leave, she paused in the doorway to point a mock-accusing finger. 'In that little black number of yours, Maddie, you'll be a hard act to follow. My poor brother doesn't stand a chance.'

'Your bro—?' Madeleine frowned. 'What do you mean by that?'

But Emma was already gone.

'You look ... fabulous.'

At the man's voice and warm press of a hand at her waist, Madeleine turned to see a grinning mouth below a Phantom of the Opera mask.

It was a popular choice for a number of men attending the ball. Some stood chatting with drinks in hand and the women on their arms in a variety of dazzling masks, while others twirled partners on the ballroom's dance floor to music from the accomplished four-piece band.

Light spilled from elegantly curved metal sconces on the walls and leadlight lanterns hanging from the vaulted ceiling, creating golden pools of light throughout the ballroom. Marble vases and urns, all intricately carved or painted with laurel wreaths, acanthus leaves, and griffins, released a potpourri of delicate fragrances from their tightly massed white roses, carnations, peonies, and bleeding hearts.

Madeleine glanced with pleasure at the elegantly

spread front table. The porcelain vase she'd chosen for the centrepiece had come from a collection of hand-painted vases and urns Kathryn McAlister had discovered locked away in a storeroom, soon after taking possession of the castle. To Madeleine's mind, the images of golden phoenixes rising through flames on the vase represented the castle's phases of renaissance, the restoration of her family's good name, and even her own emergence from beneath the millstone of guilt.

'Glad you made it, Jeff.' She grinned back at the masked man.

'Damn, how'd you know it was me?' Peeling off the mask to reveal a clean shaven, freshly scrubbed face, he ruffled his combed-down sandy hair back into its usual tousled place. 'Oh, and thanks for the invite.'

'Our pleasure. As one of our business partners we're pleased you could make it.'

'And I'm happy to be here, though I had to borrow a monkey suit,' and he tweaked the satin lapel of his tuxedo. 'The boss at the taxi rank gave it to me. Said his days of going to balls are over.' He stood tall, awaiting her inspection.

Madeleine's nose twitched as she caught the scent of camphor, a legacy of the tuxedo's long-term storage no doubt. While noticing an excess of white cuff at his wrists, and an unusual expanse of sock above his polished shoes, she refused to mention the suit's downfalls. After all, he'd gone to some trouble for the occasion.

'Pretty swish, Jeff, I have to say.'

'Excuse me, didn't you hear? I *said,*' and the plaintive voice rose, 'I'd like one of those.' The plump lady glared at Byron and pointed a pudgy finger at the tray he was holding aloft.

Tearing his gaze from Madeleine in her figure-hugging black gown and gold and black *Colombina* mask that—to his mind, anyway—had her effortlessly outshining every other woman in the ballroom, Byron hastily lowered the tray.

'I beg your pardon, madam.' Handing the scowling woman a glass of the pale gold bubbly, he dipped his head and said, 'Far be it from me to deny a parched party-goer a bout of bubbles.'

His attempt at gentle humour was clearly lost on her, for she merely huffed and flounced off, glass in hand, with an indignant swish of lolly-pink, flab-pinching satin gown.

With a longsuffering sigh, Byron whirled around to resume his butler duties. And bumped into a man, almost knocking him off his feet and dislodging the *Pantalone* mask from his face.

'Hey!' The man regained his balance with an irate grunt and growled, 'Watch it, y'clumsy fool!'

With his focus on steadying the tray and its load of precariously clinking glasses, Byron could only splutter, 'I do beg your pardon, sir.'

With a loud harrumph the man dusted himself down while Byron collected the fallen mask from the floor.

'Yeah, well, you should watch where you're going.'

Handing over the mask, Byron dipped his head and murmured, 'Of course, sir. My apologies,' and stood frowning as the ticked-off tux marched away.

'Aren't you supposed to be a shining example to our trainee waiters, bro?' Emma sidled up to peer at him through the almond-shaped eye holes of her silver *Volto* mask. 'Or are you showing them what *not* to do?'

'Very funny.' He rearranged his features, once more assuming an expressionless butler's countenance. 'Accidents do happen though, even to me.'

'Sure they do, when your mind's not on the job. Can't blame you for being distracted though, she looks stunning,' and Emma inclined her head to indicate Madeleine on the other side of the room.

'You and Mum have scrubbed up well too.'

'That's chivalrous of you, By.' Emma flashed a grin. 'All our gowns are by the same local dressmaker, and I simply *adore* mine.' Holding out the crimson organza skirt, she took a dainty twirl. 'Even if it doesn't have quite the same "come hither" appeal as Maddie's.'

When she came to a stop and realised Byron had gone back to staring at Madeleine, and probably had been the whole time, she shook her head at him. 'I take back the chivalrous comment.'

He kept staring and said nothing.

Clicking her tongue, she glanced over to where Madeleine stood chatting with the Mayor and his wife. 'She had second thoughts about wearing that gown tonight, you know. Said it's more revealing than she'd normally wear.'

As though to prove the point Madeleine gave her gown's plunging neckline a surreptitious upward tug, which only served to draw Byron's attention to her smooth-skinned décolletage. Above it, a fine gold chain glinted at her throat, and matching drop earrings twinkled under the overhead lights. Teamed with her black and gold mask, she appeared to glow as though gilded from head to toe.

To his eyes at least....

At his sigh Emma swallowed a grin and prodded him in the side. 'Hey, none of that, Mr Not-so-Chivalrous. You might be all thumbs tonight, but you're here to work, remember?'

28

From where she sat watching couples twirl around the dance floor in a blur of ball gowns and tuxedos, Connie Brande sensed she was no longer alone.

'May we join you?'

She turned to find a smiling Kathryn McAlister, and by her side a distinguished-looking man in a smart dinner suit.

'Please.' When Connie indicated two vacant chairs at her table, the man seated Kathryn before himself. Watching them, Connie was struck by Kathryn's changed appearance. Trimmer and tanned, she radiated elegance in her lilac crepe de Chine sheath gown and matching elbow-length gloves. But it was more than that. There was something brightly alive about her now, a natural glow to her face.

With a touch on his arm, she indicated the man at her side. 'May I introduce Campbell Beatty, our local MP.' As Connie shook his extended hand, Kathryn said, 'Cam, this is Connie Brande who, as I'm sure you know, bought Lorienne Castle from us.'

Connie's smile encompassed them both. 'Along with my daughter, Madeleine.'

'Pleased to meet you, Mrs Brande.' He had a pleasant voice, warm eyes and a wide smile, and just the right amount of firmness in the grip on her hand.

'The pleasure is all mine, Campbell. And please call me Connie.'

'And I'm Cam.'

Watching them, Kathryn gave a warm smile. 'Cam and I have known each other for a while now. We met when I joined the Chamber of Commerce.'

Witnessing the exchange from a few tables away, Byron smoothed the furrow forming in his brow. On spying Emma weaving through the crowd toward the ladies' room, he strode over to buttonhole her. 'Who's that with Mum?'

A quick glance at the group and Emma turned to her brother with a smug grin. 'That's Connie Brande. You know, Maddie's mother.'

'Not her, the bloke. Who's he?'

'Oh him. That's our local MP, Cam Beatty.' She backed away. 'I've gotta go.'

He grabbed her arm. 'C'mon Em, spill it. Why is our local MP cosying up to Mum like they're a couple?'

'Pay attention, By. Seems everyone's linking up with someone. Better watch out or you'll be the only wallflower.' She quirked a teasing eyebrow.

'What's that supposed to mean?'

'You'll work it out. Now,' and she jerked her head toward the corridor leading to the amenities, 'I have to *go*.'

'That'll teach you for drinking so much bubbly.'

'Who's counting?'

'Not you, obviously.'

'Like *you* never let your hair down. And how about you drop the big brother act and concentrate on being a butler?'

At a sudden thought, Emma glanced over her shoulder to where Kris stood nursing a glass. 'I shouldn't leave him by himself too long. It was hard enough convincing him to come tonight. Don't want him getting bored and leaving me in the lurch.'

'That's another thing.' Byron's eyes narrowed. 'Why is *he* still hanging around?'

Emma sniffed and stood straighter. 'He's a doctor, you know, and not just an intern or even a resident. He's what the hospital calls a CMO ... or something like that.'

'Bully for him, but it doesn't explain why he's here tonight.'

'Like I said, he's here with me.'

'Why?'

'Because I invited him, that's why. Now, if you'll excuse me.' Shooting her brother a final challenging glance, she turned on her heel and rushed off in a fragrant swirl of organza.

'I wondered why you were hovering.' Kathryn eyed her son, noting the concern on his normally oh-so-discreet butler face.

'Waiting to get you on your own.' He indicated Cam and Connie, waltzing amid other couples on the dance floor.

Kathryn smiled. 'I'm glad she agreed to dance with him. Gives my feet a rest.'

'And this date....?'

The note of interrogation in her son's voice had Kathryn fixing him with a quelling gaze. 'When Cam invited me to accompany him tonight, I was relieved. Attending functions like this on your own can be ... awkward, especially for a woman of a certain age.'

'So,' Byron persisted, 'are you and he an item?'

'I'll be seeing Cam again, if that's what you mean by an "item".' As her roving gaze alighted on Emma in Kris's arms on the dance floor she added, 'And I think the same might be said for your sister, though I hope she's not taking on a rebound.'

'What?' He blinked at the change of subject.

'Sorry, just thinking aloud.'

'Look, what about ... Dad?'

She tensed. 'What about him?'

'I thought you still ... you know ... hoped?'

Kathryn sat back, her gaze serious. 'For a long time I did have hopes. False hopes.' She smiled into his eyes. 'Which my son has now laid to rest.' She clasped her hands together. 'Let's face it, your father and I have been apart long enough for him to move to the mainland, embark on a new relationship, and even father a child. So we're not talking recent events here, Byron.'

'Sorry, Mum. It's just ... I don't understand.' He cast a quick glance around and lowered his voice. 'You cried when I told you about Dad's new ... situation.'

'Yes, and I want to thank you for telling me.'

'You're *thanking* me? For making you cry?'

'For being honest, and for giving me what I needed. Closure.' Spotting Cam arrowing toward them through the milling bodies on the dance floor, Kathryn said firmly, 'Thanks to you, I can now get on with living my life.'

Fixing her date with glowing eyes she said brightly, 'Cam, I'd like you to meet my son, Byron.' As the two men shook hands, she flicked her son a meaningful glance. 'Byron, this is Campbell Beatty, who I hope we'll be seeing a lot more of from now on.'

And the man in question flashed a broad, amenable grin.

'Your Gran's health continues to improve, and I'm sure it's thanks to learning the truth about Elizabeth. She's even talking about visiting the castle soon.'

'Wow, that's great, Mum.' As she spoke, Madeleine's eyes followed Byron as he did the rounds of the ballroom, a tray of drinks expertly suspended at head height.

'And what a brilliant discovery about the Masons and their involvement in the case! I'm so proud of you, love, and I'm sure Elizabeth's spirit can rest easy now.'

'Well I haven't had any more of those vivid dreams lately, so maybe you're right.'

When Madeleine continued gazing at Byron, Connie arched a bemused eyebrow while opting for an innocuous subject. 'I see Kathryn McAlister has a new beau.'

'So it seems.'

'She looks happy. So does he.'

'Mmm.'

At the distracted response, Connie took a sip of champagne and swept another glance around the ballroom. The crowd had thinned, with older attendees— and Connie refused to include herself in that class—having answered the siren call of their bedroom suites in the castle.

Swirling the contents of her wine glass, she once more assumed a nonchalant tone as she asked, 'Has Byron accepted the manager job?'

'He has.'

Seeing Madeleine attempt to smother a broad grin, Connie smiled into her glass.

The caterers had packed up and departed, but a few couples remained on the floor dancing to slow, end-of-night music. The kitchen and wait staff, with the job of clearing the ballroom of empty glasses, discarded napkins, burnt-out candles, and plates of half-eaten hors d'oeuvres, had to wait until after the final hangers-on left.

From where he stood, arms folded, leaning against the kitchen doorway, Byron watched the brazen cab driver in the ill-fitting tux once more try his luck with Madeleine. When he moved close to put his hands on her waist, Byron tensed and straightened. A growl formed in his throat when the cocky sod bent his head, clearly intending to kiss her.

Of all the nerve.

Byron took an involuntary step forward, just as Madeleine turned her face so the kiss landed on her cheek. He watched her move back and her lips mouth a goodbye to the cocky sod, who lurched his way out.

And with that the ballroom was empty of all but the band and Madeleine. Byron watched her sink into a chair, kicking off her shoes to rub her feet.

She was finally alone.

When the male vocalist announced that the evening

was over, Byron slipped to the stage for a word in his ear. A moment later the musicians took up their instruments again and launched into *The Way You Look Tonight*.

Seeing Madeleine glance up in surprise, Byron straightened his jacket and stepped off the stage. Once at her side he extended a manly hand. 'May I have this dance? Or is it unseemly for the Queen of the Ball to dally with a mere butler?'

Although her lips broadened into a slow smile she remained seated, stretching her toes. 'I'm paying the price for chancing new shoes,' and she indicated the high-heeled gold sandals lying on their sides on the floor. 'Wasn't expecting to be asked to dance quite so often.'

'So that's a no?'

'Hmm, dance with a butler?' She flashed an impish grin. 'You're right, that would be deplorably unacceptable ... social conventions and all that.'

Frowning, he crossed his arms over his chest. 'Duly noted.'

'For a queen to dance with a *manager,* however, would be quite different.' And she batted her eyelashes at him.

He sighed. 'I see I'll have to ask again.' Uncrossing his arms to extend a hand once more, he repeated, 'May I have this dance,' adding, 'your majesty?'

'Ah, the life of a royal ... not all it's cracked up to be.'

With a snort he bent and grasped her hand. 'Just come and dance with your new manager.'

'Very well, as long as there's nobody here to see the queen dancing in bare feet.'

'The floor's dirty, your majesty,' Byron murmured as he led her onto the dance floor. 'So you'd better put your feet on mine.'

When he took her in his arms her gown's plunging back exposed bare, receptive skin to his touch, and her hypersensitive, champagne-charged nerves responded immediately, sending the heat of skin-against-skin contact radiating through her.

'Come on, your feet on mine,' he ordered.

Swallowing, she choked, 'But—'

'I insist. It's the only way I can be sure you'll let me lead.'

'It's your funeral.'

They grinned into each other's eyes as she stepped onto his feet.

He pretended to grimace.

A few turns of the dance floor later, his husky murmur, 'You look wonderful tonight,' so close by her ear brushed warmth across Madeleine's skin.

With his strong hand at her waist they swayed, bodies pressed together, to the slow, dreamy music. It felt like the most natural thing in the world to relax and rest her cheek on his shoulder.

The singer's velvety lyrics, *there is nothing for me but to love you,* accompanied by the mellow notes of piano and saxophone wrapped them in a sweet, musical cloud, and they melted into each other.

From where she stood unseen, beneath the entwined brass letter Es above the ballroom's doorway, Connie turned with a smile and made her way to her room.

Well after the band played a long, drawn-out finale, Madeleine realised she was no longer moving. Lifting her head to smile shyly at Byron, she murmured, 'Time to go?'

He gazed into her face, tucked a tendril of hair behind her ear, and nodded.

'Are you staying tonight ... in the cottage?'

Seeing the blush infusing her face he chuckled, a low, sensual sound that made her heart give a body-thudding beat.

'Okay with you if I do?'

'Of course. Emma moved all her things out and had it cleaned. C'mon, I'll get you the keys.'

They set off, bodies pressed close, along the dimly-lit corridor from the ballroom to the castle, their eyes gradually adjusting to the deepening gloom. When muffled sounds reached their ears from a dark corner, Madeleine peered into the dimness and saw a couple in a passionate lip-lock.

And not just any couple.

'Well, well. How do you feel about that?' Even in a whisper, Byron's deep voice sounded gravelly.

'I ... it's none of my business what they do. They're both adults. C'mon,' and firming her grasp on his hand, she set off again. 'Come to think of it, they might be quite well matched. Kris is needy and Emma ... well....'

'Needs to be needed? You're right, she does.'

Once outside the door to the office he gazed down at her, his eyes dark and intense. 'Do I take it that Kris is well and truly out of the picture for you?'

'That's right.' Annoyed her voice wasn't quite steady, brimming as it was with a heady mix of hope and anticipation, she hastened to open the office door. 'I'll ... just be a sec,' and she slipped inside.

On emerging to hand him the cottage keys it occurred to her he might interpret it as a hint. But after taking the keys from her, he merely cupped her chin in a strong, warm hand and, never once taking his eyes off hers, lowered his head slowly until his lips hovered mere millimetres above her quivering mouth.

After what felt like an age of sweet agony, he pressed his lips to hers in a hesitant, achingly brief embrace. Brief, only at first....

The air around them changed, the atmosphere became charged, as if the castle itself were observing the tender scene.

Some passionate moments later, Byron raised his head to smile crookedly into her opening eyes. She replied with a slow, intimate smile of her own.

They stayed that way for some time, caught in the

joyous moment of realisation, culmination, expectation, until Byron gave a lopsided grin and rasped, 'I'd better say goodnight, your majesty. If I stay here any longer....' and he left the rest unsaid.

~

The following morning she emerged from sleep, smiling as the memories of their dance sprang immediately to mind.

The dance ... and what came after it.

Closing her eyes, Madeleine once again felt the fusion of Byron's firm mouth with hers, bringing her insides to a scalding effervescence that lingered even now....

Anticipation swelled her inner core, and she released a slow, hot breath.

At movement from the end of the bed, she glanced down to see Topaz yawning and stretching his front paws toward her.

'Hey buddy.' She sat up, and when he moved closer, scooped him into her arms and held him close. 'Well, what a night that was. I'm sure there'll be some sore heads and regrets around the ridges this morning. We all consumed too much bubbly, case in point, Emma and Kris.'

Her voice grew pensive. 'I'm relieved he's managed to move on this time, instead of ... well....' She bent her head to scratch the purring cat's throat. 'Anyway, I hope it works out for them both.'

Topaz touched her chin with what felt like a consoling

paw but was more likely to be a 'hurry up and feed me' prompt.

'Sorry buddy, you'll have to talk to your owners about your tucker. We're just roomies, remember.' Grinning, she tossed the bedclothes aside. 'And I can't stay here all day, puss-cat. I have a castle to run, renos to oversee, a new manager to get familiar with ... er ... to familiarise with his duties.'

When she spluttered into loud laughter and threw herself back, Topaz's ears flattened and he stared into the matching pair of eyes that were laughing so exuberantly into his.

Humans....

29

No elegantly gowned hostess greeted them at the door and no candlelight flickered in the room, but when Madeleine opened the heavy damask drapes, morning sunlight glowed off the antique furnishings and tapestries, bestowing the castle's dining room with an opulent but welcoming atmosphere.

'I see why you like breakfasting in here.' Byron set the tray on the dining table and took a seat opposite her, clearing his throat as he unloaded two bowls of honey-drizzled porridge and a mug of tea each.

As he passed hers across, she smiled warmly at him. 'Yum, thanks.'

Holding her gaze, he began in an uncharacteristic mumble, 'Maddie, I ... um—' only to stop at a rap on the doorframe. Cursing under his breath he turned, then saw who was standing there. 'Oh, it's you. Morning, Em.' His tone cooled a few degrees when he added, 'And Kris.'

'Hey, bro. Thought we'd pop in with this. Was in this morning's mail.' Emma waved an envelope at him as she stepped into the room, Kris in tow.

Gazing at him standing a tactful distance just inside the door, Madeleine couldn't help thinking how awkward this must be for Kris ... or was it? He certainly didn't appear discomforted. If anything he looked ... content?

Yes, content.

Not a word she'd have used to describe Dr Kris de Voss before now.

Interesting how things work out sometimes....

'It's for you, from Dad.' Emma passed Byron the envelope. 'Getting a letter—or anything—from him,' and a critical edge crept into her voice, 'is something of an occasion. So I thought you'd want to read it straightaway.' She waited for him to speak, and when he remained silently staring at the envelope's handwritten address, she turned to Madeleine. 'Hope you don't mind us barging in like this, Maddie?'

'I'm getting used to it.' Madeleine gave a lopsided grin. 'So,' and she indicated the letter, 'your dad prefers sending handwritten mail?'

'This is something of a first, which makes it super intriguing.'

Emma's words appeared to jolt Byron into action.

Clutching the letter more firmly he rose and turned to Madeleine. 'I'm just gonna nip out for a bit.'

'Okay.'

'Back soon.' When he bent and kissed her on the mouth, a possessive gesture she figured was at least partly for Kris's benefit, she grabbed the front of his shirt to keep him close and smiled into his eyes. 'Not too long though, or your brekkie will get cold.'

At his smiling nod she let go of his shirt and he left, tapping the letter against his hand and casting Kris a narrow eyed glance on the way out.

When Emma made as if to follow, Madeleine said, 'Could we have a quiet word? Just you and me?'

Emma eyed her before turning to Kris. 'I'll meet you in the Lodge shortly.'

Once they were alone, Madeleine beckoned her to Byron's vacated chair. 'So,' she said in a low voice after Emma settled herself, 'you and Kris...?'

'Yeah.' Emma gave a shy smile. 'Me and Kris.' Her smile became a nervous wince. 'I ... hope that's okay with you?'

'More than okay, I'm thrilled for you both.' Picturing them together, she added a thoughtful, 'You make a great couple,' and smiled. But when Emma gushed, 'That's what his mother said, too,' Madeleine stiffened. 'You've met the formidable Mrs de Voss? Already?'

'Not in the flesh ... yet. Kris arranged a video conference with her yesterday, and I sat in on it.' Emma gave an indulgent smile. 'We're going to visit her in a few weeks' time.'

'Wow, you guys are fast workers.' Madeleine watched colour rise in her friend's cheeks. 'So, what did you think of Mrs DV?'

'A bit ... yeah, formidable ... at first, but I've decided to like her.'

'Smart move.'

Emma's voice lifted. 'She told Kris she thinks he's made a better ... er ... good,' and she winced an apology, 'choice this time.'

Madeleine brushed off the apology. 'Well done you. And what did she say when you told her where you work?'

'Didn't seem all that interested. Was more worried about my plans for the future.'

Madeleine's lips twitched. 'Can *I* ask what those plans might be?'

Emma's blush deepened and she looked away. 'Not sure I'm ready to share.'

'You didn't share them with Mrs DV either?'

'Well ... yeah, I did ... kinda....'

'Oh I see.' Madeleine tapped her lips. 'You thought it wise to oblige your future monster-in ... er ... mother-in-law.'

Emma's initial scandalised expression morphed into a guilty grin, and she spluttered into giggles.

Laughing with her, Madeleine realised with a heady rush that one day they might be more than friends — even sisters-in-law. She took a deep breath and was about to speak when Emma beat her to it.

'On the subject of couples, you do know your secret's out?' Feigning nonchalance, Emma lifted a hand and examined her nails. 'Not that it was a surprise to some of us.'

'My secret?'

'About you and my brother.' Emma flicked her a sideways glance from smiling eyes.

'Oh, um ... you ... know about that?'

'It's pretty obvious. And his is my brother.'

'Of course.' It was Madeleine's turn to blush. 'And how do you feel about that, or is it a secret too?'

'I'm totally rapt.' Emma's grin widened. 'I've never seen my brother so happy. What you said about me and Kris making a great couple goes the same for you two.'

They sat smiling at each other, and then a loud tummy rumble set them both chuckling.

'Breakfast calls.' Emma rose to leave. 'And unlike you,' and she flashed Madeleine a wink, 'I don't have a butler waiting on me.'

As if on cue Byron strode into the room, still tapping the now open envelope against his hand.

On her way out Emma touched him on the arm. 'I'd like to hear what Dad had to say, so I'll catch up with you later.'

'Okay, Em.'

As he approached, Madeleine fixed him with a level

gaze. 'So, what did your Dad say? Something important, by the look on your face.'

'Yeah.' He opened the envelope. 'Important to me, anyhow.'

When he perched on the edge of the table beside her, Madeleine felt a quiver in the room's atmosphere, as though the castle didn't approve of such an undignified seating position in its formal dining room.

It was a quirky thought she kept it to herself.

Only the castle knew....

Byron extracted and unfolded the single sheet of writing paper, then passed it to her while summarising its contents. 'He says they're all fine, and that the farm's doing okay despite the Government's "efforts" on behalf of primary producers.' He pointed to the relevant paragraph. 'Efforts he describes in rather colourful language.'

'And?'

'He goes on to say he's glad I went to the trouble of finding him.' Byron cleared his throat. 'And that he's proud of the man I've become.'

She saw pride, gratitude, and a host of other emotions cross his face, and resisted the impulse to hug him as he continued

'Dad wants to stay in more regular contact from now on, and says Emma and I should get to know our little half-brother. Oh, and he gave me a piece of advice. Advice he wished someone had given him back when we were still a family, so he said.'

'Which was?'

'To grab every opportunity for happiness and not let pride or anger get in the way.'

She nodded her approval and handed back the letter. 'So have your parents worked things out now?'

'You could say that.' Slipping the folded letter back into the envelope, he shoved it into a pocket. 'Dad's settled with his new family, and Mum's getting on with her life, with a new man who seems decent enough.'

'All good then.'

'Yes.' Fixing Madeleine with a searching gaze, Byron said in a voice heavy with emotion, 'And I have every intention of taking Dad's advice.'

'Oh?' Her own voice grew breathless. 'How so?'

His gaze intensified. 'By grabbing onto this opportunity for happiness.'

The look in his eyes set joy exploding in her chest, and in the expectant stillness of the historic room—which surely had witnessed many romantic *tête-à-têtes*—the ticking of her wristwatch seemed loud.

Byron's words cut through the tension-filled vacuum. 'I have something to say, something I've been trying....' He paused, bent his head to take a deep breath, and then lifted his chin to gaze into her eyes. 'I love you, Madeleine Brande.'

The hairs on her arms stood on end as emotions collided within her, scattering her thought processes to the four winds.

In the awkward silence that followed, a crease formed in Byron's brow. The crease deepened into an anxious frown as the silence dragged on, and he gave a hard blink.

Seeing that, Madeleine gulped and moistened her lips. 'Byron?' The word came out as a croak and she cleared her throat.

'Yes, Maddie?' Hope illuminated his eyes.

Lips quivering, she managed to whisper, 'I love you, too.'

Dropping to the floor beside her chair he pulled her into his arms, pressing her against his chest and resting his cheek on her honey-blonde hair.

With the urgent beat of his heart so close to her own, she closed her eyes as her arms slipped around his neck to squeeze him tight. And when she pulled back to gaze at him, he bent his head and claimed her mouth.

When they finally parted, she rested her cheek against his shirt and murmured, 'I just realised something.'

'Yeah?' His voice rumbled under her ear. 'What?'

'That I've only ever said "I love you" to one other man.'

'Really? Well, it's the first time I've said it ... to anyone apart from Mum, of course.' After stealing another quick kiss he rose to pull a chair close to hers and dropped into it, taking her hand in his. 'So who was this other lucky bloke? Not the uber-fickle,' and he pulled an incredulous face, 'Dr de Voss, I hope?'

'No.' Madeleine gave a dismissive snort.

'Please tell me it wasn't the cabbie?'

'J-eff?' She spluttered at his mock horrified expression. 'Are you kidding? No, it was my Dad.'

'Well that's alright then. Hey, tell me about your father. You've heard all about my family, it's time I knew more about yours. After all....'

At his unspoken meaning she had to clear the lump in her throat before answering. 'Okay ... but remember that we lost Dad when I was only five years old, so all my memories are those of a child.'

'Yeah, go on.'

'Dad had beaut ideas for adventures and games. I don't know of any other girl who had a quicksand pit made for her in the back yard.'

'A quicksand pit?'

'Just a small one.' She grinned. 'He made it so I could rescue my doll "victims" from the gooey clutches. Dad said everyone should experience being a hero at least once.'

Byron gave an amused snort. 'I guess a quicksand pit makes a change from the traditional dollhouse.'

'I had one of those too, but I liked the quicksand better. Dad knew I would, he knew me better than anyone.' Emotion thickened her voice. 'He was *my* hero.'

Gazing at her in silent empathy, Byron ran a caressing finger down her cheek and tucked a loose strand of hair behind her ear.

Raising her head she blinked at the clock. 'Hey, shouldn't you be meeting with Carl by now, planning tonight's menu?'

'Normally yes, but this morning I made my first executive decisions as manager.'

'Did you now? And what did you decree, oh managerial one?'

'Firstly, that Carl could take the day off, which actually pleased the ornery sod. And secondly, that castle guests could try a different cuisine tonight, namely Italian.'

'You'll arrange for Jeff to take them to Gino's?'

'Yep.' He tapped the end of her lightly freckled nose with a finger. 'That's a brilliant arrangement you've made with the cabbie dude, I must say.'

'Oh!' Jerking straighter in her chair, Madeleine grabbed his arm with an urgent hand. 'We must go to Gino's ourselves, together, the first chance we get.'

'We *must* go? Not that I'm against the idea, but why the rush?'

'Ada saw me having coffee with Jeff, and I think she got the wrong idea.'

'I see.' Mischief joined the passion glinting in his eyes. 'You got caught out and now you want me to fix things for you.'

'Caught out?' She gave his arm a playful punch. 'We were only talking. I wanted to find out about his family's history.'

'Why are you so interested in a local cabbie's family?'

'Turns out they're descendants of George Mason, father of Philip Mason.'

'And Philip Mason is...?'

'*Was* Genevieve Lorienne's beau.' At his raised eyebrows Madeleine said with a chuckle, 'Long story. It'll keep for later.'

'Let's see now,' and Byron counted on his fingers, 'there's Jeff, along with some Philip dude, and let's not forget poor old cast-off Kris.' With an affected sigh he dropped his hand. 'I don't know ... with you pretty girls it's "off with the old, on with the new" at the drop of a hat—' With a throaty laugh he ducked another badly aimed blow.

'You're lucky you called me pretty, otherwise....'

'Otherwise what?'

He didn't give her a chance to answer.

30

'I've decided that Genevieve meant to do the right thing by Philip.' Madeleine paused to sip her coffee. 'It was that awful disease that robbed her of the opportunity.'

They sat at the large island bench in the Lodge's kitchen, crumb-covered plates at their elbows and scents of toast, grilled cheese, and espresso coffee hanging in the air.

'Fair enough.' Byron dipped his head. 'So, Madame of Mystery, you've managed—'

'*Mistress* of Mystery, thank you very much.'

'Oh, humble apologies your mistressness.' He gazed at her from under his brows, the message in his eyes and the grin forming on his lips sending her stomach into spirited calisthenics.

'Mistress Madeleine,' he went on, 'has not only

managed to track down Philip Mason's descendants—who turned out, in a huge stroke of luck, to be cabbie Jeff's family—but also uncovered what George Mason did to the Loriennes in the name of vengeance, thereby solving a mystery about her own ancestor. Kudos to the Mistress of Mystery.'

With a regal dip of her head, Madeleine beamed at him through the steam billowing from her mug.

'Your mother's right about your nose for mystery, Maddie. It certainly makes life interesting.'

Oh, how she loved the way her shortened name rolled off his tongue....

Shrugging, she leaned across to caress away the moustache of coffee froth from above his top lip. 'Can I help it if I have an active imagination?'

Her low, intimate voice had him swallowing and clearing his throat. 'Active? That's one way to describe—'

'Hey!' She clicked her fingers. 'I meant to ask earlier ... that dinner at Gino's — what about tonight?'

He sat back to eye her with amusement. 'Oh yeah, that's right. You want me to fix things for you.' After a loaded silence he gave a bark of laughter and leaned in to drop a kiss on her lips. 'No need to give me that look, I'm happy to have dinner in town. Our new butler-in-training is ready for his first solo flight here anyway, and needs to be up to speed in time for the Spectres Ball.'

∼

Sitting in a shaft of sunlight staring at her laptop's screen, Madeleine breathed the fresh scents of herbs flourishing in pots around the once dank and moss-drenched, now rejuvenated and inviting, castle courtyard. Made over by the team of castle renovators, and with help from Kathryn McAlister's green thumb, the courtyard was now the delightful sanctuary Madeleine had envisaged.

Gazing at the nearest flowering plant, whose leafy arms stretched upward as though to show off its rosy pink blossoms, Madeleine drew a contented sigh. The so-called Apple Blossom Rosebud pelargonium was a favourite of Queen Victoria's, Kathryn had told her, and therefore a 'most appropriate feature plant' for the castle's growing collection.

Turning her attention to the email she was drafting to her mother, who was once again on the mainland spending time with Gran and attending the odd business meeting, Madeleine grinned. Connie's absences only made her more insistent she be kept up to date on the castle's operations and renovations, along with any significant personal happenings in her daughter's life.

Like the fact she was now 'spoken for' and happier than she could ever deserve to be.

Imagining her mother's reaction to that piece of news, delivered oh-so-casually amid a description of her 'Matterhorn-high' ironing pile, Madeleine chuckled. There was bound to be an excited phone call within minutes— even seconds—of her finger pressing SEND.

And a phone chat would be handy. She needed to find out if her mother planned to attend the upcoming Spectres Ball, a fundraiser for a local not-for-profit organisation being held in the castle's ballroom. Along with enjoying the odd soiree, Connie would no doubt be keen to celebrate her daughter's newfound happiness, so her answer was bound to be a firm yes.

'I'd better see off the remaining guests. Don't go anywhere.'

'Yes boss.' Grinning, Madeleine watched Byron stride over to where his mother stood, a smiling Cam at her side, in conversation with the ever-jovial Capaldis.

Recalling how Gino and Ada had greeted Byron's announcement that he and Madeleine were now in a 'committed relationship', with loud clapping of garlicky hands, effusive two-cheek kisses, and floury hugs all round, her grin softened.

Bending her head with its elegant up-do, she tucked an errant strand of hair behind her ear, and as the vocalist began crooning *Unforgettable*, turned her gaze to the party debris in the streamer-strewn ballroom.

'Right, that's everyone.' Flopping into the neighbouring seat, Byron sighed and unfastened his bowtie. 'Your Mum left a while ago, but I was starting to think those party animals,' and he indicated the departing group, 'would never leave.' As he undid the buttons on his tuxedo jacket and loosened the neck of his white dress shirt, he caught her watching and gave a bemused grin. 'What are you smiling at?'

She set down her wine glass. 'Dance with me.'

'What, again?'

'Yes, again.' Already on her feet, she ran smoothing hands down the hip-hugging satin skirt of her antique-gold, off-the-shoulder mermaid gown. 'No excuses. It's not like you've had to do the butler thing tonight.'

With a mock groan he refastened his jacket and rose to take her in his arms, murmuring in her ear as he led her into a slow waltz, 'Luckily for you I can take being bossed around by beautiful women.'

Pressing her cheek against his shoulder, she closed her eyes as a picture floated into her mind; of the love-struck teenagers, Genevieve Lorienne and Philip Mason, and a distinguished Edward Lorienne and wife Elizabeth, joining them on the dance floor in a haze of billowing ball gowns and elegant suits.

When she murmured dreamily, 'All's well with the world,' Byron gazed down into her smiling face, and while his eyes softened, his lips firmed.

After the song ended he led her to the nearest table, signalling covertly to the vocalist, who nodded at the other band members. As they began a smooth rendition of *The Way You Look Tonight,* Madeleine sank into a chair with a sigh.

'They played that song last time too. Must be their

finale number—' She ended the sentence with a gasp on seeing Byron take a small box from a pocket inside his jacket, and set it on the table in front of her.

A plush jeweller's box.

Face aglow and heart wildly thumping in her throat, she sat gaping at him, the box, and then back at him.

When he indicated it with a dip of his head, she reached for the box, her senseless fingers almost dropping it twice before managing to open it.

From the midnight-blue satin interior, a breathtaking cluster of diamonds, embedded Victorian style in a filigreed, rose-gold band, winked up at her.

She raised her head, and met Byron's intense gaze above an uncertain grin.

Swallowing, he took a breath and said firmly, 'According to Gino, this is something I should do before someone else gets in on the act. As it was,' and he gave a rueful lift of a dark brow, 'de Voss almost beat me to it.'

Taking the box from her, he removed the ring and held it over her left hand. 'I meant what I said about not letting happiness slip through my fingers, Madeleine Brande.'

'Don't you mean,' she croaked, 'de Brande Barlow?'

'Not for long if I get my way,' and his words held a silent question.

When she gave a wilful shake of her head his face fell, and then she smiled. 'I'd settle for Madeleine Brande-McAlister though. I've always had a thing for hyphenated names—' Her remaining words were smothered by his bark of triumphant laughter.

'I should've known,' he drawled, 'after all the trouble you went to reclaiming your family's original surname.'

She grinned. 'Topaz can be a Brande-McAlister too.'

'Topaz?'

'That's the name I gave your castle cat.'

'What castle cat?'

'You know, the tabby...?'

Byron shook his head. 'We never had a cat here. Must be a new addition.'

'But he....' At the look in Byron's eyes she said quickly, 'Oh, doesn't matter now.'

With a dip of his head, Byron slowly, reverently, slipped the ring on her finger and rose to sweep her up, into his arms. 'You, my love, deserve every single syllable of whatever name you choose.'

From where he sat watching, eyes half-closed in a contented feline smile, Topaz gave a flick of his tail and melted away, leaving only a trail of tabby mist.

As Byron carried Madeleine from the ballroom a draft of cool night air followed them along the corridor, wafting past the castle's lovingly restored rooms. Tipping her head back and closing her eyes, she fancied she could hear whispers on the air, telling of redemption, renewal, and joyous new beginnings....

If you've enjoyed reading *The Long Road to Loving Byron*, I hope you'll consider posting a review on your retailer's site. Maddie and Byron will love you for it!
Alicia